The Book of Cain

JEFF LOWE

The Book
of Cain

Little White Cabin, LLC
Woodland, Alabama

Little White Cabin, LLC
197 County Road 531
Woodland, AL 36280
publisher@littlewhitecabin.com

ISBN 978-1-949585-00-1

Cover design by Ava Lowe

This is a work of fiction. Any resemblance of characters or plot to real
people and events is purely coincidental.

To Maria

Acknowledgements

I would like to acknowledge my daughters, Armida, Tyne, and Ava Lowe for their encouragement and support in reviewing, editing, and publishing The Book of Cain. Their contributions were invaluable in turning this dream into a reality.

Chapters

1. Leper 1
2. A Good Marine 11
3. Predator 18
4. River Cat... 25
5. Infection 33
6. The Red House 41
7. New Nod 46
8. Hooked 54
9. The Sour Lemon 68
10. All About the Green 88
11. The Pain Pit 95
12. Samuel Blue 113
13. Hobo.. 124
14. Laura 135
15. Sister Ada's Shack 149
16. You, Aunt Violet....................................... 155
17. The Cult.. 172
18. Prophet 177
19. The Hero of Harlington 186
20. Indigo Bunting 194
21. Slave Girls 203
22. Muse 215
23. The Mark of Cain 221
24. The Third Panel....................................... 232
25. I Had a Sister 239
26. Jailbreak 248
27. Revival 258
28. Baptism 271
29. Cain's Testimony 276
30. Heal, Mama 279
31. Eris 285

1. Leper

THE KIDS CALL IT "THE LAZ," as in: it's the laz place you ever want to be on the road from school to prison.

The Lazaretto Alternative School stands on an island in the middle of the Prevene River, with an almost Alcatraz-level of seclusion. The compound was built more than a century ago to be a leper colony, and darkened by the rain, its stone and brick buildings utterly defied all attempts to make it look like something else.

An early morning squall had blown through shortly before I arrived. The winds were still stiff enough to whip the tree branches and the parking lot was slick and puddled, but the rain had stopped and the storm cover had broken so that patches of blue sky showed here and there. To the east the sky was red, turbulent gray above, and to the distant west, after a stretch of blue, great white cumulus clouds were looming high.

I don't recall seeing the rainbow at that point.

My name is Lillian Last. I am a psychiatrist. I had been to a lot of "alternative" and "special" schools, juvie homes, detention centers, and such places in my work with troubled teens, and I have witnessed the ways that environmental factors can influence their treatment, good and bad. If you have a kid with a paranoid fear of being strangled, you don't treat him on the gallows. But that was exactly the sense I got of this ghastly place.

To enter it from the parking lot on the west riverbank, I had to walk across an ancient iron footbridge—the only access into or out of the place that I could see—through a locked gate surrounded by an impassable fence like a dragon's collar halfway across.

A tiny guardhouse next to the gate was no longer in use. Instead, employees could open the gate using a key card while guests like me could use the intercom to talk to the receptionist inside. As she buzzed me through, I looked down into the river below. The water was brown and swirling from the hard rain. In it I saw something tumble, swept along by the current. I didn't know what it was at first. Then I saw the teeth and the open mouth. It was the bloated carcass of a dog.

I don't believe in omens, or I didn't then, but the sight of that dog filled me with a sense of doom as I entered. The principal and school administrator had not yet arrived, so I asked the receptionist to show me to the office of Elton Ricks, the staff therapist assigned to my patient. As she led me down the hallway I noticed that among all the standard self-esteem and motivational posters on the walls were framed black-and-white photographs of residents and staff from back in the leper colony days. Some were quite graphic in their depiction of the physical ravages of the disease from back when there was no cure. I could only imagine the effect it had on the fragile psyches of the children here, and I mentioned that to Elton Ricks when I met him in his office.

"Well, as I understand it," he said, "this company was able to purchase the property at a well-below-market price on the condition that we honor its history."

"As a leper colony," I said.

"Yes. So we're obligated to keep the name, The Lazaretto, and certain relics like those photographs."

Elton Ricks was a pudgy, pasty, prematurely balding man with a well-trimmed beard and thick glasses who looked like he should be wearing a tweed jacket even when he wasn't. He had a sour countenance and seemed on edge.

"I'm sorry, I don't mean to challenge you, Mr. Ricks," I said, "but I'm just concerned about the effect all these environmental factors may have on the children here."

"Well, Doctor Last," he said, "I may actually share your concerns in that regard. But I'm not the architect or the interior designer and I don't control the money around here. I'm just a lowly therapist. But I can tell you this. The client you're here to see?"

"Richard Tyler."

He gave a sarcastic laugh. "Yeah, good luck calling him that. You've read his file?"

"Of course."

"Then it ought to be clear to you he is not a child. He's seventeen going on thirty-five and he is a dangerous, unstable young man. He's been here way too long and in all that time he has not made any progress, or even any effort, in therapy. Not an inch. Not an iota. And he still won't even acknowledge his real name. Do you know what he calls himself?"

"Yes, it's in his file."

Ricks stood up and started pacing back and forth be-hind his tiny desk. "Cain. He calls himself Cain, Dr. Last. You know who Cain was, don't you? The first mur-derer. If you read his file, you'd realize he really was try-ing to kill that Kernell kid. It wasn't just some dustup between teenagers. Did you read the list of injuries?" He took a paper from the file folder on his desk and read from it. "Broken jaw, four teeth knocked out, broken or-bital bone, four broken ribs, one of which punctured a lung, ruptured spleen, crushed testicles and a dislocated patella, not to mention too many cuts, abrasions, and bruises to count. Then the cops came. Four of them. Three wound up in the hospital. Three grown adult po-lice officers. And your kid was sixteen years old. Six-teen! They said it was like trying to subdue a rabid dog. One of them actually pointed his gun at him, and the kid lunged at him and the cop actually pulled the trigger and guess what? The kid lucked out. The gun jammed some-how. And you know what your guy did? He took the gun right out of the cop's hands. The cop said he used this lightning fast move, and next thing he knew the kid had his gun. Then the kid, your guy, says, "You can't kill me. I am Cain," and he handed the gun back to the cop. Lucky for everyone involved, one of the cops hit the kid with his stun gun right about then and they were able to restrain him. They thought for sure he was on PCP or bath salts or something."

"There were no drugs found in his system, according to the toxicology report," I said.

"I know that," Ricks said. He was getting more anxious and angry as he made his case. "But that's really the point, isn't it? It was an unprovoked attack on a total stranger. And it wasn't drugs that made him do it. Which means whatever it is that drives him to do this sort of thing can't be fixed with a little substance abuse treatment, unfortunately. Look, here's the point: We can't help this client. We've tried, and he simply will not cooperate in his own treatment. All of us, every therapist employed at The Lazaretto, has signed on to the decision to remove him from here."

"So you think he should be just shipped off to the adult prison population?"

"That's what the court order requires, Doctor. That if he doesn't show substantial improvement in socialization and attitude and moods, as determined by us, the therapists at The Lazaretto, by his eighteenth birthday, then he's to be transferred to the adult prison system to serve out his time on the original charges. And to answer your question directly, yes, I do. I think he should be transferred out of here now, today. In my opinion he should have been tried as an adult, convicted, and sent to the adult system right away. He simply doesn't belong here. He scares the kids, he scares the staff. He scares me. It's not fair to any of us."

"Mr. Ricks, has Richard Tyler ever actually attacked anyone here?"

"Yes. He attacked several other students. I thought you said you read his file."

"I did. According to the report in the file, he was coming to the aid of a staff member who was being attacked by those students."

He rolled his eyes and sighed. "That was Sarge."

"Sarge?"

"Yes. To be honest, I can't even remember his real name off the top of my head. Everybody has always called him Sarge. He's an ex-Marine or something. But let me tell you. He's biased in favor of the Tyler kid. I don't know why. Maybe it's a tough guy, macho thing. Sarge used to be the head of our rapid response team— until his support for your guy went a little too far for our comfort, so he was demoted. The guy we've got leading the team now is a lot more realistic about the danger your boy poses. He wants him gone too."

"I'd like to talk to Sarge before I see Richard, if that's all right."

"Fine. Whatever. Look, Dr. Last, I must confess, I'm at a loss to understand why you're here. In all other cases, the staff therapist makes the decision as to the client's disposition. We don't require some over-credentialed shrink, pardon my indelicate phrasing, second-guessing us. So. Why are you here?"

"I'm here by orders of the Governor."

"That much I know. But nobody else gets this kind of privileged treatment. So why for this kid? Nobody really knows anything about him. There is a huge gap in his life that no one knows anything about, and he refuses to tell anyone. He may as well have been raised by wolves.

Why is the Governor interested in him? What's the connection?"

"Does it matter?"

"Come on, Doctor. Is it those two people from Harlington? It is, isn't it? That sheriff and the kid's aunt. They're constantly bugging us, especially the aunt. They have some kind of political pull?"

"Sheriff McKenzie and the Governor were in the Marines together."

Elton Ricks slumped into his chair. "I knew it." He shook his head and scowled. "The Marines. Jesus. The governor, the sheriff, Sarge, and Cain. Does the phrase 'toxic masculinity' mean anything to you, Doctor? And his aunt, what's her name..."

"Violet Tyler. I've talked to her."

"Yes, well, you know who doesn't talk to her? Her nephew. Your boy. Richard Tyler. Refuses to talk to her. Has since the day he came here. She writes him letters every single week. He doesn't reply. She calls. He doesn't take the call. He refuses to have anything to do with her or with that sheriff. Look, these may be nice people, but they don't know this kid. According to his file, his mother took him away from Harlington when he was, what, five years old? They didn't keep up with him. They didn't even know where he was until he got arrested for beating up the Kernell kid. And they never would have found out about that, either, because he refused to identify himself except to say, 'I am Cain.' And then one of the detectives working the case recognized that burn scar on his chest to be a cult symbol. And he checked the files and got in touch with Sheriff McKenzie who had apparently investigated the cult. That's the only way they even found out who he was. And by the way, have you seen that scar? It's absolutely hideous."

"Mr. Ricks..."

"It was fresh when he was arrested. Freshly burned into his skin. I'm telling you, he never should have been sent here. The Lazaretto isn't a prison, it's a school. It is not set up to handle that sort of problem. And he shouldn't be getting favoritism because of political connections, that's for sure."

"Mr. Ricks, Sheriff McKenzie and Violet Tyler are just being good advocates for the child. The fact that the other kids here don't have support is not Richard's fault."

"If they're such good advocates, why doesn't he accept them? And why don't they just become his legal guardians and make decisions for him?"

"Apparently because his mother is still alive. She would have to..."

"His mother!" Ricks laughed. "Doctor Last, here's something that is not in his file that you should know. I have talked to the cops. Do you know what they think? They think Richard Tyler killed his mother and then dumped her body somewhere before he went and tried to kill the Kernell kid. It's an active investigation. That's why it's not in the file."

"Well, Mr. Ricks, thank you for your time and the information. It's very helpful. You said on the phone the other day I could use your office for my session with Richard. Is that offer still on the table?"

He stood up. "Sure. I'm taking the rest of the day off. I don't want to be here if that powder keg explodes, that's for sure. And he may. No, let me rephrase that. He will explode. And people will get hurt or killed. It's just a matter of when. I'll tell you this, Doctor. The other therapists and I have talked and we agree. If Richard Tyler is still here by next week, we're all quitting."

"You're kidding."

"I am totally serious."

"Did Richard physically assault any of the therapists?"

"Does he have to?" Ricks said. "He's already shown he's capable of extreme and unprovoked violence. None of us wants to be in a room alone with him. How can we do effective counseling if we have to have rapid response standing right there in the room with us? Do you know what he said to the cop when he was in the squad car after they arrested him? This isn't in the file either."

"What did he say?"

"The cop asked him why he beat that kid up. And you know what he said? He said, 'indigo bunting.' Now what the hell is that supposed to mean?"

"An indigo bunting is a bird."

"I know an indigo bunting is a bird! But what does it mean? Either it's some kind of cult code word or the kid is just unhinged. He hasn't changed since he got here. You wonder why the therapists are afraid of him, even though he hasn't actually bashed their skulls in? I'll tell you why. Whenever we try to counsel him, he just sits there, in that chair where you're sitting now, all quiet, but tense and twitching. He doesn't answer any of our questions, he just glares at us, like he's sizing us up, and you know what it feels like? I'll tell you. It feels like he's a predator and you're his prey. It feels like you're sitting in the same room with Travis the maniac chimpanzee who's about to go ape and bite your face off. If we adults feel like that, how do you think the kids here feel? He needs to go. And he needs to go now."

He let out a tired sigh and then picked up a handset and spoke into it. "Sarge? This is Elton Ricks. Can you come to my office? Cain's shrink is here. She wants to talk to you."

"OK, it's all yours, make yourself at home," he said. He stood and stepped toward the door. "Look, Doctor, we get tough kids in The Lazaretto all the time. Strong kids, impulsive kids, kids who like to fight, but in all those other cases we're confident that if we need help we can call rapid response and they can come in and get control of the situation. But not with him. Not with Cain. He's a different breed. Even the people on the rapid response team are afraid of him. Except Sarge. Sarge is a fool. Ask the others. They'll tell you."

2. A Good Marine

SARGE WAS BUILT like the proverbial fireplug, about five-foot-seven and stout with what my father called "old man's muscle." By the gray in his crew cut and the chapped leather of his face I'd guess he was about sixty, and when he shook my hand he said "Ma'am" with a dry, military courtesy, but I could tell he could easily crush my hand if he wanted to. Unlike Elton Ricks, whose eyes didn't stop flitting about during our conversation, Sarge looked directly at me, almost as if he were challenging me.

"So they call you Sarge," I said. "What branch of the service were you in?"

"Marines, ma'am," he said.

I nodded and held his gaze. "My father was a Marine," I said.

"Oh? Well, that's good. I hope he taught you well."

"He tried, in the time he had. He was killed in action in Vietnam near the end of the war. I was seven."

Sarge's demeanor suddenly changed, as I knew it would. He stood and saluted me. I stood, went around the desk and hugged him. "From my dad to you, semper fi," I whispered. "Thank you for your service."

"Yes, ma'am, thank you, ma'am. God bless you and your dad."

"Sarge," I said as I sat back down, "I've been sent here to evaluate Richard Tyler..."

"Look, Doc, he's a good boy, he really is. These people here, they just don't know how to handle a kid like that."

"A kid like what, Sarge? How would you describe him?"

"He's tough, Doc. He's tough and he's disciplined. All these other kids here, they're a bunch of weaklings, I mean, in terms of moral fiber, physical strength, you name it. They'd spend all day playing video games if you let them. But Cain... I mean Richard, he works out every day, every damn day rain or shine. Hell, you could put him in any of the hardest programs in the Marines, or in the Army Rangers, Navy SEALs, you name it, he'd make it. Today. He's that tough. Plus he can swing a wrench like nobody's business. You name it, he can fix it, boat engine, commode, washing machine, whatever. And he keeps his room neat as a damned pin. And no one forces him to, he's done it since day one. You can't do that stuff without discipline."

"The therapists here say he won't talk to them."

"I don't blame him. I wouldn't either. Buncha pussies. Pardon my French."

"You do understand that he needs their approval to go free when he gets out of here, don't you Sarge? Otherwise he'll go to prison."

Sarge shook his head disgustedly. "What's wrong with people nowadays? When I was young I got into some serious trouble, just like he did. And you know what the judge said? He said, Mr. Gallantine, you got a choice: jail or the military, which is it going to be? So I went into the Marines, and I turned out fine. That's the way they did things back then."

"I know, Sarge, but that's simply not an option here. Times have changed. Richard committed a very serious act of violence to get here. And according to his record he beat up some kids here, is that right?"

He pointed his stubby finger at me to make his point. "That boy may have saved my life that day, Doctor. There was this kid, Ernesto Reyes, I think his name was. He thought he was a tough guy, a gang-banger on the outside. Tried to start that gang crap in here. He had one of his followers start some trouble in class, so the teacher calls me in. And just as I'm putting that kid in a hold, this Reyes creep smacks me in the back of the head with an iron pipe. Just about knocked me out. Suddenly I've got four of these tough-guy kids all whaling on me. You know who steps in then? Cain. He was in that class. It took him all of about thirty seconds to lay these dudes out one after another. Saved my bacon. And what do these administrators do? Punish him. Why? Zero tolerance for fighting! I mean, what the hell?"

"Sarge, is it true you were demoted for your relationship with Richard?"

He nodded. "You heard about that, huh? Look, when I first saw Cain I could tell he was a tough guy and I told him in no uncertain terms, boy, if you're looking for trouble, you come to the right place. I will put you down like the punk you are. Well, once he fought by my side, and I didn't ask him to, he just did it, that was it. We were brothers. I wanted to do something for him. So I brought in a heavy bag and a speed bag so he could work out. That's all. They said I was encouraging him to be violent or some such crap. So they demoted me from chief of the rapid response unit, where I had served with distinction for fifteen years."

"Apparently the therapists are afraid of him. And they say the kids are afraid of him too."

"These kids?" he scoffed. "These kids worship Cain, let me tell you. Hell, that's why the therapists don't like him. He's taught a lot of these kids how to fight. He's given some of these kids more real self-esteem by doing that than all these therapists have with all their cocka-mamie talk sessions. And they can't stand it. That's what's going on here, in my opinion."

"Sarge, does Richard ever talk to you? Has he ever opened up about his past?"

He shrugged. "No, not in so many words."

"How do you mean?"

"Well, I mean he's obviously learned a good bit, like how to fight, how to fix things, do chores and whatnot, and he can read and write, unlike some of the kids here, so that tells me he's had some kind of education from people who know what they're doing."

"But he hasn't told you specifically who these people were, or what his life was like before the incident that brought him here?"

"Well, yeah, I suppose that's right. He's not a yapper, for sure."

"Has he even used or responded to his actual name, Richard Tyler? Or has it all been just Cain?"

He scratched his head. "Well, Cain, I guess."

"Sarge, you've read his file, haven't you?"

"Yes, ma'am."

"You know about how badly he beat that other boy back in Pico County? In an unprovoked attack?"

"He made a mistake," Sarge said. "One mistake, for crying out loud. Besides, that kid was probably a real jerk. His father was a big shot abortionist. Disgusting way to make a living if you ask me. I doubt the apple fell far from the tree."

"Sarge, that kind of talk is not helping your case or Richard's, do you understand?"

"Aw, I was just yapping. Never mind me. Cain never said anything about that."

"Does Richard ever talk about his mother?"

"No, why?"

"The police apparently have a theory that he killed his mother before he attacked the Kernell boy."

"Killed his... Ah, that's bunk. He wouldn't do that. He's a good kid."

"When he was apprehended he had a fresh burn mark on his chest. Did he ever tell you how he got that?"

"No."

"According to the police, it's some kind of cult symbol."

"That's ridiculous. Cain's not in any cult. He's too freaking independent. But give him a chance and he'll be a good Marine. Just like your old man and me. Just give him a chance, Doc."

"Sarge, he's not Cain, he's Richard. The fact that he won't even answer to his real name tells me there's a serious problem."

"Aw, come on, Doctor. It's a nickname, that's all. A lot of kids go by their nickname. Hell, I do."

"Sarge," I said, "I see the tattoo on your forearm. It's a crucifix, isn't it?"

"Yes, ma'am. I am a Christian. Born again. Bible-believing."

"Then you know who the biblical Cain was."

"I do."

"And you've read Richard's file. You know of the incident from when he was a little boy. How he lost his brother. I would think his insistence on being called Cain, this many years later, might concern you."

Sarge lowered his eyes, thinking. He shook his head as if at an impasse. Then he looked at me again. "OK, what do you want me to do?"

"I want you to tell me what it would take to convince Richard to open up and talk to me."

He thought about it for a minute, then shook his head. "The grace of God," he said. "A miracle."

"All right," I said. "Thank you, Sarge. Will you please bring him here now?"

"Sure," he said. He took the door handle then turned back to me. "You know that old movie about Spartacus?"

"Yes. Kirk Douglas."

"You know how when that Roman asked the group who was Spartacus, and all those other guys stood up and said 'I am Spartacus' to cover for him? I guarantee you, these kids would do that for Cain. That's what these people are afraid of."

"Yes, well, if I remember my history correctly, Sarge, the Romans killed Spartacus and crucified all his men. I really don't think that's a productive way to think about Richard."

"Roger that," he said. "OK, I'll get him."

3. Predator

WHEN SARGE LEFT to get Richard Tyler I plugged in my recorder and reviewed his file.

I understood the fear Elton Ricks and the other therapists felt. I understood it only too well. I had been violently assaulted by a disturbed teen I was counseling once. It took a long time to recover from that trauma and get back to work, in part because it overlaid an earlier, hidden trauma that I had never come to grips with.

When I was a young woman I suffered a miscarriage. I say "suffered" now, but back then I wouldn't have used that word. I told myself it was just a common medical event, nothing to worry about, certainly nothing to derail a career, and I dismissed any need to grieve. I got divorced, changed my discipline from surgery to psychiatry and specialized in treating troubled teens. Boys, mostly. Often, boys who had suffered from toxic relationships with their mothers. But it was only after the assault, in counseling, that I realized that I had always seen myself as the mother of a boy. And my mothering instinct, warped as it was by my miscarriage and the grieving process I denied myself, motivated me in my work.

In fact, I wrote about toxic mother-son relationships and their influence on the mental stability and criminality of teenage boys. That book was what prompted Violet Tyler to contact me to help Richard.

After my assault, my own psychiatrist advised against my getting back into this work. But here I am. Aware of my inner motivation, but not beholden to it. I am no one's mother. I offer this autobiographical note only to contextualize Richard Tyler's actions and the likelihood of a hidden motive that may be revealed and successfully treated, and thus deliver him from the hell that is prison.

I do fear, of course, that he may be suffering from a true identity disorder. A lot of kids might play at being Cain for any number of reasons. But to actually believe you're the reincarnation of the first murderer? Religious delusions are not my area of expertise. And treating teenagers is hard enough without having to tiptoe around the sensibilities of the people who hired me to do it.

And what if Richard saw me as a mother figure? That's not unusual with these kids. My own counseling revealed how I would unknowingly act out my own mothering urges with my patients, and I learned how to avoid that. So I would be careful not to exude that with Richard. But what if he did kill his own mother? How dangerous is that for me? I had long felt that nothing in my life, not my miscarriage, my divorce, or the death of my father, was as traumatic as the assault. And yet I could not sanction the idea of asking Sarge or another rapid response unit member to stay with us. It would have to be Richard Tyler and me, alone.

Having spoken with his aunt, Violet Tyler, I had reasons for both comfort and trepidation. Violet had, apparently, raised Richard in the first few years of his life because his mother rejected him. Then, after Richard's younger brother died in an accident, his mother took him away from Harlington. They stayed away without any contact for ten years, when Richard suddenly showed back up in Harlington, by himself and with some indication that he had already begun calling himself Cain.

At that time Sheriff McKenzie, a friend of the Tyler family, was investigating a cult that was suspected of kidnapping and murder. Richard was there for less than a day, but in that time he had some interaction with the cult—and though Sheriff McKenzie and Violet Tyler both called the boy's actions "heroic," their descriptions simply did not seem plausible to me. I wanted Richard to tell me his version.

Then Richard disappeared from their lives as abruptly as he had come. They had no further contact with him until after Richard's assault of the Kernell boy when a Pico County detective contacted Sheriff McKenzie about the cult symbol. Without that, the courts would have processed Richard Tyler as a John Doe, as he had no school record, no medical record, no fingerprints from any juvenile record, no social contacts, and the fact that he would only identify himself as Cain.

An unsolicited tip from a mystery caller led detectives to where he lived in an old trailer nestled in the woods off a remote county road. There was some very odd, and in some cases gruesome, evidence of strange activities that went on there, but investigators could not piece together a clear picture of his life, nor was his mother found.

Richard refused to help himself during the court proceedings, and he refused to acknowledge Sheriff McKenzie and Violet Tyler, both of whom tried their best to convince the court to go easy on the boy.

Violet Tyler dearly loves her nephew and it is not an exaggeration to say she hates Richard's mother and blames all the boy's problems on her. "Absolutely evil" are the words she used to describe her former sister-in-law. However, I've been around quite long enough to realize how skewed perceptions can be when family fault lines reach earthquake conditions. I resolved to take Violet's opinions with a grain of salt until I could get another perspective either from Richard or his mother.

If she's alive, I thought. If Richard had not murdered her. This possibility was beginning to trouble me very deeply. I almost had a panic attack when Sarge knocked on the door.

Sarge didn't introduce us, but just led the boy in and said, "Ma'am, your patient is here."

My heart was pounding. I stood and offered my hand, desperately trying to tamp down the trembling I felt. "Hello," I said as cheerfully as I could, "I'm Doctor Lillian Last. It's nice to meet you."

Richard's hands were large and callused, palm and knuckle, like the hands of an old-time ditch digger or bare-knuckle fighter, and the muscles of his forearms looked like steel cables under the skin. His handshake was a lot like Sarge's, though he did not restrain his power quite as much. It hurt, though I'm relatively sure he didn't intend that. Nor did he introduce himself.

Sarge said, "Do you want me to stay?" and I was just about to respond when I realized he was talking to Richard, not me.

Richard just shook his head, and Sarge left the room and closed the door. "Please," I said, "have a seat."

Of all the teenaged patients I had ever seen, Richard Tyler had by far the hardest, the most severe look about him. All the ways people had described him—seventeen going on thirty-five, tough, strong, fighter, dangerous predator—seemed to fit. He had the bad-boy look that mothers love in their sons and some teenaged girls find irresistible. But I empathized with Elton Ricks and the other therapists. A lot of kids you counsel look anywhere but directly at you. They roll their eyes, look to the side, look up at the ceiling, down at their feet, out the window (that's a favorite), but avoid eye contact. Richard looked directly at you, either right into your eyes or scanning your face and body as if sizing you up as an opponent. It was, to say the least, unsettling.

I have tried hard to forget the boy who assaulted me, to stop projecting his look, his movements, his voice, on my other patients. But alone in that office with Richard Tyler, my fear got the better of me and I recalled him. And I thought: Richard Tyler could do to that boy what that boy did to me. "Cain" was by orders of magnitude more dangerous and intimidating than the boy who nearly killed me.

As I felt the panic grow I became desperate to find something, anything, that would reveal some softness, some humanity in him. I said, "I talked to your Aunt Violet. She says hello."

Immediately his gaze seemed to drift out of its predatory focus, as if he had turned it inward. The faintest hint of a smile appeared, and a small but deep scar on one cheek gave him a dimple there. He turned his head toward the window and said barely above a whisper, "Hello, Aunt Violet."

Elton Ricks had kept the blinds drawn over the window, likely to keep his "clients" from getting distracted with the view. Richard's smile was small comfort to me and I was still feeling trapped, even claustrophobic (which I'm not) in that closed room. I stood and stepped to the window. Then I raised the blinds.

In the west, opposite the rising sun, was a rainbow. Trying to sound light and cheerful I said, "Oh my, look. A rainbow. Isn't it wonderful?" I turned back, fully expecting to meet his predatory glare, but his countenance had utterly changed. Gone was the hard, dangerous man. Here was an innocent five-year-old boy, staring at a rainbow that seemed to fill him with wonder in the purest sense of that word. I just about melted. He could have been my own child.

I had no reason to expect that I would succeed any more than all the others who had tried and failed to convince this troubled young man to reveal his mysteries.

In fact, I quite expected to fail. But before I had even begun to try, with no prompting at all from me, as he stared at the rainbow as if in a trance, Richard Tyler began to talk.

4. River Cat

FIRST OF ALL, I remember the cicadas.

They were those kind that sleep underground for years and years and then pop out all at once. I remember they had a reddish color, with shiny red eyes, and they were everywhere, on the trees, on the ground, even on the surface of the river. They were making a hellish racket, a buzzing coming from all around that was so loud it just about drowned out the sound of the outboard motor on our fishing boat.

There were three of us in the boat: my dad, me, and my little brother. I was four-going-on-five and my brother was one. My mother was on the shore by the edge of the water, drawing. She's an artist. I remember she was wearing a white dress, and she had black hair. She was barefoot, I remember that. It was sunny, blue skies, puffy clouds, warm but not hot.

There were some other people on the riverbank there too, a girl and a couple of adults—a man and a woman. Later on I learned who they were, but that doesn't matter at this point in the telling. Right now, I just want to stick to what's actually in my own memory from that day, just so you can judge if I'm being honest. I'm not shading anything or making up tales to cover for, you know, what somebody else might have done.

I'm not the liar my mother says I am.

I remember my dad was full of what you might call happy energy, taking his boys out fishing for the first time. The river was wide and slow and deep there, and kinda brown and murky in color. There were fish, lots of them. Catfish. You could see them swoop to the surface and grab a cicada in their mouths and then disappear underwater. Some of them hit with a little splash and others took it easy and slow, like they were grazing or something.

"Dad, look!" I said, and I pointed at one after another as they hit the surface. Man, I was so excited, I couldn't sit still.

"River cats," my dad said. I remember him saying that. "River cats."

I was just about as happy as a kid could be, but for having to share the boat with my brother. He was too little to learn to fish. He was a mama's boy. Kinda small and weak and too pretty for a boy. Not rough-and-tumble like me. She loved him and she didn't love me, and I'm not just making that up, even she would tell you that today if you could find her, so it's a straight fact, and I'm here to tell you the truth.

Anyway, I wished it was just me and my dad. I wished my brother wasn't in that boat that day. I wished that every day for a lot of years after that.

So what happened was: Dad was in the back of the boat, leaning over the motor. Not sure, he might have been trying to clear a fishing line or something that had gotten tangled in the propeller, that part I don't exactly know. Anyway, his back was to us and he was paying attention to what he was doing.

My brother was sitting next to me. He had on a little life jacket that didn't fit him well and diapers that didn't fit either. Pretty sure I was out of diapers by his age. Like I said, a mama's boy. Suddenly he stood up in the bottom of the boat and pushed his diaper down and stepped out and at the same time wiggled out of the little life jacket he had on, and he stood there naked in the sun.

"Dad," I said. He glanced over his shoulder at us for just a second.

"Just hold on to him, Son," he said. "I'll be right there."

I grabbed him by his sides. "Stop wiggling, you little jerk," I said. "Aw, come on. Dad!"

"You can do it, Son," he said to me. "You're the strong one."

I loved that. It made me proud. And I was. I was strong. My brother was kinda small and a weakling, even for a one-year-old.

And then my brother stopped wiggling and looked right at me. Big blue eyes, black hair, like my mother. And he kinda got this weird look on his face like something important was about to happen, and he said something. I'll never forget what he said. He said, "Poop!"

He started to squat a little. Oh, no way, man! You're not going to do that right here, not on me, not in the boat, come on! You stupid kid!

And as my Dad leaned over the motor with his back to us he said again in a happy voice, "Just hold on to him for a minute Son, you can do it, you're the strong one."

So here's what I did. I picked him up and I moved him so his behind was hanging over the edge of the boat, you know, so he could poop in the water and not in the boat. But he squirmed and pushed with his legs until his feet dipped into the water. Even so, I could have held him there until he did his business, I'm sure I could have, just to show my dad I could.

And my brother looked at me, right in my eyes with his baby blues and he had a little smile like he loved and trusted his big brother even though I was mad at him. He was a beautiful kid, really. He had my mother's looks.

Then something swirled in the water right next to the boat. At first it looked like a cloud of black water billowing up from the bottom. But then it turned solid and slick and I saw, like, a flash of colored light like a rainbow in the middle of it and too late I saw it had a face and eyes and whiskers and as it broke the surface it opened its mouth real, real wide, wide as a garbage can, and... and it took my brother right out of my hands.

And then down it went. So smooth there was hardly even a splash. That huge, slimy body, long as the boat and wide as I could reach, and the back fin passed and the tail fin gave one swish, and then nothing but a swirl in the water.

And just like that, my brother was gone.

I don't know that I can really tell you how I felt right then. For a while I couldn't yell or even breathe. It was like I was frozen but my skin felt like it was on fire. And then there was this high-pitched sound like a siren going off in my head and I was screaming and stamping my feet so that my dad had to turn around.

"What's wrong?" he said, but I still couldn't make words, I could just point and scream. Then he saw that my brother was missing, and his face twisted all weird and desperate. Like mine, I guess. Finally my words came out: "River cat! River cat took him!" and my dad let out this wild shout and dove into the water.

The people on shore noticed and started yelling. The man there waded into the water, then swam out and grabbed the edge of the boat.

"Hey!" he yelled as my dad surfaced, "What's happening?"

"He fell in!" my dad yelled. "He fell in! Help me find him!" He took a breath and dove under again.

The man told me to sit down, and he swam the boat back toward the shore. When he could stand on the bottom, he shoved the boat toward my mother. She had waded into the water and was screaming, "What's happening? Where's my baby?" Then the man swam back out to help my dad search for my brother.

My mother grabbed me by my arms. Her fingers were like claws digging into my skin. Her face was all, you know, rage and desperation. She shook me and screamed into my face, "Where's my baby? What did you do to him?"

And I just kept bawling, "River cat took him! River cat took him!"

And she was screaming and I was bawling and she yelled, "You go get him back! You go get him back!" and she threw me in the river. I couldn't swim. But the other woman who was there, the woman who was not my mother, she picked me up from the water and carried me to shore. I kept crying, "I'm sorry, I'm sorry, I'm sorry…" She held me tight and pressed her cheek against mine and she kept saying softly, "Hush, now, it's all right, it's all right…"

And as that woman walked up the riverbank I could see my mother splashing in the shallows, following my father and the other man as they kept moving down-river, searching for my brother, and she kept screaming at them, demanding to know what was happening, crying out for her baby.

I was in that nice woman's arms, bawling and saying "I'm sorry" again and again and again, and I was already starting to replay the incident in my mind—as I would a million times in my life. And I was sorry. I really was. It was my fault. I knew it was. I did something really bad. And stupid. I knew I'd be in big, big trouble. My poor little brother. I was the strong one, I should have protected him.

Man, I was wailing. "He said poop! I'm sorry, I'm sorry, I'm sorry…"

But with all that horribleness, whenever I replayed that scene in my mind, one strange and special thing stuck out. That fish had a mark on its face. A rainbow that ran from one eye over to the other eye in a smooth curve. A perfect rainbow with all the colors and everything. It was brilliant, man, and it shined like it had its own light. You could say it was just the sunlight shining on it or whatever, or maybe the kind of thing you see when there's oil in a rain puddle on the street. Catfish skin is kinda oily, they say.

But it wasn't that. It was a mark on the fish. Nobody ever heard of a river cat with such a mark, but this one had it, right between the eyes. I saw it flash underwater just before the fish broke the surface. And I would think a million times that it was that rainbow mark that made me freeze, like it hypnotized me or something, and that's why I hesitated instead of jerking my brother back into the boat. After all, it didn't move all that fast. It wasn't like a barracuda or a shark, it was almost, I don't know, lazy.

I hated ever to admit it, but that rainbow was really beautiful.

Don't get me wrong. I never lost the feeling that it was my fault. I mean, I was supposed to be the strong one.

The woman carrying me stopped and turned to face the river, mostly so I wouldn't have to look at it. But I saw her. My mother. Kneeling in the river water. Wailing. She turned to look my way. People always said my mother was beautiful. But you don't know what ugly is until you see the way she looked at me.

Let me tell you something, I held tight onto that rainbow in my mind, tighter even than I held onto the woman who was carrying me. I know it was you, Aunt Violet. Now I do. I didn't then, or for a long time after. I just wish you would have kept walking up the riverbank and never came back.

5. Infection

FOR A WHILE AFTER THAT DAY, a lot of people asked me a lot of questions about what happened to my brother. A bunch of annoying adults in suits or robes or uniforms and no matter how many times I told them, "river cat took him," they always just twisted the question a little this way or that and asked it again.

At first I tried to get them to understand. "Well how long was it?" Long as the boat. "Well how big was its mouth when it opened it?" Big as a garbage can. "And the fish took him after you dropped him in the water?" No, it took him right out of my hands! Ask my dad, he was there! Where's my dad? Where is he?

So I clammed up when I realized they didn't believe me, and they clammed up whenever I asked about my dad. And my dad didn't come to help me. I was desperate for him to come and help me, but he didn't.

My mother was there, though. Crying, sobbing, yelling at people, yelling at me, cursing my dad who wasn't there, breaking things, chasing other people away, lying on her bed, sometimes moaning for her lost baby, sometimes just lying there with her eyes open like she was dead.

She wasn't like those other adults who tried to tiptoe around my feelings. "Stop lying!" she'd say to me. "That didn't happen! He was my miracle baby! Things like that don't happen to miracle babies, they only happen to bad boys like you! You know what happened, you know what happened and you're going to tell the judge, do you understand? Your father murdered my baby because he was jealous! And you, you lousy, rotten little boy, you're covering for him with that stupid fish story because you're jealous too, you're jealous of your brother!"

At first when she did that, I'd cry. "No, Mom, river cat took him, river cat took him..."

And she'd press her palms over her ears and yell, "Shut up, shut up, shut up! You're lying! You're lying! Stop it..."

"Where's Dad, Mom? I want my dad..."

"Your father is wherever men who murder their children go. He should be in jail, but they can't put him in jail because of you and your lies! Stop covering for him! Stop lying!"

I'd be bawling by then. "It's true, Mom, river cat took him..."

She screamed and started crying real hard, like the sobbing a little child would do, like I did when she yelled at me, and when she could get the words out she said, all whiny and pitiful, "Why are you doing this? Why? Can't you see you're hurting your mommy? You put this... this terrible, ugly thing in my head and I... I can't get it out... I can't... You were supposed to protect your little brother. You were the strong one. Why didn't you protect him?" And she'd go into her bedroom and shut the door, and I could hear her in there mourning her baby, and I was out there all by myself.

And then my mother left. Not for a long time, but for a bunch of days, I think, maybe a week. In that time the nice lady who comforted me at the river took care of me. It was all white clouds and blue sky and easy breathing then, you know? But then something happened, and I know you didn't mean it to, Aunt Violet, I mean, it wasn't your fault, but, well...

I think it was some kid's birthday party or something, I can't really remember. We went out to a restaurant. It had dragon designs and colorful lanterns and all that. The smell was wonderful. We were all standing there in the entrance area, waiting to be seated. I was in the back of the group. And in front of me there was a tall man and he was holding a little girl in the crook of one arm. She was no more than two years old, I would guess.

A couple of adults moved to go to their table and that's when I saw the big fish tank. It had a light in it and a fake castle and pretty rocks and stuff, and bubbles. I saw a couple of great big colorful fish swimming in it— one was gold and another was white with red splotches.

And then I saw the dull gray one just lying on the bottom. It had wide set eyes and a wide mouth and long dark whiskers. A catfish. And up above I saw the little girl the man was holding. She had a small plastic baby doll in her hand and she was kinda waving it over the top of the fish tank.

The little girl dropped her doll in the water. It bobbed on the surface. The little girl reached down for it and as she did, the catfish rose toward it and opened its mouth.

It was like I had some kinda spasm, man, I mean, it was like electricity, like being shocked. I screamed. I ran up and heaved my body against the man to shove him away from the fish tank. I hit him so hard in the leg his knee buckled and he fell against the tank and the tank toppled over and smashed on the ground and all the water and fish spilled out. And that catfish on the carpet started walking on its spiky fins right toward me, right across the broken glass, writhing its body with this slurp-thunk, slurp-thunk kind of noise.

I must have looked like I was possessed by demons or something, the way I was carrying on. They took me to the hospital in an ambulance. The doctor said it was a panic attack, but they couldn't let me go with the people who brought me, since they weren't my parents. And you tried and tried to find my father, but finally had to contact my mother to come get me.

And my mother did come, from wherever she had been. I hated seeing her walk toward where we were in the emergency room. And she took me home. And that was the last time I saw you for a long, long time, Aunt Violet. A long, long time.

My mother seemed to be a lot calmer than when she left. Maybe she was medicated, I don't know. Her voice sounded kinda like she was on drugs or something. But we were there in our house, just me and her. She told me to sit down in front of the TV. She said, "Now. You have a certain fear, and you have given that fear to me. Like an infection. And this fear is preventing you from telling the truth, and it's... Well, it's very hard for your

mommy. My therapist says that the only way to over-
come a fear is to confront it. And that's what we're going
to do. You and I. Together."

She turned the TV on and started a program. Then
she went about turning off all the lights in the house. It
was night out, so the house was really dark except for the
TV light. I couldn't read back then, but the narrator's
voice was saying the show was going to bring us into "the
strange world of walking catfish."

"Now," she said, "all the experts that have looked into
our case have said that it is impossible that a catfish
could have... done what you say. It's simply impossible.
They don't get that big, for one thing. Especially not in
this river... it simply doesn't have... the capacity... to sus-
tain... a fish of that... that size. Somebody else would
have seen it. People fish in that river all the time. And
no one else has ever seen it. Nobody. Ever. So... we'll
just watch this documentary and... you will see that real
catfish are just... our friends. They're nice. They don't
hurt people. And when we're done, maybe you can tell
the truth about... about what happened... to your
brother."

As soon as the program started, my mother sounded
like she was about to vomit, and she said, "You go ahead
and watch this. I'll be right back," and she ran into the
bathroom.

I don't know how long I watched it. Not very. Because pretty soon it showed this catfish swimming in a
pond. And it swam up to the bank, and it just kept going,
right across the mud and onto the grass with this slurp-

thunk, slurp-thunk kind of movement I saw at the restaurant. And what made it worse, the cameraman must
have been walking backwards right in front of the catfish
because it looked like the catfish was walking right toward me and in a second was going to walk right into the
living room and gobble me up.

I panicked again. I screamed and bull rushed the TV
and knocked it over. It crashed and broke on the floor,
and I tripped and fell on top of it, and I sliced both my
palms when I put my hands out, you know, like, by reflex. It was completely dark then, and I was crying out,
"Mom! Mom!" and feeling all over the walls for the light
switch.

It seemed like it took her forever to come out. Finally,
the lights came on and my mother was there, yelling, and
her voice wasn't druggy any more, it was sharp and angry, and she said, "What? What is wrong with you?"

And I stood there, crying. My hands hurt really bad.
I looked down and saw the blood, and it was all red and
oozing, and I squealed like a little pig and cried harder.
I held my bloody hands out toward my mother. Like any
five-year-old would.

But she wasn't looking at me. She was looking at the
walls. It looked like a crime scene. Dozens of bloody
little handprints that I made as I was searching for the
light switch, and long smears of blood, all over her nice
white walls.

Finally I guess she noticed me. "Come with me," she
said. She sounded annoyed, like I was taking her from
something more important.   We went into the

bathroom. She got out some bandages and ointment and dropped them on the counter by the sink. "Wash your hands with soap and water first," she said. "Then dry them. Put some of this ointment on and then put the bandages on."

She turned to leave. "Mom, can you do it for me?" I said with those catching breaths little kids have when they sob.

"No." She walked out. Left me there by myself.

Five years old, give or take, and I bandaged my own hands. It wasn't easy. But in my mind, I heard my father say, "You're the strong one." And I did it. When I came out of the bathroom she was kinda pacing with her arms crossed or her hands on her hips, back and forth, back and forth, studying the bloody handprints like she was in a museum, looking at a painting.

She turned and looked at me, but different this time. I thought she'd be angry. She wasn't. "You did this," she said.

"I'm sorry, Mom, I'm sorry..."

And the way she looked at me was so weird, almost like something good had happened, like she suddenly got some idea, and she said, "Go to bed. I need to go out for something."

And just like that, she left me alone in that house with my own bloody handprints and my bandaged hands. I cried for a while, and then I felt really, really tired. I went into my bedroom, lay down on my bed, and spent the rest of the night trying to run away from walking river cats in my dreams and winding up in a place with blood on the walls.

I guess they were dreams. Maybe not, though. Given what I was about to wake up to, I mean.

6. The Red House

WHEN I WOKE UP THE NEXT MORNING, all the walls and ceiling of my bedroom were blood red and there was a bad smell in the air. I just about panicked. I thought the river cat tore me to pieces sometime during the night and sprayed the whole room with my blood. I mean every square inch of the room except the floor was red.

I pushed to sit up and my hands stung bad. I looked at my hands. Some blood had soaked through my bandages and crusted, but not that much. I touched my body and legs, and I was actually surprised to find everything intact.

I went out into the hallway. Everything was red there too. And in the living room, and the kitchen.

Finally I went to my mother's room but her door was locked so I knocked and called out, "Mom!... Mom!" but she wouldn't get up. I tried to go outside, but my hands hurt and I couldn't grip the doorknobs. I tried the windows, but they were jammed shut too.

I'd call out, "Dad!" Nothing. And I'd call out "Mom!" Nothing. And I'd do it again and again, until finally my mother cracked her door open. And I could see that her room was still white, the only place in the house that wasn't red.

"Mom!" I said, "What's going on? Where are we?"

She just said, "This is what it was like for your little brother, to live and die inside your river cat. How do you like it?"

"I hate it!"

"So does he. So you should let him out."

"I don't understand, Mom!"

"Stop saying river cat took him. Start telling the truth. Your father killed him because he was jealous. That's all. Tell the truth. That's all I want. And I'll let you out."

I was bawling, "OK, OK, OK, I will, I will..." but I couldn't. As much as I wanted to get out, I couldn't. Whenever I started to talk about it, I sank right into the memory, like it was really happening all over again, and the truth just tumbled out. I couldn't help it. No matter how hard I tried, I couldn't lie about it.

And so I stayed in the red house until I thought I was going crazy. Days. Weeks. Months I was locked up in that red house. I begged my mother, I pleaded with her to let me out. I had nightmares about the walking catfish. Every time it rained or the wind made tree branches rub against the house, I thought it was the walking catfish out there, coming to get me. I looked out the window just to get some color in my eyes and to watch for my dad. I still hoped he'd come and get me.

One day my mother saw me staring out the window like that. The next day she dyed all the windowpanes red.

You know what it's like living like that? Red. Red, red, red, everywhere, all the time. I bet you don't. I wouldn't wish it on you or anybody.

I don't know why I didn't just pick up a skillet and throw it through a window to get some light or to escape. I'd end up breaking plenty of things when I was older, but I guess I just didn't think of it back then. Five years old. I had already broken the TV so I couldn't watch it. I'd daydream. Or, I'd try to. But my mind always went to the same time and place. And as bad as it was, remembering how I lost my little brother and how all my mother's sadness and anger was my fault, I'd feel that nice woman holding me and telling me it would be all right, and I'd see that rainbow, and it would give me a little peace.

When she was in the house, my mother mostly stayed in her white room and left the red house to me. But that didn't make it any easier on her. She still cried and moaned all the time, or lay there like she was dead, or yelled out, all angry and cussing my dad and his family and God and everybody.

I could tell she was having problems with people on the outside. She spent a lot of time on the phone, arguing with them. I wasn't sure what it was all about, but I got the feeling that someone was going to come for me. Maybe my dad. Maybe you, Aunt Violet. And then the day came that my mother suddenly slammed the phone down and said, "That does it! We're leaving!" And she told me to go get my clothes and stuff and put them in the car.

I wanted nothing more than to get out of the red house, but she was really angry, and I was worried. I said, maybe for the last time, "Mom, where's Dad? I want my dad!"

And she said, "Your father is a crazy man. He has gone totally insane. He's a wild man, an animal. He's not going to help you. Ever. Now load the car like I said."

I went about it slowly, back and forth between my room and the car in the garage, but my mother was in a fury, just dumping everything into the car in a huge clutter, creating mounds of stuff in the trunk and on the seats.

That night my mother was outside when I heard her scream and yell at somebody. She ran into the house and locked the doors. She yelled out, "I'm calling the cops!" and she got on the phone, and soon was yelling at the dispatcher to send the police.

Somebody outside began shaking the door handles, trying to get in. He was yelling like he was hoarse and I couldn't make out any of the words or even recognize the voice.

I kinda crept up to a window and peeked out but I couldn't see anything through the red tint. Suddenly whoever it was slapped the windowpane with his hand. I fell backward and crabbed away. Then he slammed his fist right through the window. Shattered glass rained onto the ground at my feet. I screamed.

The man yelled something that sounded like, "Raahhh-raaarrrhh..." and reached in through the broken pane to fumble for the latch. Just then the flashing lights of the patrol car came, and I could hear them yell as they rushed at the man and pulled him away. I could hear them scuffling in the bushes. Then the commotion drifted away and I heard car doors slam, and the patrol car drove away. It was quiet again.

My mother was standing there, breathing hard and shaking. She looked at me and said. "Get in the car. We're leaving."

"Where are we going?"

She didn't answer me. I honestly did not know if that was my dad outside the house that night. If it was, then my mother was right. He was crazy, and wild. If not, then... I don't know. I didn't know what to think. My brain was fried. Five years old, man, going on six. It was too much. I was exhausted. I needed to get out of that red house no matter what or with who.

So I got in the car. I got in the car with my mother, and we left that red house and that town and that whole scene. If I only knew what I'd be getting into, maybe... I don't know. What could I know? I was just a stupid little kid.

7. New Nod

WE DROVE A LONG, LONG TIME. I was so happy to be in the colors of the world again, I just watched the world go by, seemed like for hours.

We drove into a bad storm, and she finally pulled over into a rest stop and laid her head back and took a nap. There was a family in a van parked down the lot a ways, and they looked nice and happy. They reminded me of the nice family I was with when I had my first panic attack at the restaurant. I looked at my mom and I thought, I don't want to be with her. I got this real strong urge to sneak out of the car and go to that family, tell them I was lost or something, maybe they'd take me back to where I was from. To my dad, or to you, Aunt Violet, though I didn't remember you then. I went so far as to start turning the door handle.

But it had stopped raining and all of a sudden, there was a rainbow in the sky. Huge and beautiful and glimmering. I stared at it like some kind of gift from heaven, and I didn't even know about heaven then. It just, I don't know, filled me with peace, I guess. And I looked at my mom and she seemed peaceful, and I didn't hate her. And I got this feeling, like, everything's going to be OK. And I didn't open the door.

My mother woke up and we kept driving and driving and then at some point we pulled off the main roads and onto some back roads that snaked around through the country until finally she pulled off onto a dirt driveway and drove up to this junky old trailer in the woods. We got out.

Then she turned toward me and she said, "So what you're telling me is you killed your brother."

I said, "What?"

"You say your dad didn't do it. You say you picked him up on purpose and you held him over the side of the boat on purpose and then a giant fish just came up and took him, just like that, like you just gave my baby to that fish. So you did it. It's your fault. That's what you're saying."

Maybe I should have denied it, or said it was an accident or something, but the fact is I always felt real guilty about it and I knew it was my fault because I was the strong one and I should have protected my little brother.

So I just dropped my head and I said, "I'm sorry, Mom."

She stood there with her hands on her hips glaring at me. "You're sorry. That's just great. You killed your little brother. That's what you're telling me. You, not your father, you. OK, fine. That's just fine. Do you know what they call boys who do that? Your father's family, those religious idiots, they have a name for people like you. For boys who kill their brothers. Do you know what it is?"

I shook my head no.

"Cain." She stood there and let it sink in. "Cain," she said again like it should have meant something to me, but it didn't. "In their stupid storybook, Cain killed his little brother, you know why? Because he was jealous of him, that's why. Cain's little brother was pure and good, just like your little brother was pure and good.

"And then guess what happened to Cain," she said. "He had to leave his home and go far away. He couldn't have any friends or nice things. Everybody hated him. People wanted to kill him for what he did. He had to be a fugitive and a wanderer forever."

I guess my lip started to tremble or something. She said, "Don't give me that crap.

You confessed to killing your brother, you killed my precious baby. So until you convince me that you lied, until you tell me the truth and not some stupid fish story, you will stay here, this will be your prison, and you will not be allowed to have any friends or any nice things, do you understand? No friends, no school, no toys, no nothing. You will be Cain. From now on that's your name. Cain."

I don't know why that hurt so much, but I started to cry. "No, Mom, that's not my name, my name is..." And I swear to you I could not remember my own name. And that just made me cry harder.

She looked at me like she had just made some kind of breakthrough. "Cain," she said. "You are Cain." From that day on, that's the only name she ever called me by.

She walked into the trailer, slammed the door behind her. I stood there trying like hell to remember my name, but every time I dug into my memory to fetch it, it came all unraveled in the red house. Just like I couldn't remember it was you on that riverbank, Aunt Violet. That damn red house. It's hard. It's real hard.

Anyway, so we moved into this crummy little trailer in the sticks. My mother called the place "New Nod" for some reason. Put a little sign with that name above the door, though I couldn't read it then. To this day I don't know how she found the trailer or what exactly brought her to that spot, but when you're little you don't think of things like that anyway. It was just home.

I got a little room on one end of the trailer with a bare light bulb in the ceiling and a window that wouldn't lock. I slept on blankets on the floor. My mother's room was on the other side of the trailer, and it had a proper bed and furnishings. But at least she didn't paint the place red, I was real glad about that.

She did something kinda similar, though. She threw out a bunch of my clothes that were dark colors, and she brought home some used things that were all white. Like especially a couple of overalls that were too large for me. And then she dyed them all orange. I asked her why, and she said, "Prisoners wear orange, Cain, so people know they're criminals and they're bad." And that's all she said about it, and I never asked any more. From that day on for a long time I just wore prison clothes.

She put me to work, for sure. She told me to do all kinds of chores at the trailer, cleaning and cooking and whatnot, and not to leave the place, because prisoners aren't allowed to go anywhere.

I was actually thankful to my mother for moving us out of the red house. I mean, dingy as it was, that trailer was paradise compared to the red house. And I tried to show her I was thankful. I did my chores, and I got real good at them too, but I was always an outdoors kid and I promised myself I'd never get stuck in a place like the red house ever again. My mom would lock the doors with padlocks on the outside but my bedroom window wouldn't latch and she hated coming into my room anyway, so I came and went through the window while she was gone.

So I explored. First just around the trailer, but as time went by, farther and farther out. I mostly stuck to the woods and fields and places where there weren't any people, since my mother had me believing they'd try to kill me if they saw me since I was a fugitive and prisoner and brother-killer and whatnot. I always took a kitchen knife with me, just in case I met up with a walking catfish, which I still had a real fear of. And I'd climb trees and throw rocks—I discovered I had a good arm, strong and accurate enough to hit a bird or a squirrel on occasion.

That went on a good long while. I couldn't read a calendar but seasons came and went, I know that. As for my mother, well, she left me home alone while she went out in the car, and sometimes she'd bring home groceries, but never any people, no friends or anything like that.

All that time, I don't think my mother had a job. Maybe she had money saved up from where we lived before, I don't know. She tried to do her art, but there's no way she could have made any money at it, not then.

She'd start a drawing and then she'd get all angry and she'd rip it up or stomp it into the ground. Every time.

First time she seemed to be able to finish one was kinda weird. It wasn't a drawing or a painting, more like a sculpture. She made me help, and I was real glad to, you know, it was almost like a real family thing, my mother and I doing something together like that, and I figured if I helped her maybe she wouldn't have to stomp it into the ground, maybe she'd be happy, maybe she'd love me for it.

She brought home this book and a balloon and she blew up the balloon and she took some flour and water and made some white gooey stuff like paste. And then she'd tear a bunch of pages out of the book and she'd hand them to me and make me tear them into strips. And every time she'd hand me a stack of pages she'd say here's the book of this or that. For some reason I can remember a couple: Book of Genesis, Book of Exodus... those were the only two I remember, there were a whole bunch and I lost track. And after I tore them into strips she dipped them into the white paste and stuck them onto the balloon. And when she was finished she said, "and now we have the Book of Cain."

And it looked just like a catfish. She even painted it, only not gray like a catfish, but orange like my clothes. And then she gave me a stick and tied my leg to something so I couldn't get away, and she dangled that fish over a tree limb by a rope and kinda jerked it around, and I had to hit it, and I was scared of that thing, like, terrified, and I beat it real hard and it broke open and out fell a bunch of little plastic baby dolls. And I just kinda looked at them, they were just like the baby doll that the little girl dropped into the fish tank at the restaurant before the red house.

My mother had been laughing and yelling, like, "Kill that fish, little Cain! Kill it!" And then when I busted it open and all the little dolls fell out she stopped laughing and she fell down and she was crying real hard. You know, sobbing like a little child. And she scooped up the baby dolls in her arms and cried some more.

I felt real sorry for her, but I felt, I don't know, real, real angry too, and I got the urge to... I don't know, put her out of her misery, or mine, maybe. I had the stick in my hands and my blood was pumping, man. It felt good to bash that fish open like that. I can't tell you how good that felt. I guess I got the urge to bash my mother with it. I guess that's the truth of it.

It was a cloudy day, and pretty windy and warm, I guess it was summer. You know the kind of crazy weather you get in the summer sometimes. And suddenly it rained pretty hard but just for a little while, a minute or so, and then the wind blew the clouds apart and my mother was sitting there in the mud holding her baby dolls and crying and I raised the stick and I'm pretty sure I would have hit her. And she looked at me like she wanted me to hit her. She wanted me to end it for her.

But it happened again. I saw the rainbow. And the rainbow wouldn't let me. All that poison just drained out of me. I stood there looking at that rainbow a long time, until it went away, wherever it is rainbows go. And when I looked down again my mother was gone. She had gone into the house to lie down. She had one of her headaches that lasted a long time. The balloon fish got all wet in the rain and it came apart. So it got destroyed same as all her other artwork.

You asked me about this scar on my cheek, Aunt Violet. It had to do with another piece of my mother's art. I helped her with it, too. This one she ended up keeping. I promised I'd tell you about it, so here it is.

8. Hooked

ONE DAY, I RECKON I WAS SEVEN, maybe close to eight—I
don't know, we didn't celebrate birthdays and I didn't go
to school, and my birthday was one of the things I lost in
the red house—anyway, I was out exploring and I got
pretty deep in the woods when I took a step and the
ground gave way under my foot.

I gave a shout and backed away from it, then I looked
around like anybody would when they don't want to get
found out. I was at a place where the woods opened into
a little meadow full of sawgrass and thistles and wild-
flowers, and on the other side of the meadow was a tiny
old abandoned house with broken windows and weeds
growing in the gutters.

I had stepped on an old piece of plywood that had gotten covered over with leaves. Underneath the plywood
it was really wet and my shoe and sock were drenched,
and it smelled horrible. I let my curiosity get the better
of me, I guess, and I shoved the plywood aside.

There was a big hole, I don't know, maybe three feet
by six feet or so, and it was full of this dank, nasty water
with scum on top. I found a stick and dipped it in an
arm's length or so and did not hit the bottom. And that's
when I thought, man, if there's a place in the whole
world where a walking catfish would come out of, this
was it. So I started to run off, but then I remembered

the plywood and I went back and shoved it back over the hole.

I was terrified. I just knew that it went deep into the earth and all the way back to the river and some night a 500-pound walking catfish would come slurping out of it and follow my tracks to my home. I just knew it.

I just didn't know it would be that night. I know, you're probably not going to believe this, but it's true.

That evening came a big storm that lasted most of the night. Thunder, lightning, wind, hard rain, the works. I didn't sleep a wink. And then the winds died down, the thunder got more distant, and the rain got soft. And then it was quiet. And I lay there and I listened. For a long while I didn't hear anything and I think I was just on the verge of drifting off when I heard it. Slurp-thunk, slurp-thunk, first dim then stronger, stopping and starting, stopping and starting, and as it got closer, the sound of twigs breaking and branches moving.

Any normal kid would have been able to run to his normal mother and jump in her arms, but I had to lie there, crying, and trying to do it without making a sound, and squeezing my kitchen knife so hard my hands trembled.

There was a weird sound like breathing, or wheezing more like it, as if the thing was tuckered out from being so long out of the water. I lay there staring up at the window, quiet and still as I could be. And then the thing started moving again, and its slurp-thunk, slurp-thunk kinda trailed off and then was gone.

It's going away, I thought, and I cried for a while, and that let out the tension a good bit. And then the dawn broke and the morning light came in my little window and I was never so happy to see it.

I stayed in my room for a while after the sun rose, just in case, then I got up, unjammed my door and tiptoed out. My mother's bedroom door was open. She was still asleep.

As I watched her I realized something. I had missed an opportunity. Instead of cringing and crying in my bed last night I could have taken that knife and gone outside and I could have killed that fish when it was right outside my window. I could have been the strong one. I might even have been able to cut my little brother's skeleton out of it. Sure'nuff, that would show my mom.

Then I thought, maybe it's not too late, you know? I put on my clothes and shoes and I grabbed that knife and I went outside.

It took a while of looking, but I found the tracks, or what I figured were the tracks. Something really big had slithered to the house from the direction of that plywood-covered hole in the woods. I could see a big mark right under my window where something had been. But the tracks didn't go back where they came from. They went in a different direction.

"You are the strong one." That's one thing I could pull right out of my memory, and in my dad's voice, too. I held the knife out in front of me. I took a deep breath and a step, then another and another, following the slithering track and looking all around to see if I could spot the river cat as I went.

I followed those tracks through the woods past where I had explored before. I was in new territory. Everything was still drenched from the storm, and sometimes I'd think I'd lost the track in some stretch of rocky ground, but then I'd always pick it up again on the other side.

I was looking real close at one place on the ground that had the clearest track I had yet seen. And then I heard something. A soft sound like a wheezing a little ways away.

I glanced forward and I saw a narrow stretch of mown grass and a concrete curb. Then a blacktop parking lot. And there were a bunch of cars in the parking lot. And there across the parking lot was a little white church with stained glass windows and a high-pitched roof and a steeple with a cross on top.

The wheezing sound was coming from inside. I listened for a bit and realized there was singing too. I sat there all wet and muddy and I took it in. I never remembered going to church, and really, I didn't even know it was a church at the time, but I got the real strong feeling I had been in this kind of place before and it was nice.

Still, it was a strange sight, especially the stained glass windows. It was still pretty early and the sun was low and on the other side of the church, and the sunlight was coming through, shining through the windows from the other side.

I wanted to get a better look so I snuck across the parking lot between the cars, closer to the side of the church. One window, in fact one place on that window in particular, seemed to just draw me, like I couldn't look away.

I was right underneath it when I realized what it was. A fish, or rather a simple figure in the outline of a fish, like a cartoon fish. And I stared at it amazed, and I even wondered if the river cat had left it there as a clue. It was way on the bottom of the window, not much higher than eye-level where I stood and as I stared at it suddenly I became aware that it was staring back.

It had an eye. A real eye, and it was looking back at me and moving and then it blinked. I jumped back and fell on my behind, and that's when I saw the whole face of the kid on the other side of the window laughing at me.

I was caught. I ran into the parking lot and hid behind a car. And there it was again. This car was a van with a door on the back and there was a dent in that door and right there in the dent was another one of those fish symbols. I couldn't believe it. It was about the size of my hand and made of some kind of silvery metal or plastic and was just dangling there by one little nub.

I heard the church doors open and voices of people starting to spill out into the parking lot. I grabbed the fish symbol and pulled it off the car. Then I turned and ran into the woods and all the way back home.

My mother was up, sitting at the kitchen table when I got back. She saw it even before I moved to hide it behind my back. "What have you got there?" she said.

I shrugged and shook my head.

"Put it on the table," she said.

I was still carrying the knife so I placed it on the table. "Not that," she said. "The other thing." I pulled it out from behind my back and I looked at it for a moment, then I set it on the kitchen table. I expected her to get angry and yell at me, but she didn't. When she spoke her voice was low and soft.

"Where did you get that?" she said.

"I don't know."

"It's not nice to lie to your mother."

Her tone was so unusual, so soft and easy, I didn't clam up. Instead I blurted out, "It was a white house with colored windows. And there was this broken car..."

"They call that a church, dear," she said softly. She never, ever, ever called me anything sweet like that. It almost made me melt. "You've been to church, you know, a long time ago," she went on. "When you were little."

"Can we go again, Mom? There's kids there too."

"Do you know what that fish symbol means?" she said.

I shook my head.

"Do you want to know?"

I nodded.

She smiled. My mother smiled at me. She did. And she was beautiful. And I was happy. "You wait here, dear," she said.

She went into her bedroom. I heard her rummaging in her drawers for a bit and when she returned to the kitchen both her hands were closed like she was holding something in each one. She sat down in a chair and told me to stand in front of her. She was still smiling this sort of easy smile.

"I'm going to show you how I learned about that fish symbol," she said. "Now close your eyes and open your mouth... Oh, go on, you can trust your mama. Close your eyes and open your mouth."

I felt like I was on a roll, I guess. I got through the storm, the walking catfish hadn't eaten me, the morning was beautiful, I was brave enough to follow what I feared, and lucky enough to find that pretty little church, and now my mother was smiling. At me. Good God, smiling at me. It was a new day. I closed my eyes and opened my mouth.

She said, "In your father's religion, which is called Christianity, they like to call themselves fishers of men. And what they do first is they give you something sweet."

She put something in my mouth. I tasted it with my tongue first, and sure enough it tasted sweet. It was a jelly bean. I chewed it up and swallowed it and laughed as I opened my eyes. It had been so long since I had a piece of candy.

"Oops, don't open your eyes yet," she said. I closed them again and opened my mouth. "Because fishers of men have patience and they want to make sure you're really, really tempted by their kindness." And she put something else in my mouth. It was a malted milk ball covered in chocolate and I just had to giggle from the way it melted in my mouth as I sucked on it.

My mother giggled softly with me and said, "Now keep your eyes closed because there's more to come. OK, now, open your mouth again."

I did. I closed my eyes and opened my mouth. Let me tell you I was a happy kid.

"Yes, those church people, those Christians, you know those people in your father's family, they're all church-going Christians, and they gave me sweet, sweet things, just like I gave you, and now I'll give you what they gave me, and this one they said was the best of all, way better than jelly beans and chocolate. Are you ready? Here it is..."

I don't know how to describe it, Aunt Violet, I really don't. The pain, I mean. How bad it was. And sudden. Like hornets, or a copperhead, I don't know, a black widow. Right in my cheek, so bad my knees buckled and I screamed and opened my eyes. My mother was backing away from me and there was a string going from her hand to my cheek and she was shouting, "Blood of the lamb, boy, blood of the lamb! You like the taste of that? Isn't it sweet?"

And then she yelled, "Fishers of men! Hey, we caught another one, let's reel the little sinner in!" and she gave a yank on the string that pulled on my face.

There was something hard in my mouth like a piece of metal and I reached up with my hand to find a sharp point on the outside of my cheek. I was trying to scream, "Stop, mama, stop!" but I couldn't make out clear words. Then I tasted something hot and definitely not sweet in my mouth and I saw all the blood on my hand. In my panic I tried to turn and run but the string pulled on my mouth and I couldn't go anywhere.

My mother was standing across the room holding the string taut, still yelling "fishers of men, fishers of men, reel'em in, reel'em in!" I grabbed the string in my fist and pulled back. Then I saw the kitchen knife I had laid on the table. I grabbed it and cut the string and tumbled backward. I could feel the metal thing on my tongue and clacking against my teeth and I ran from the kitchen into the bathroom and shut and locked the door.

I think there was only one thing that kept me from passing out from the pain and panic. Whatever it was in my mouth, I had to get it out. There was a little footstool under the sink so I pulled it out and climbed up on it to look in the mirror. My eyes were so full of tears, I couldn't see clearly, so I rubbed them with the back of my hands, but that just smeared blood in them and made it worse.

I fought through the panic and trembling, and I pulled a washrag from the sink and wiped my eyes with it. There was blood all over my face and neck and down my shirt. Then I saw the fish hook. Great big one. Piercing my cheek from inside out. The sight of it made me sick to my stomach. My tears really started flowing, and

I had to wipe them away again. I was wailing. I didn't know what to do.

"You're the strong one." It was like my memory pushed my dad's words up just then. I stared at my face in the mirror and I started to get angry. I reached up to touch the fishhook, but my hand was shaking too much, so I rested it on the sink again and waited, trying to settle down.

Then I raised my hand again, still shaking but not so bad, and I pinched the hook with my fingers where it was sticking out of my cheek. Just touching it made the pain stab through my whole face and down my neck. I saw right away the hook had a huge sharp barb on it and I wouldn't be able to back it out the way it went in. So I started drawing it out the other way. It hurt like anything and my tears welled up again, but then it stopped. Inside my mouth the loop in the top of the hook where she tied the string was bigger than the hole in my cheek and didn't want to slide through easily. A couple of times I started to pull on it and it wouldn't come through.

I started to cry more. I didn't think I'd ever get it out. I almost called my mother for help, but I knew she wouldn't and that made me angrier. So I put my finger in the bend of the hook outside my cheek, I took a deep breath, and I gave one big heave. It came through. It was finally out. I pulled some more until the rest of the string was all through and I threw the hook aside.

I don't think I had been so angry in my whole life. I didn't really think about what I was doing. I picked up the kitchen knife that I had dropped on the floor and I went out of the bathroom to hunt my mother. As I stepped into the kitchen I slipped on my own blood on the floor and fell on my butt.

I got back up. The door leading from the kitchen outside was open, and I pushed the screen door and stepped out. My mother was sitting in a lawn chair with a drawing pad on her knee and a pencil in her hand. Her back was to me.

I squeezed the handle of the knife as I approached her. When I was standing right behind her I raised the knife above my shoulder, and just as I was about to ram it down, I saw it.

A rainbow. For real, I'm not making this up. A rainbow, big and bright and clear in the sky. You can say it was just another coincidence if you want to, nothing special, just a regular old natural thing seeing as how we just had a storm not too many hours before, but let me tell you it saved my mother's life and I doubt she even saw it. I don't think I could have killed her with a stick that time before, back when she made the Book of Cain. But a knife? A knife would have done the job.

Let me tell you something. If it wasn't for that rainbow, my mother would have been dead. I'd have murdered her.

But you know what? The anger drained out of me, and all that was left was the pain. I breathed in one of those choking kind of breaths you get when you've been crying real hard. And the blood in my mouth went down my windpipe and I coughed, and when I did I sprayed my blood on her clean drawing pad.

I dropped the knife on the ground and went back in the bathroom and I spit in the sink until my wound stopped bleeding. That took a good long while. I had a bad headache along with the throbbing in my cheek and I went to my room to lie down.

I jammed the wedge under my door so she couldn't come in. My mother didn't treat my wound or take me to the hospital, so naturally I got an infection which just about killed me.

My face swelled and turned colors and hurt like hell for a good while and I felt like I was burning up and tired and achy and sick all over and I lay down and I guess I dreamed. But it wasn't like a normal dream, it was a lot more real, like I was really living in a different world.

I lived through the incident at the river over again in my dream, and everything that happened was perfectly clear and accurate as to my memory, what with the buzzing red-eyed cicadas everywhere and the fish eating them and my dad leaning over the back of the boat, and my little brother saying "poop" and me getting angry and holding him over the side of the boat and the river cat taking him, and that shiny rainbow mark on the fish's head.

The only thing different, and I guess not really different, just clearer maybe, was when I was on the riverbank and the nice lady was holding me and I saw my mother in the water and she looked so ugly and mean, only in my dream I could see—no, I could feel—how terribly,

terribly sad and miserable and lost she was, and it was like I could feel how much she hurt, the way her heart was breaking at losing her beautiful baby like there was no goodness and no love and no light in the world.

And then my dream got even more dreamy and weird. There was a rodeo in the woods behind our trailer and the walking river cat was going slurp-thunk, slurp-thunk in the mud and my dad was riding it like a cowboy and waving his hat and he didn't have a shirt on and he was all "yahoo" and stuff, and there was a cowgirl riding a pony around them. And then my dad gave the river cat a kick with his spurs and the river cat spat out a glob of something like a plug of chewing tobacco that went flying in the air and the cowgirl raced her pony over to it and caught it in her hat and went galloping into the woods with my dad riding the river cat slurp-thunk after her like they were both heading for the pot of gold at the end of the rainbow.

And meanwhile my mother's horse had fallen over and trapped her beneath it, and it was dark and shadowy where it fell, and I ran over to her and tried to pick it up off her but it was too heavy and she kept saying, "Please, please get it off me, help me, help me..." And my dad called out from the woods, "You're the strong one! Help your mother!" but I felt so darn weak, my legs were like rubber, and no one would help me no matter how much I called.

Then my fever broke and I woke up.

When I went to the kitchen I saw my mother had taken the bloody sheet from the drawing pad and fixed it to the fridge with a magnet. And she wrote some words on it, though I couldn't read at that time. She wrote those words in my blood.

She also took the bloody fishhook and dangled it from the magnet by its string in front of the artwork, and she took that fish symbol I stole from the van at the church and hung it in the crook of the fishhook, like the fish had been caught. For a second I had the urge to rip it all down, but I didn't. I don't know why I didn't, I really don't. And it stayed there on that fridge for a long, long time.

9. The Sour Lemon

YOU KNOW WHAT THEY SAY, AUNT VIOLET, about whatever doesn't kill me makes me stronger? I suppose that was true for me. Getting hooked didn't kill me. And the infection I got from it didn't kill me either. I guess I kinda bucked up a little, you know, in a couple of ways. One, I got rid of all those orange prisoner clothes. Swore I'd never wear another stitch of orange again. I raided the charity clothes box by the gas station for more clothes. And two, I guarded against my mother. I never closed my eyes in front of her again, and I carried the kitchen knife all the time, even in the house. And I let her know I carried it, too.

But now, my mother, she was a different story. She had an infection too, or so she said. That fish story I stuck in her head that she couldn't get out, well, it's like she was slowly burning up with the fever from it, you know? Like it was killing her real slow. That's how it seemed to me, anyway.

She kept trying to do her art, but nothing came of it. I remember she'd stand in the kitchen, studying that bloody artwork she hung on the refrigerator door. It made me feel queasy at first, thinking she might be getting juiced up for another go at me.

But that didn't happen. Instead, she'd study it for a while, just like she did with my bloody handprints in the red house, and then she'd get up and go in her room and rummage about for a bit, then she'd come out with her drawing pad and maybe her easel and she'd go out in the yard and sit down like she was about to draw something. Sometimes she'd just hover her hand over the paper and not make any marks, and other times she'd make a few lines, but she never finished a drawing. Almost always she'd wind up crying and growling and going into a rage and she'd rip up the paper and fling the pieces around or stomp the shreds into the ground with her feet.

And then she'd come back into the kitchen and stare at the bloody painting again and sooner or later she'd say, "Pain is truth," or something like that. And then, sometimes, she'd stagger out to the car and drive off. I don't know where she went. She never took me with her.

Once after she drove off I decided to go into her bedroom. Now, she would always lock her bedroom door from the inside so I couldn't go in, but in my watching her I learned that there was a little hole in the outside of the doorknob, and she'd just shove a nail in there to unlock it.

So that's what I did. And after I rummaged around a bit I found this big black leather case that was flat and rectangular and with a zipper around it. It was under her bed.

I pulled it out and opened it. There were lots of drawings, mostly in pencil and a few watercolors, some on big sheets of paper and some small, but let me tell you I was amazed. They were beautiful. More beautiful than anything I ever saw before or since. There must have been a hundred portraits of my little brother, and of other people I didn't recognize, and there were nature scenes and some things I didn't know what they were but they sure were beautiful.

They were all in good shape but one. It had a tear in it and some crumpled spots and part of it was smeared with mud. It was a picture like you were looking down into the water and there was a fish with his mouth wide open and it was at the surface, just about to swallow a cicada. And the only color on the whole thing was the red eyes on the cicada. And you could see kinda swirly reflections of puffy clouds and trees in the water. It was like a photograph, only more beautiful.

I knew right then this was what she was drawing on the riverbank the day the river cat took my brother. And I don't know why but suddenly I got this pang in my heart for my mother. I mean, all that beauty she put into those pictures, and all that beauty she could see in the world back then—all become nothing.

And I felt low again. It was all because I couldn't hold on to my brother. Because I was stupid and held him over the side of the boat when he was about to poop. Shoot, I'd let him poop on my lap if I had to do it over again. Sure enough, I deserved to be punished. Stupid Cain. Stupid, butterfingers Cain. Let a slimy fish take my brother right out of my hands.

Those pictures of my brother were so real and so beautiful that I began to imagine him growing up with me. When I'd go out exploring I'd pretend he was with me and I'd teach him how to throw rocks and climb trees, and I'd protect him if we got attacked by dogs or bullies or walking catfish. I think that's one of the reasons I got so good at throwing rocks, because I was showing off for my imaginary brother.

I even started having conversations with him. Well, I'd do the talking, the most he'd ever say was "poop," and that got kinda annoying. But he was the only one I had to talk to in those days, so I put up with it. I remember one time my mother heard me yakking away with him and she yelled, "Who are you talking to?" and I yelled out, "Mister Poopyhead!" and me and my brother laughed like anything. But mostly I didn't want my mother finding out about him because I didn't want her to hook him like she hooked me. He couldn't take it like I could. I was the strong one.

I wasn't the only one with an imaginary friend, though. My mother had one, too. I think she did, anyway. I remember the first time I noticed it. I can't remember what she was doing at the time, but she suddenly stopped and stood real still with her head kinda cocked to one side like she was listening for something. She got this, I don't know, dreamy look on her face, and then she walked into her bedroom, real soft, almost like tiptoeing so she could listen for whatever it was she was hearing.

She left her bedroom door open, like she didn't even notice me standing there watching her. And then she put on this thin nightgown, and she was naked underneath, and she opened the windows in her bedroom and she took the screens out and she stood there letting the breeze blow on her. And she whispered or kinda like moaned, real low, and I could hardly hear her, but it sounded like she was saying, "Come in now, I'm ready for you... Please come in... Please..." And then she lay down on her back on her bed, and she covered her eyes with these sleeping shades, and she just lay there whispering something like, "Oh, spirit, come and take me."

I could see her chest move up and down as she breathed. I could see her lips move, just barely, like she was talking to herself, or maybe to her imaginary friend, but not out loud, not like me and my little brother did. She got so limp and relaxed, it was almost like she was a different person. I stood there a long time, real quiet so I wouldn't bother her, watching. She didn't know I was there. I could see why other people thought she was beautiful. She was. She looked, I don't know, delicate, I guess. Like someone I was supposed to protect. Or love, maybe, I don't know.

Real quiet, I sat down on the floor and leaned back against the door jamb and just watched her. It was peaceful. I think I dozed off. And I had a dream, or something like a dream, that someone or something was about to come in through the open window. And that scared me and I must have made a grunt or a little shout or something when I woke up, because she kinda jerked her hands up a little, and I hightailed it outta there before she could get her mask off and catch me spying on her.

I could hear the slap of her bare feet on the floor and she groaned and cussed and I could hear her kinda whimpering, "I'll never be happy again," over and over and finally she yelled out, "I've got to get a job." Well, she really said I've got to get a effing job, if you know what I mean, and she said it like it was just about the worst thing she could think of to say.

And she did. She got a job at some place called the Sour Lemon and she worked evenings and late into the night. I didn't know what she did, but she always wore some kind of costume. I can't remember what the first ones were, there were a bunch of different ones at first, a nurse, I think, and a school teacher, and they always had like short dresses that showed a lot of skin on the legs and all.

I don't remember ever seeing her drink before that, but she came home drunk a lot in those days. Woozy, slurring her words, stumbling around. I'll never forget one time I saw her headlights come up the driveway, and then the car stopped and the headlights went out and she got out and just as she slammed the car door another set of headlights appeared coming up the drive.

She looked toward them and turned toward the house in a hurry, fumbling in her purse for her keys. But she was drunk and fell down and the stuff in her purse spilled out. A man got out of the other car and went after her. She tried to fend him off but he threw her to the ground and jumped on top of her. I could see them in the headlights.

I was out the door in a heartbeat. I was wearing a pair of workboots that I had stolen from the "Cure Poverty" bin and my first kick landed square in his throat. He kinda huffed and I pushed him off of my mother and jumped on him as he rolled onto his back. Real quick I straddled his chest and touched the tip of the kitchen knife to the inside of his eye and I kinda leaned on it like I was just about to plunge it right through his eyeball into his brain.

It was like I had become more animal than human and when I opened my mouth the only thing that came out was this wild scream. I had my face right next to his, and my teeth were bared and my muscles were all tight and twitchy, and I saw his fear. I knew then what people mean when they say a dog can smell your fear. I knew it from the dog's point of view.

I let him up, though. He stumbled back to his car. Then I hit him in the head with a rock just as he got in the car, but I let him go. My mother had gone inside the trailer and locked the door behind her. I had the place pretty well secured from intrusions with doors locked and sticks in the windows and all and unfortunately for me my mother didn't open her window and call for her imaginary friend, and she didn't open up no matter how hard I banged on the doors and windows, so I spent the night in her car.

I don't know if it was because of that incident, but after that she changed her costume. She stopped wearing the nurse and school teacher outfits and started coming home dressed in some black leather thing, with fishnet stockings and spiked heels and a dog collar and some kind of mask. And she carried a whip.

I didn't know anything about that sort of thing back then, and to me it just looked stupid. But that's what she wore to work for a good long while so I guessed it was effective for whatever kind of job she had.

Whatever job it was, it paid in cash. And it's funny, you know, how you can learn to count money before you can even read. I did, anyway. She brought home all kinds of bills, a lot of ones and fives at first, but later more twenties and quite a few fifties and hundreds. It made it easier for me to do laundry and shop, but it got so I couldn't sleep. I'd spend all day doing chores, exploring and stuff, and at night I'd turn the lights on and wait for my mother to get home, and always fearing another weirdo stalker would show up like before, only this time less drunk and more dangerous. Constantly listening for any crack of a twig or crunch of car tire on the gravel. I tell you what, Aunt Violet, it was wearing me out.

But my mother, I don't know, it was like she was dying. Like she just couldn't shake that fever she had from the fish story I put in her head, that infection, she called it. She was turning yellow. I mean actually yellow in color. Her skin, even her eyes.

At first I thought maybe it was part of her costume, you know, like they dyed her skin yellow for working at the Sour Lemon. But it wasn't bright like the picture on the matchbooks she brought home from work, it was dull and I thought maybe she had some kind of disease, but I didn't know what to do about it.

I remember waiting up for her one time and when she came home I said to her, "Why are you turning yellow?"

And she was drunk, and she glared at me and she said, "You did this to me."

Well I was tired and hungry and fed up with all of it and I just kinda pointed the kitchen knife at her and I yelled, "Shut up! You just shut the eff up!" only I didn't say "eff," Aunt Violet, I cussed her out with every cuss word I learned from her. And she bent down toward me and she put her throat right against the knife blade and she said, "Go ahead, Cain. I know you want to." Her breath stunk of booze or vomit or something and I just turned away from her and went into my bedroom and slammed the door and jammed it shut.

Not long after that it all came to a head, like a boil filled with yellow pus. My mother was away at her job. I was taking a shower when all of a sudden the lights went out. And then almost at the same time the water cut off. My first thought was I was being stalked. I stood there in the bathroom and listened. I heard all kinds of sounds—maybe they were natural and maybe not, I couldn't tell, and my heart started to race.

I stayed quiet. I could hardly even breathe. I felt around for the clothes I had left on the floor and put them on over my wet body. I started to panic even more when I couldn't find the kitchen knife I carried. I was on my hands and knees feeling around for the knife, trying to stay quiet, and I was getting dizzy with fear. I could hardly feel the floor.

Still on my hands and knees, I crawled to the kitchen in the dark, feeling my way along the wall. I thought maybe I had left the knife in there. I put my hand on the refrigerator door to steady myself and as I stood up something sharp jabbed my palm.

I jerked my hand away, then slowly put it back. I could feel the sharp point and barb of the fishhook on my mother's bloody artwork. And I could feel the fisher-of-men symbol, and the drawing paper with my dried blood on it. As I touched it I felt the old wound on the inside of my cheek with my tongue.

Two years or so it had been hanging there. I was only about seven back then. I was older now. You're the strong one. The panic eased off. Anger came, and I let it fill me. Enough, I thought. I had had enough.

I stopped looking for the knife. I opened the kitchen door and stepped outside into the darkness.

The place where she worked was about two miles away, straight up the county road, a little past an abandoned gas station and among some car repair shops and whatnot. Since I didn't have my knife, I gathered as many throwing rocks as I could and stuffed them into my pockets. The big yellow lemon was lit up when I got there. The parking lot was full of cars and you could hear music and somebody talking into a microphone whenever the door opened.

I can't say I really had a plan. I was just mad. When the lights and water shut off like that, I just got really spooked and anxious. I had been rolling on too little sleep and too much worry for too long. I was frazzled and I wanted it to stop. I didn't know what went wrong and I didn't know how to fix it, all I knew was I might be the prisoner, but it's my mother's prison, so she should fix it. And the more I rolled this stuff over in my brain the angrier I got and the more determined I was to go in there and just drag my mother home to fix it. I even thought I should have brought the fishhook and dragged her home that way if she put up a fuss.

I don't need the fishhook, I thought. I'm the strong one, and when I picture her eating good food at a restaurant when I had to eat from the dumpster or go without, and now without lights or water, well, I'd drag her back by the hair if I had to.

I didn't count on the place having a bouncer, though. I didn't even know what a bouncer was back then, all I know is when I went to open the front door this huge dude with a shaved head and whiskers on his chin and tattoos up his neck held the door shut and said, "Hold on there, son. Where do you think you're going?"

"I gotta get my mother," I said, and pulled on the door handle again.

He laughed and held the door shut. "Your mother? What makes you think your mother's in here?"

"She works here," I said. "I gotta get her. Let me in." Just then a couple of adults came up and he opened the door to let them in. I tried going in on their heels but he caught me by the back of the shirt and dragged me back out.

"I told you, you can't go in there," he said.

I wriggled out of my shirt and made to go in, but he grabbed me hard by the arm, so I bit his wrist real hard and he gave a howl and picked me up and threw me onto the pavement. He cussed me and threatened to break my face if I didn't beat it.

So I turned away from him and walked a few steps, then pulled a rock out of my pocket, and in one motion turned back and threw it as hard as I could. Bam, got him right in the temple and he went down. I ran past him and into the building.

I could not believe what I saw in there.

The lights inside made everything look yellow. A lot of people, mostly men, mostly drunk, hooting and hollering and gawking at two people on the stage. One of them was my mother, dressed in her black leather outfit, only minus a piece or two and showing more skin than when I saw her in that outfit at home. The other was a man, and he was on his hands and knees and he had some kind of ball stuck in his mouth, and when my mother cracked the whip on his back he writhed and the crowd let out a roar.

I can't tell you why, I was only nine years old or so, but I hated it. And before I knew it I was jumping up on the stage and grabbing my mother by the arm and yelling at her, "Mom! Come on, we gotta go! Mom, come on!"

And just then the bouncer came rushing up shoving people out of his way and bellowing like a mule, "Lemme at that little sonofabitch!" Well, he was calling me lots worse than that, but I'm trying not to cuss for you, Aunt Violet.

I let go my mother's wrist to escape the bouncer and my mother looked at me with this horror on her face and then she wailed like a cornered cat and just went ape on the whole crowd with the whip—and believe me, it wasn't just fun and games, she was full blown fishhook bonkers and drawing blood from some very surprised, and then very angry customers.

I had a good portion of rocks left in my pockets and I slung them at the bouncer. But I had never thrown in a crowd like that and some hit the target and some hit other people and that just riled them up even more. And when I ran out of rocks I picked up drink glasses from people's tables and heaved them, all the while I'm screaming, "Mom! Come on! You gotta come home!"

Well, this guy comes running out of a back room, I guess he was the boss or something, and he comes at my mother and jerks her by the hair, and there's shouts from the crowd from people she had whipped for him to hold on to her so they could wallop her, and it looked like she was going to get it bad.

Just then a man jumps up and drops the boss with one punch. And the bouncer, who was already bleeding from a couple of places on his face where I had beaned him with rocks and whatnot, he attacked this guy and the guy gives him a swift kick in the groin, and when the bouncer doubled over from that, the guy hit him an upshot with his knee that knocked him out cold.

This guy wasn't a big guy, he was a good bit smaller than the bouncer, but man, could he fight. All the while this guy was kinda keeping my mother to his back like he was protecting her. But the crowd's still drunk and pissed and stinging from her whip and they're pressing forward. So the guy reaches into his pocket and he pulls out a switchblade and snaps the blade open.

And my mother, she kinda slumps over him and he hoists her over his shoulder and he motions to me to come along. Then he makes his way toward the door, jabbing and slashing at people to keep them away from us.

He carried my mother over his shoulder through the parking lot to her car, and he pulled a key for it from somewhere under the fender and opened the door. Then he threw my mother in the back seat and told me, "You ride shotgun."

Well I didn't know what the heck that was, but I jumped into the front seat next to him as he started the engine and tore out of the parking lot with the tires squealing and gravel flying, as people slammed their fists on the car and threw bottles at us.

I don't know, maybe I shouldn't have trusted him the way I did, but if you've ever been in a fight where it's like you against the world and somebody takes your side, well, that somebody's not a stranger, he's a friend. You just know it. And that's how it was with me and him.

So I showed him how to get to our place, and we drove there. He drove fast, and all the way he was glancing in the mirrors to see if anybody was following us. My mother was passed out in the back seat. But he didn't seem much worried. In fact, he kept looking at me, then back to the road and laughing and saying stuff like, "You're her kid? Damn! The Belle of the Baal has a kid. Who'da freakin' thunk it? Hah! Man, I tell you what. If that don't take all." And he'd laugh and shake his head and say, "You know what, it figures. It figures, if that woman had a kid, he'd be like you. Run into the lion's den and raise holy hell. Fearless, man, absolutely fearless. Woman like her deserves a kid like you."

As we pulled into our driveway he said, "So where's the fire?"

"What fire?" I said.

"Whatever fire it was made you come running into the club to get your mother. What was so all-fired important?"

I told him about the lights going out and the water shutting off, and how we had stalkers and all and how tired and starved I was and I couldn't take it anymore. So he said, "Sounds like there's been a problem paying the bills. Which is strange, seeing as how she gets more cash stuffed in her... uh, in her purse than all the other girls combined. Well, we'll fix all that tomorrow. Right now let's get your mom into her bed and I'll make a run to get some supplies."

Before he left he said, "Your mother calls me Sailor. I'm in the merchant marine. I work on ships for a living. What's your name?"

"Cain," I said. It just came out. I didn't even think about it.

"Cain," he said. "Cain. Like the one that killed Abel?"

"I don't think that was his name," I said.

He laughed again. "Look," he said, "You stay in the house, lock the door, don't open it for anyone until I get back, OK?"

"OK." I was a stew of emotions waiting for him in that dark trailer. Something about seeing her in that place made me even madder at her than I was before. That guy I saw her whipping on that stage? That was the same guy I had to chase off just a month or two prior when he attacked my mother in the driveway that night. It was all just bad, you know? Everything about it, the way she was dressed and acting in front of all those people, I just couldn't stand the thought of it. But this new guy, Sailor, it was like, I hadn't had a friend in forever, and now I have one and he's old enough to be my father, and so I had this strange giddiness mixed up with the disgust I had for my mother.

When he came back he knocked and said, "Hey Cain, it's me, Sailor," and I let him right in. And I was happy to see that my instincts were proving right. He brought some propane lamps we could see by, and some flashlights with new batteries, and bottles of water. Best of all, though, he brought some hamburgers and French fries and soda for me and him, and to me, that was like heaven.

As we were eating I started telling him about how I hated seeing my mother at that place and how I didn't want her working there anymore, and he made me finish eating then tell him again, because he couldn't understand a word I was saying with all the food in my mouth. And so I did, and when I got to the part about that guy on stage had come here and attacked my mother, and I had to fight him off, he got a real serious look on his face and he said, "That was Gerald. Son of a bitch. All right. I'll take care of him. You won't have him to worry about anymore."

"But she shouldn't be working there at all, Sailor," I said.

"Cain, my boy, I've told her that myself on many occasion," he said. "Look, obviously she hasn't told you about me, just as she never told me about you. But she and I have been seeing each other for a while, now. Hey, I hope you don't mind. But I'm with you, she's way too good for a place like that. But she's stubborn, you know. Anyway, what else can she do?"

"She's an artist," I said.

"That she is," he said, nodding. "That she is. And you know what? Those people at that club just don't get it, man, they sit there and watch a performance artist of the first degree create these incredible works of art, and all they see is a damn stripper."

I wasn't even sure what he was talking about, but I was pretty sure we weren't saying the same thing. "That's not what I'm talking about," I said. "Just a minute." And I ran into her bedroom where she was still passed out on the bed in her getup and I reached under the bed and pulled out the big black leather case that had all her artwork, and I dragged it out to him and opened it.

"Look here, this is what I mean," I said.

He looked through all of it. "Oh my God," he kept whispering. "This is amazing... Look at that... Good Lord..." But when he finished he said, "These are all dated, and there's none in the past few years. Does she still do this?"

I shook my head "no."

"Why not?"

"Because it doesn't hurt," I said. "I don't think she can do art anymore unless it hurts," and I touched the scar on the inside of my cheek with my tongue.

He looked at me funny for a good long time like he was trying to understand what I meant. And then he kinda nodded, and he said, "So that's why she whips people," and then he shook his head again.

"Look," he said, "your mom's a great artist, but the fine art market's tough, especially in a place like this. She could make more money, you know... hurting people the way she's doing it now, although they won't be letting her back in that club any time soon."

"What about that?" I asked, and pointed at his forearm. "Didn't that hurt?" He looked down at the tattoo on his arm. I said, "I'll bet she could do a better job than that."

He looked from his arm to her artwork to me and stared at me as a grin slowly grew on his face. "Well ain't you just the little entrepreneur," he said.

"The what?"

He laughed. "You got a head for business," he said. "I believe you have just solved the problem. I could definitely get her started in the tattoo business, maybe piercing, too. Hey, I'm all about the green. There's good money in the intersection of pain and art, as you have so eloquently pointed out. Lot of guys I sail and ride with, I could send her way, as a beginning customer base. Yeah, that would work."

He was pacing as he talked his thoughts out. Then he stopped and looked at me. "Look, son, I think the world of your mom," he said. "I got no family, no one to support with all the money I make going to sea. I'm going to set you and your mom up good, I swear it. Tonight I'm going to sneak back to the club on foot, get my bike back, and then I'll come back here. And just to show you I'm a gentleman, I'll spend the night in your mom's car. Then tomorrow we'll get the utilities paid for and turned back on, and we'll start getting that tattoo business set up, if we can convince your mom that's the way to go. She can be kinda stubborn, you know."

The way he looked at me in the glare of the propane lamp, something caught my attention. His eyes. They were green. Really green. Something about that made me trust him. I'm not sure why. I seemed to remember my dad having green eyes, but I couldn't be sure. My time in the red house burned out memories like that.

He turned to walk away. "Wait a minute," I said. He stopped and looked at me. "Can I go with you?"

He smiled and shrugged. "Sure, why not? Won't take us long. Your mom'll be safe here."

It took us probably twenty minutes to walk to the club. I feared there'd be a gang of angry people waiting for it, but the parking lot was almost deserted. When we got to his bike he put me on the back of the seat, then he got on and started it. I don't think I'd ever heard such a roar. He turned back to me and yelled, "You ever done a donut?" And before I could answer he was peeling around in circles with this hellish rumble and gravel flying everywhere, cracking against parked cars and the windows of the club while I held onto him like a monkey. And then we headed home.

I guess you could say that's when my mother's fever broke. And I guess you could say Sailor saved her life. But her infection wasn't cured, not by a long shot.

10. All About the Green

SAILOR WAS AS GOOD AS HIS WORD. The next day we got the power and water turned back on, and then he set about fixing us up in a bunch of different ways. He said to me, "All right, Cain, when I'm ashore I'm the old man and you're my chief mate. I'm going to teach you how to take care of things so your mom can focus on her art, OK?"

First thing, he tried to show me what bills were and how to write checks, but I had to stop him and tell him I couldn't read or write, that my mother wouldn't let me go to school.

He shook his head and laughed at that, and he said, "Hey, last place you should go if you ever want to really learn about life is school. They take boys like you and turn them into girls, man. Drain the fighting spirit right out of you. Turn you into sheep to be sheared. Hell with that. Everything useful I know I learned out in the real world, and you can too. And besides, you'll have another advantage. You know what that is?"

I shook my head.

"No school means you'll be a man with no papers. No record for the government and corporations and all those ruling-class sonsabitches to control you by. Unlike all those suckers that go to school, you'll be free, and that, my friend, is something that no sheepskin can buy you.

"I'll teach you to read and write, arithmetic, all that, don't you worry," he said. "Plus I'll teach you stuff every man ought to know but not a single one of them panty-waisted high school and college pansies know: how to fight, how to work with your hands, how to make money, how to really appreciate life, you know what I mean? You'll do fine. Don't you worry. You'll do fine."

Sure enough, just like he said he would, he brought a steady stream of visitors, friends of his to teach my mother how to use the tattoo equipment, or to be guinea pigs for her early efforts. And it was just like I suspected. Unlike when she tried to draw on paper, she could do this. As long as she knew her subjects were feeling pain, she could draw.

Her first customer, if you could call him that, was Gerald. He was the guy that my mother was whipping at the club that night, the one that tried to rape her in the driveway. I remember when I told Sailor about that, he said, "That's Gerald. I'll take care of him," I thought he was going to kill him or something.

Instead, Sailor and a couple of his buddies brought Gerald to my mother's studio and they made him lie down on the table, naked, and he said, "Now, Gerald here has been given the choice between the top of this ink table and the bottom of the swamp, and he has chosen to be inked, haven't you, Gerald?"

And Gerald, he was a freak anyway, he had this weird mixture of fear and pleasure going on at the same time and he just kinda nodded like a bobblehead dog.

"Wise choice, Gerald," Sailor said. "And Gerald has chosen the unlimited package, which is very, very expensive, haven't you, Gerald?"

"Yeah, yeah, unlimited, unlimited," he agreed. "Go ahead. Please hurt me. Hurt me real bad."

Like I said, a freak. I left the room about then because he was looking, I don't know, let's just say stiff and slimy in all the wrong places. But my mother worked on him for probably a couple, three days, and sometimes judging by the sounds I heard coming from that room, I knew he wanted to change his choice to the bottom of the swamp.

When she was finished with him he kinda limped through the foyer dressed in a pink bathrobe. Sailor said, "OK, Gerald, pay the man." And Gerald looked confused, so Sailor pointed to me and said, "He's the man. Pay him." And Gerald pulled out this stack of bills and started counting, but Sailor said, "Hey. Don't count it. Just pay him." And Gerald gave me the whole wad.

"I want you to look at this young man," he said to Gerald. "This is the same kid who kicked your ass here one night when you tried to rape his mother. But he's only going to get bigger, and stronger, and meaner, and I'm teaching him everything I know about dealing with creeps like you, you catch my drift?"

Gerald whispered, "Yeah," and nodded.

"All right, then. You can go. It's been nice doing business with you." There were about four or five of us there and as Gerald turned to leave, Sailor said, "Oh, Gerald. One other thing."

"Yeah?"

"Why don't you show us the work?"

Gerald untied the bathrobe and let it drop to the floor. Nobody spoke for a minute or two. I don't think anybody even breathed. You know when people use the word "stunning," they don't really mean it? Well, if you've ever seen a bunch of tough old tattooed sailors and bikers sit there with their mouths open, staring like they'd been slammed in the head with a bat, you'll know what it really means to be stunned.

There was a tall, cheap mirror on the hallway closet door and Gerald started turning around slowly, looking at himself in it and saying, "Is it beautiful? Is it beautiful?"

I can't even describe it. I really can't. Yes, it was beautiful. Like Sailor said, you couldn't really even compare it to a tattoo, any more than you could compare the trailer we were in to the Empire State Building or the Taj Mahal.

It was beautiful, but the more you looked at it, the more you knew there was something really, really disturbing hidden in it. Like, it could give you nightmares, you know? Or worse. Like the devil was looking back at you.

One of Sailor's crew was good at photography, so Sailor had him take a bunch of pictures of Gerald's tattoo. Then, before sending him on his way, Sailor told him, "Gerald, don't ever tell anyone where you got that tattoo, or who gave it to you, you understand?" And Gerald nodded uh-huh. And Sailor snapped open his switchblade and put it to Gerald's throat and he said, "Do you really understand, Gerald?" And he said yeah, and he meant it, because he knew Sailor would do it.

When he was gone, Sailor looked at me and the wad of bills in my hand and said, "We are definitely going to have to start charging more. A lot more."

Sailor started pacing, and talking out his thoughts. "This is a game changer, man, a total freaking game changer. She's an artist, you know what I'm saying, a true artist! She's not going to be doing tramp stamps, that's for damn sure. You're not going to tell her what to draw, she's going to decide what to draw, you got no say in the matter. But there's a market for what she does, I can feel it. Low volume, high value. It's like having Michelangelo ink you, I mean, just think about it. We're going to get those pictures in tattoo magazines, hell, in fine art magazines. Look, there's a lot of rich masochistic freaks in the world that would pay top dollar to get inked like she did Gerald. Top freaking dollar."

And so that's how my mother got into the tattoo business, and how I got educated.

By the time Sailor left to go back to sea about three months later life had changed a lot for us. I had been in solitary confinement, basically, for a long, long time, and suddenly there were people around every day.

Sailor and several of his friends drilled me in reading and writing and arithmetic, and they were amazed at how hard I worked at it, being the kind of rock throwing, tree climbing boy I was. Sailor wanted most to make sure I could take care of the bills and my mom's business finances before he left, and he thought it was a testimony to my "love for my mother" that I worked so hard at it.

I didn't know what to think of that. I really looked up to Sailor, so I guess... I don't know. I guess I left room for it in my mind.

Really, though, there were two things I wanted. I wanted the lights to stay lit. And I wanted to read what my mother had written on that bloody artwork she made after she gave me my lesson with the fishhook. I knew all along she had written some words, but I didn't know what they said.

And so, on the day Sailor was packing to leave, I stood there in front of the refrigerator and I sounded out the words. They said:

TELL

THE

TRUTH

I turned around and saw Sailor looking at me. I never told him about the fishhook and I don't know what my mother told him, if anything.

He said, "Look at it this way, Cain. Way out here in the middle of Nowheresville is a woman who may be the greatest artist of our age. I mean, we may not understand it completely, because true artists, they see and feel life deeper and more clearly than the rest of us. And they know that pain is part of the deal. It has to be. The rest of us, well, we're like pieces in one of her art installations. And you know what? We ought to be thankful that our lives could be used like that."

I looked at him like I didn't know what the heck he
was talking about. Because I didn't.

"And I'll tell you something else," he went on. "I've
watched you and your mom for quite a while now. And
I've learned this. You, Cain, have a special role to play.
You know what it is?"

I shook my head no.

"You are her muse."

I just stared at him.

"I know. You don't understand it yet. But someday
you will. And then..." He shook his head. "Not sure I
want to be around when that happens."

11. The Pain Pit

AND SO FOR THE NEXT SEVERAL YEARS Sailor split his time between New Nod and the sea. He'd ship out for a few months, and then he'd be home for a few months, and all the other seamen and bikers in his crew would come and go too. I still didn't have any friends my own age, but I liked having them around.

He was careful about that, though. Not just anybody could come around. In fact, he set it up so all our mail went to a post office box and no deliveries came directly to New Nod either. And when it came to customers, or anybody outside his crew, he turned New Nod into a "blindfold-only" destination. He'd have one of his crew meet them in some town a good distance away and they'd blindfold them for the drive in and out.

Let me put it this way. The stuff that went on at New Nod wasn't exactly legal, and Sailor and his crew weren't exactly in the law-abiding business.

I learned a lot, I really did. Not just reading and writing and numbers, but working on engines and mechanical stuff, managing money, and how to fight. Between Sailor and others in his crew, I had people who could teach me just about every kind of fighting technique— street fighting, really, no holds barred. And how to use a knife. That was big. Sailor was a knife guy. Switchblades. I became one, too.

He set up an area he called the pain pit. That's where they taught me to fight, in part by learning to endure pain. The guys I trained with were all older and bigger than me, and so I got beat up a good bit in the process. Busted lips, black eyes, blade nicks, wrenched joints, choked til I passed out, that sort of thing.

The pain pit wasn't just for my benefit, though. Sailor set it up outside my mother's studio window so she could watch. I could always tell when she needed artistic inspiration because Sailor would drag me over to the pain pit for some training he called "bloodletting."

That kind of pain I could take, because I was a rough-and-tumble kid from the get-go, and I really did learn from it. And by the time I was fourteen I was giving as good as I was getting. But there was another kind of pain I had a real hard time with.

Sailor'd say, "All right, Jason, listen for the siren." That's the only time he'd call me anything other than Cain. I don't know why. And I never did hear a siren. They'd chain me up in the pain pit by myself and then they'd leave. My mother's studio window would be open. She'd be working on some young woman. And the way that girl would moan and scream, man, it just tore me up. It was torture. I'd cry and yell at my mother to stop it and leave her alone, and I'd yank on my chains, but there was nothing I could do about it.

The worst time was with this girl, Estelle something-or-other. She was from New York City, maybe twenty years old, bored and rebelling against her rich parents. She stayed there a couple days before my mother started on her, and I guess you could say my teenage heart beat pretty hot for that girl. So I had a real hard time chained up in the pain pit while my mother worked on her. A real hard time.

When it was over, Sailor said it was my mother's best work. My mother said, "Take her over to Cain. Let him see her." And she watched from her window as Sailor walked Estelle over to where I was chained up and dropped her robe to the ground.

Estelle's face was red and wet with tears. She was trembling. I can't even describe the artwork, I won't even try, except to say it was the most hellish, heart-breakingly beautiful atrocity I had ever seen, and I knew, I just knew that poor Estelle would regret it every day she lived.

And Estelle looked at me with the saddest eyes I'd ever seen and she said, "Cain? Is it... OK? Is it... is it beautiful?"

I wanted nothing more in the whole wide world than to break my chains and use them to slaughter my mother and Sailor and his whole crew, but I couldn't, I wasn't strong enough, and I was desperate, absolutely desperate to ease Estelle's pain, so I forced myself to nod my head and say, "Yeah," but I couldn't stop from bawling like a baby and I watched through my tears while Sailor got Estelle back in her clothes and put the blindfold back on her and put her in the car and had his driver take her away. They left me chained there until I stopped thrashing and wailing.

Estelle, or her ignorant parents, paid fifteen thousand dollars for that work. Sailor grinned as he held the cash and said, "Fifteen grand for three days work. Hey, I'm all about the green."

But not everybody in his crew was so positive about it. There was this one gal, Wendy. She was a tough biker chick, lots of tattoos and piercings and whatnot, but she was always sweet to me, almost motherly. She had watched the whole deal with Estelle and me until she just couldn't take it anymore and she broke the cardinal rule of New Nod. Never insult the queen.

She just started yelling at my mother, "What the hell is wrong with you? Are you insane? Why do you always have to treat this boy that way? That's no way for a mother to treat her son! He's a good boy..."

My mother flicked out this knife-edge voice of hers and said, "Get out."

Wendy just kept on. "No! What you just did was absolute torture and child abuse! You rag on him constantly, you put him down, you never have a nice word for him, you don't send him to school, you don't let him have any friends, what the hell is wrong with you?"

"I said get out. Sailor!"

Wendy was so angry she was red in the face. "I'll tell you what I think. I think you ain't really even his mother. You don't act like it. He don't look nothing like you. He don't act like you. I think you abducted this child and brought him to this god-forsaken place just to abuse him. I ought to contact Child Protective Services and tell them about this hellhole."

Just then Sailor came storming around the trailer, snapping his switchblade open as he charged Wendy. In a flash he knocked Wendy down onto her back and was straddling her with the edge of the knife set against her jugular. He was hot, man, you could see his veins popping out and he was snarling like a dog, not even saying any words.

Wendy's biker boyfriend, a squat guy they called Fat Fred dropped to his knees next to them and was begging Sailor not to do anything rash, not to kill Wendy, she didn't mean it, just let her up and we'll take off and not come back, I swear...

Sailor was a flinch away from slicing Wendy's throat, and I looked at my mother and I said, "You kill her and you'll never get what you want from me. Ever."

She had never heard anything like that from me. It was the closest I ever came to hinting that there might be some wiggle room in my fish story. She blinked and rubbed her temples with her fingertips. She said weakly, "Let her go, Sailor," and she walked into the trailer.

Sailor dog-growled at Fat Fred and Wendy and said, "I know where you live. Even when you're on the road, I know how to find you. I know your families. If I ever see any Child Protection people, or cops, or anybody else sniffing around here, I will come for all of you, do you understand?"

"Yeah, Sailor, we understand," Fat Fred said. "We ain't telling nobody nothing. Ain't that right, Wendy?"

"Yeah," Wendy said. Poor woman was scared to death and could hardly breathe.

"Tell Sailor you're sorry, Wendy, and we'll up and go and not come back."

"I'm sorry, Sailor," she said. "I'm real sorry. I swear I won't say anything. It ain't none of my business. I swear. I'm sorry."

Sailor got up, closed his knife and stuck it back in his pocket. Fat Fred and Wendy took off on their bikes and sure enough, they never came back. That's how it was in those days. The crew that hung around New Nod got fewer and fewer, and the ones that did remain were Sailor's hard core followers who knew the deal.

But something Wendy said stuck in my mind. It was like a light turning on, but with a dimmer switch, starting real low and getting brighter the more I thought about it.

What if my mother was not really my mother? What if she escaped from some insane asylum and kidnapped me from my real family? I mean, Wendy was right about me not looking anything like my mother. And sure enough, my mother never really acted like my mother, treating me the way she always had. And the thing of it was, in my pure memory of the day river cat took my brother, there was another woman there on the river. The nice lady who picked me up and comforted me. And what's more, I seem to remember even before that—now this isn't a true memory, but more of an impression— that this nice lady or someone like her used to hold me on her lap and love me like a mother. I know who that was now, Aunt Violet, but I didn't then.

I wrestled with this idea for a while until I just had to do something to find out. One day Sailor took my mother out. I went into her bedroom and started rummaging about. Well, not rummaging, really, I mean I was careful not to mess things up. I wasn't sure what I was looking for, just any kind of evidence about my past. And sure enough, I found something.

I didn't have to look hard or long. It's not like she made any real effort to hide it. On the floor of her closet was a small metal box. It was locked, but the lock was really simple and cheap and picking that sort of lock was just one of the things Sailor and his crew taught me over the years. My mother knew that. It took me about thirty seconds to get it open.

If Sailor had never come into our lives I may never have learned how to read, and never would have learned to pick locks, so this would not have happened. But in that box was a divorce and custody decree. Now to start with, I wasn't sure what I was looking at—not only because I didn't have that kind of knowledge, but I didn't recognize any of the names.

Keep in mind, I didn't know my own real name. Living in the red house had zapped a lot of my memory from way back when, and ever since we moved to New Nod my mother had only ever called me "Cain" or "boy" or whatever. I didn't remember my father's name. I didn't know my mother's name, I only ever called her Mom and Sailor only ever called her "Sweetheart" or "Sugar" or "Woman" or some such fake thing. And ever since Sailor came into our lives he changed the utilities into some

fake name and so that's how the bills came in, and I
didn't have any old bills to go by back when they might
have been in my mother's real name.

But I figured it was about us and it had something to
do with life in the old place because it was covered in
weird doodles that only my mother could have drawn
and hateful, angry words pressed hard into the paper so
you could feel them on the other side. And from what I
could make out, the judge granted the woman her peti-
tion for divorce from the man who had abandoned her,
and gave the woman full custody of "the only remaining
child."

The other paper was a restraining order issued by the
same judge. It required the ex-husband and one other
person, someone named Violet Tyler, to stay away from
the petitioner and not to contact her under any circum-
stances.

I thought briefly about confronting my mother with
this, but I figured neither she nor Sailor would let me get
away with that. And then I got an idea. I'd write a letter
to the judge. Sailor had a long time ago given me the
sole responsibility for checking the mail at the post office
box so I would be able to take care of the bills and all
when he was at sea. I had the judge's name and address.
If I wrote to her and got a reply, nobody at New Nod
would be the wiser.

So that's what I did. In my letter I wrote:

Dear Judge Witt,

I am writing to ask for your help to get information about me and my family. I saw some papers signed by you that gave custody of a boy named Richard Tyler to someone named Eris Morton Tyler and she got divorced from Robert Tyus Tyler, who was her husband but he was missing. I think I am Richard Tyler, but nobody calls me that anymore. I would like to find out who my real mother is, and I would like to get in contact with my father, if you can help me I would appreciate it.

Thank you very much.

p.s. The paper said Richard Tyler was their only living child. I had a little brother who died when I was a kid. I'm pretty sure it was before my parents divorced. I don't remember his name. I hope this helps.

Also, if I am not Richard Tyler, please let me know and I won't bother you anymore.

I stuck it in the mail. And then for a while I felt like I was holding my breath and making twice daily visits to the post office.

About two weeks later something weird happened. It was evening, after supper if I recall, and it was just me and my mom in the trailer when I thought I heard something outside. A rattle and a hiss, not like a snake, but something mechanical, like pressurized steam or air escaping a hose. It was faint and I assumed it was Sailor, but then I remembered he had gone off for supplies and I had not heard the car return. I was just about to get up and look out the window when there was a knock at the front door.

We didn't keep set hours for my mother's tattoo business, I mean, sometimes she'd work til sunrise if she was on a roll and the customer didn't pass out, but we always required appointments. The way my mother did business, we couldn't risk getting the attention of the health department or the licensing department or the cops or anything like that.

So I went to the door and without opening it, called out, "What do you want?"

Whoever it was said something that was kinda muffled through the door and knocked again. I took my switchblade out of my pocket and held it behind my back. Then I cracked the door. "What do you want?" I said again.

The guy said, "Are you Richard?" He was tall and gangly with grimy hair and whiskers and he didn't look like a tattoo customer or a cop or authority of any sort. A sting went through my gut at the sound of the name, which had been on my mind ever since I wrote to the judge.

"There's no Richard here," I said, and made to close the door, but he shoved his foot in the way and leaned on it with his shoulder.

"Can I... can I talk to you?" he said. If anything, he sounded more wired and anxious than I was.

My mother walked in from her studio—she called it a studio and not a tattoo parlor—and she said to me, "Who is it? A customer? Let him in, I need to work."

My mother always got real antsy whenever a day or two went by without the opportunity to needle pain on some human canvas. She was like a junkie who needed a fix.

"It's not a customer, Mom," I said, and told the guy, "Go on, get outta here."

"Oh yes!" he called in so my mother could hear, "I'm a customer. I'm a customer, can I come in? Please?" and he pushed on the door.

My mother saw me holding the door back against him and got pissed. "I said, let him in," she told me. She walked up and looked at the guy through the crack in the door. "You a cop?" she said.

"No."

"Nah, you don't look like one." She pulled on the door, but I held it in place.

"Mom, Sailor said..."

"Never mind Sailor," she said. "I'm the boss, not him. Come on in, fella."

"Fine," I said, and I backed up as the man walked into the room. In a weird way, I wanted the guy to come in. I knew I could have kept him out if I wanted to, but I had to see what this "Richard" stuff was all about. Maybe nothing. Just a mistake. But coming so soon after my letter and what with this guy just showing up and not even looking like a tattoo customer, well I just had to know what was going on.

This dude was different, let me tell you. Most customers, man or woman, they kinda stare at my mother. Sailor said she was an eyeball magnet. I don't think this

guy even looked at my mother. He never broke eye contact with me, and he had this really weird, sort of desperate stare. My mother didn't notice any of that.
Junkie needs her fix. She just said, "OK, fella, follow
me," and went into her studio.

Without taking his eyes off me, the guy said, "OK, I'll
be right there. I just need to go get my wallet. I left it in
my car." But he didn't go. He just stood there, staring
at me.

"It's really you, isn't it?" he said to me. He had this
crazy smile.

"What are you talking about?" I said.

"It's you. I mean, Richard Tyler. You're him. You're
Richard Tyler."

I put my thumb on the button of my switchblade behind my back. "Who are you?" I said.

"I..." he glanced at the studio door and back to me. "I
need you to come with me. It's really important.
Please."

"Like hell," I said.

"We need you," he said, and his face lost the crazy
smile, but not the crazy. "You've got to come."

"Come on!" my mother called from the studio. "Let's
get started!"

"Here," he said, "I need to show you something," and
he pulled a scrap of paper out of his pocket and stepped
to me. I fell for it, and suddenly he threw his arms
around me in a bear hug, lifted me off the floor, and
headed for the door.

I don't know. If this was a normal fight I would have been ready for that, but this guy just didn't look like the kind of guy you'd expect that sort of thing from. He looked more like some down-on-his-luck college professor, but one that had gone nuts and pushed a shopping cart around and dug in dumpsters and whatnot.

So I didn't react as fast as I should have. Boy, I tell you, we had a go at it. It's amazing how strong a guy like that can be when he's nuts. And this dude was nuts, man. Hollering and squealing and yipping as he tried to carry me out of the trailer. The way he had my arms pinned I couldn't use my knife, but just as he went to squeeze through the half-open door, I bit him on the nose and gave him a good knee to the groin.

We fell and as we hit the floor his grip loosened just enough for me to get my right arm free and I stabbed him in his left side. You could hear the wind come out of him and I pushed out of his grip. I jumped to my feet with the knife at the ready, but he had lost his steam.

He was sitting there, leaning against the wall, holding his side, looking at his blood like he couldn't believe what just happened. My mother had walked into the room to see what the commotion was about. She wasn't panicking or anything. She was just kinda staring at the guy who had started to plead, "Help me... I'm bleeding..."

She had a weird look on her face. Almost a smile. It was like she was studying him the way she studied my bloody handprints on the wall in the red house. Then

she walked back to her studio and returned with a piece
of drawing paper.

"Help me," he said.

She squatted down and pressed the drawing paper
onto his wound. Then she came to me and said, "Give
me your knife." I did. I don't know why I did—maybe
the guy wasn't a threat any more, maybe I just didn't
want the evidence in my hand, I don't know—but I did.

Just as she disappeared into the kitchen with the
bloody paper and the knife, Sailor came home. "What
the hell?" he said.

I was still breathing hard but I told him, "This guy
came in and attacked us, Sailor, I had to cut him, I had
to."

"Is she OK? Where is she?"

"Mom's OK, she's in the kitchen. He didn't touch her.
Just me."

"Who is he?"

"I don't know."

Sailor drew out his own knife and switched it open as
he squatted by the guy and held the blade to his throat.
"Don't you even move," he said.

"I'm bleeding," the guy said.

"Shut up." Sailor looked at me. "Where's your knife?"

"Mom took it."

"OK," he said. "I'll deal with that later. Is he alone,
or was there someone else with him?"

"I don't know," I said.

"Hey," Sailor said to the guy and slapped him on the
cheek. "Are you alone?"

"I'm bleeding, I need a doctor, please..."

"All right," Sailor said. "You and me are going for a ride. If you want a doctor, you'll tell me what I want to know." Then he turned to me. "Cain, clean up the mess. Every drop of blood. Use bleach. Wipe down anything he might have touched. Clean it up and burn the rags so there's no evidence anything happened here, got it?"

"Yeah, I got it."

"Tend to your mother. Keep the doors locked til I get back. You say your mother took your knife?"

"Yeah."

"All right. Here, take mine. Use it if you have to. You did good, Cain, really good. You protected the castle. I'm proud of you."

And with that he dragged the bloody guy out of the trailer and was gone.

I spent a good portion of the rest of the night cleaning up and worrying about the guy I stabbed. I mean, what if he died? I'd be a murderer. Again. I didn't think the cut went that deep, but still, if I nicked the liver or lung, that'd be it. Plus, it wasn't some ambulance crew that took him away, it was Sailor. And Sailor wasn't likely to deliver any more first aid than it took to get information out of him.

But mostly I worried who the guy was, and how he knew about me, and what he'd tell Sailor. At some point in the night, all the cleaning and worrying tuckered me out and I dozed off.

My mother's scream woke me up around sunup. "Cain, you little bastard! Get out here! Cain!" She was never one to refrain from cussing, but man, I thought Sailor himself was going to blush the way she was going on.

When I got out the front door into the yard she was livid. "You did this! This is your fault! You did this, didn't you! Damnit!" As she yelled she was pointing at the front of the trailer.

Somebody had spray-painted a symbol on it. I stared at it in shock. I couldn't even speak. It was like that cartoon fish I found at the church, the one that made my mother so mad she fishhooked me, only it was different. This one had its mouth open and in its mouth was what looked like a cartoon baby, like a stick figure. It's body was going down in the fish's throat and its head was a circle with a little curly-cue on top for hair and a sad mouth. There were two "x" marks for eyes, like it was dead.

"You did this, didn't you?" she yelled again.

"I didn't do it!" I shouted. "It was that guy! I... I heard something before he came in, like spray painting, it wasn't me, it was him!"

"Liar!" my mother yelled. "It's your fault! This is all you! This is your doing! Look at it!"

"I didn't do it, I swear! It was that guy!"

"You brought him here, didn't you! If it wasn't you, then how did he find us? Tell me that. How did he find us? What did you do?"

"I didn't bring him here! How could I..." I looked at Sailor. "What did he tell you? Did he tell you anything?"

He shook his head. "I didn't get much out of him. Dude was pretty much nuts. Plus he was dizzy from loss of blood. Just babbled about saving the river or something. He was alone, though, I'm pretty sure of that."

"Everybody just shut up," my mother said. She stood there with her eyes shut like she was thinking. You could see her jaws clench. Then she said, "I'm going for a drive. When I get back I want this cleaned up. I don't want to see even a hint of it on this house."

She got in her car and sped off. Sailor said, "I better follow her, just in case. I already got the stuff out, but I think it's best if you clean it up. There's the sandpaper, there's the paint and roller. Sand it off, then paint over it. I'll be back."

"Sailor," I said. "Is he, you know…"

Sailor gave me one of his outlaw grins. "Don't worry about him," he said. "Just keep your eyes open, make sure there aren't any more of them."

I thought I'd be in a heap of trouble when they got back. I mean, surely the guy got a hold of my letter somehow, and surely Sailor dug that information out of him one way or another, and surely my mother would have dug it out of Sailor. She was his queen. He'd never say no to her.

But when they came back they didn't mention it. They were calm. When I was able to talk to him alone I asked Sailor what he learned from the guy and what became of him. Sailor just said, "Ah, just a crazy fool and a case of mistaken identity. Just drop it. We got a new

customer starting tomorrow, that'll get your mother's attention back on her art. That's what's important."

Later that day he told me, "Look, Cain, your mom
wants a bit of a break from old Sailor, so I'm heading
back to sea for a while. Watch over your mother while
I'm gone. Oh, and by the way... Did you see what's on
the fridge?"

"The fridge?"

He smiled and shook his head. "Panel number two in
the triptych of Cain," he said. "Check it out." Then he
saddled up and roared off on his bike.

I didn't know what the heck he was talking about, so
I went into the kitchen. And there it was. On the fridge,
right next to the old fishhook blood painting. The drawing paper that she had pressed against the weird guy's
bloody wound, where I had stabbed him. Dangling from
the magnet by a string was the switchblade I had used.
And words, written in his blood:

VENGEANCE

IS

MINE

12. Samuel Blue

ABOUT A WEEK AFTER THAT, which was three weeks after I sent the letter, I got a reply. But it wasn't from the judge. When I first saw the letter I recognized the postmark and return address as being from that town, Harlington, but it was handwritten and didn't look official. The letter inside was in a girly kind of cursive, which I had some trouble with, but it wasn't long and I got through it. I remember what it said:

> *Dear Richard,*
> *I can't believe I'm hearing from you, after all these years! My name is Laura McKenzie and you and I were friends when we were little. I have always wondered where you went and what became of you after you left! We have so much to catch up on!*
> *I think I can help you get the information you're looking for, except I can't help you get in touch with your father, because he's still missing. If you want me to help you, please write to me at the return address I used. Better yet, if you can call me, use the number at the bottom of this letter. But please, please, please don't tell anyone that you got this letter. I could get in huge trouble. I work part time at the judge's office in the courthouse, doing things like opening and sorting mail, which is how I saw your letter. If they find out I*

intercepted your letter, I could get fired, or even prose-
cuted! So please keep this between us. You can trust
me, and I know I can trust you.

Some people might say it was pure luck that I was in
that place at that time to find your letter. But like your
Aunt Violet says, "Not lucky. Blessed."

Anyway, please, please, please write back or call me.
We have so much to discuss!

Your friend,

Laura

p.s. I know what happened to your little brother. I
was there too.

I can hardly describe how Laura's letter made me feel.
After the thing with Estelle, I thought I'd never cry again.
And yet, this letter brought a tear to my eye that I had to
wipe away with my sleeve.

I put the letter in my pocket and I went outside on a
fast walk in the woods. Now and again I'd stop and open
the letter and read it. Laura's words sang to me like a
bird. Pretty soon I found myself at that stinky old spring
with the plywood over it, the place I always feared the
river cat would come walking out of. The woods there
opened onto a little meadow and across the meadow was
that abandoned old house, and in the sky above it was a
rainbow. I kid you not. Big and perfect. Gleaming.

Everything felt just absolutely right in the world, let
me tell you. I was smiling, man, and then I just let out a
shout. Just for the hell of it. Just for joy. And you know
what, Aunt Violet? I heard a shout back.

For just a second I thought it was an echo, but it wasn't. It was an old voice, and kinda weak, and it shouted again, "Hey! Can you give me a hand?"

So I walked across the meadow toward the house. An old man was lying on the ground with a big tree branch pinning his leg down. "Friend," he said, "can you give me a hand? The storm last night must have weakened that branch, and it come down right on me. I can't move an inch. Lucky it didn't kill me, I reckon."

The branch was big, but it had a part that turned upward and I was able to get my shoulder under it. I gave it a shove, but my feet slipped in the wet ground and down I went. The old man gave out a tired, hoarse laugh. "It's a big one, my friend," he said. "We may need a tractor."

I looked around and found a couple of rocks to jam into the ground under my feet for traction. Then I gave the branch another shove, and man, it took everything I had, I was grunting and straining, and the bark was digging into my shoulder, but finally I lifted it enough that he could wiggle out.

"Thank you Lord! Thank you Jesus," the old man said, and he sat up and began feeling his shin with his hands. "You are an answered prayer, my young friend, an answered prayer. When I realized I couldn't get out from under this by myself, I prayed God would send me someone to help. Way out here, no one could hear me but God. And he did, he sent you. Such a blessing you are. And so strong! How'd you get to be so strong at such a young age, my friend?"

"I don't know," I said. "Born that way, I guess. How's your leg?"

"Well, I don't think it's broke, praise the Lord," he said. Then he leaned back on his elbows and just looked at me for a while. "Everything happens for a reason," he said. "Had that tree limb not fallen on me, I'd be long gone lonesome George. Instead, here I am and here you are, and now the world has two friends it didn't have before. And look up there. Look at that rainbow. Ain't it beautiful?"

"I love rainbows," I said. I don't think I had ever said that out loud before. It felt good.

"Yeah," he said. "It's a sign, you know. Of God's covenant."

I didn't know what he was talking about, and I must have looked like it.

"Rainbows are a sign of God's love for us," he said. "A sign that everything's going to be just fine." I looked from the rainbow to the old man, and he said, "I believe God brought us together for a reason today. It's up to us to figure out what that is."

I still didn't know what he was talking about, but it didn't matter. For the first time in my life that I could remember, I felt like I had a true friend.

"Hey," he said, "what do you say we have a stew? If you look over there I got a bag with some taters and carrots, they're from a dumpster but they're pretty fresh. And there next to it is a groundhog, he's pretty fresh too, I saw a car hit him last night and I picked him up right away. I was going to make the stew last night, but the rain kinda put a damper on that."

So that's what we did. I used my switchblade to skin and cut up the groundhog and the vegetables, and he had a cigarette lighter I used to light a fire from sticks I found around the place and broken lumber and furniture from inside the house. That's also where we got the stew pot.

We let it cook for a couple of hours and we just talked. I was slower to open up so he talked about himself first. His name was Samuel Blue and a long time ago he had a good job and a wife and two children, girls, and they lived in this very house. And then one hot summer day he drove to work and when he finished the day he went back to his car and there was his younger daughter, still strapped in her car seat in the back seat of the car, dead. He was supposed to have taken her to a day care, which is something his wife normally did, but she couldn't that morning for some reason.

There was a court case and a jury convicted him and he spent some time in prison for it. His wife divorced him and never spoke to him again or let him see his other daughter. When he got out he never tried to get another job. He just rambled, a hobo from that day to this.

"I guess I was always a wanderer," he said. "I used to sing and daydream too much. That's how I forgot about my child in the car." He was quiet for a while and when he looked at me there were tears in his eyes. "The only reason I am alive today," he said, "is that I know the good Lord has forgiven me, even if no one else has."

Well, I reckon I couldn't stay shut up then. I started talking. And I didn't stop til I had told Samuel Blue everything—about the river cat and my little brother, and how that broke up my family, and how my mother changed my name and took me to this place she called New Nod, and how I had never been to school, and about getting fishhooked, and about Sailor, and writing the letter to the judge, and Laura McKenzie writing me back, and everything. It all came tumbling out like a dam had broken. I had never talked to anybody in my life like that.

And Samuel Blue believed every word I said. Like when I told him about how I couldn't hate the river cat that took my brother because of the rainbow mark, and how it seemed to move so smooth and all, and how I could never find the right word to describe that, he gave me that word. He said, "That's called grace, son. Grace. God's grace. What happened, happened for a reason. You're not to be condemned for that."

And when I told him about my dreams, like the one about the rodeo, he looked at me like I wasn't crazy at all and he said, "Those are prophetic dreams. That's why they seem so real. They have meaning. The Lord speaks to some people through dreams. He's speaking to you. But you don't need to be in a rush to figure it all out. It'll come to you in due time."

When the stew was done we ate in silence. It was the most delicious meal I ever had. When we were finished,

Samuel wiped his mouth with his sleeve and said, "I know why the Lord brought us together this fine day."

"Why?"

"What's the name of that town you came from, where you wrote to the judge?"

"Harlington."

Samuel Blue chuckled. "Harlington. I know that place. Know it well. And here's something else I know from riding the rails so many years. You know the railroad that goes through here, maybe a half mile yonder? Well, that line goes straight down to Harlington, and not only that, but there's a southbound freight train that, when it passes through here, it slows way down and it makes it easy to jump, and when it gets to Harlington there's a bend where it slows way down again and it's easy to jump off. I've done it many times. That train comes through here just after sundown. You need to be on that train. Go find what you're looking for.

"And here's what else tells me it was the good Lord brought us together today. That Laura girl, you're going to have to contact her, tell her you're coming. She sounds like a sweet gal." He reached into his pocket and pulled out a cell phone, one of those cheap folding kind. He said, "Yesterday I was at a park and this lady was trying to use her phone and she was getting all peeved because she couldn't do something with it and her husband was there and she said, 'That's it, Harold, I'm getting a smart phone! Right now!' and she went marching back to their car she was so irritated she just threw that cell phone in the garbage can.

"Well I fished it out and to tell you the truth I didn't even know why. It's not like I need a phone. But something made me fish it out. The Lord did that, I'm convinced. Guided my hand into that dumpster. And I'll bet..." he flipped it open, smiled, and held it toward me, "it's got a nice strong signal. Now who would have thought, out here in the boondocks you'd get four bars like this? You see a cell tower around here? I don't."

He handed me the phone. "Take it," he said. "Call her. Tell her you're coming. You'll be there in the morning."

I guess I kinda froze. Sailor and his gang used what they called "burner phones" and I helped them out in their business on occasion, so it's not like I didn't know how, but, I don't know, I couldn't even remember ever talking to a girl of my own age. I must have looked pretty helpless to Samuel.

I'm glad he didn't try to persuade me. I don't know what I would have done. Instead, he said, "That's all right, I reckon God put the phone in my hand, not yours, so this is my job. You got that letter she sent you?"

I pulled it out of my pocket and handed it to him. He dialed the number she wrote and in a few seconds he said:

"Hello, is this Laura McKenzie?... Laura, my name is Samuel Blue and I'm calling you on behalf of a mutual friend of ours, name of Richard Tyler. I believe you wrote him a letter recently." He smiled and nodded while she spoke. "Well, he's busy making some other preparations, otherwise he'd be calling you, but he would like to take you up on your kind offer to help him find some information about his background... Oh no, no, nobody else knows but me and you and Richard. The secret is safe, yes... Anyway, Laura, Richard is planning to come down... Yes, actually come down there... When? Well, he's going to ride the rails, hobo style, and he should be there in the morning. Will you be available to meet him?... Well, if it's like it used to be years ago, there's a place where the tracks cross a road, and there's a signal arm on the road, I believe it's the only signal arm in Harlington, and there's a little old water tower and a catch pond... Oh, you know it, wonderful!" He covered the phone and whispered to me, "She lives close by there." Then he continued his conversation with her. "Yes, that's right, the southbound train comes through right around sunup and it slows down as it crosses that road because there's a sharp bend... Yes, that's right, well it's nice to see you know the area so well. That's right, tomorrow morning... Well, I'll tell him that, and he's really looking forward to seeing you, too... What does he look like?... Well, he's a handsome young man, I must say, and he's got hair the color of Alabama red clay and he's, well, let's say he's unusually strong for his age, but it's more wildcat strength than bull strength you might say, and oh, he's got a scar on his... let's see, his left cheek that kinda sorta gives him a dimple there when he smiles. Dimple on the left cheek, that's right... OK, then, you be sure to meet him there, OK? All right, fantastic! God bless you, girl... Good bye."

When he finished he looked at the phone and shook his head in amazement. "Look at that," he said, and showed me the face. "Battery's dead." He got up and hobbled over to his rucksack leaning against the house, then he pulled something out and came back and handed it to me. It was a book.

"What's this?" I said.

"That's the Bible," he said. "I've carried that Bible for years. It's brought me a lot of peace and wisdom along my path. I reckon it'll do the same for you on this journey."

"You think it'll bring me good luck?" I said.

"Nope. It's like she said in the letter. You're not lucky. You're blessed. Always remember that... Just a minute," he said. He hobbled back to his rucksack and brought back a pen. He opened the Bible and wrote this on the inside cover:

To my very dear friend, Richard
Jesus can save anyone, even Cain
No longer a wanderer
You are now on the path to Glory!
God bless and keep you
Your friend, Samuel "Singin' Sammy" Blue

Then he handed it to me and said, "You know, this kinda puts the urge to travel in me. I'd come with you, but this bum leg of mine would just slow you down. You need to do this on your own, anyway, I reckon. But when you get back, I want to hear all about it, OK?"

I looked from the Bible to him and I felt this surge of emotion I can't really describe, even today, except to call it love. And I felt really anxious that I'd leave it and never find it again. "You'll be here?" I said.

"I'll be here."

"Promise?"

"You have my word on it, son." And then that old man hugged me. The last time I remember someone hugging me was the day I lost my brother and I wasn't even five years old, and that nice lady on the riverbank picked me up and tried to comfort me.

"And when you get back," he said, "indigo bunting ought to be here. I'll show him to you."

"Indigo bunting?"

"Indigo bunting's a bird. The most beautiful bird you've ever seen. Little bitty thing, but the deepest blue you can imagine, and when the low sun shines on him, he just sparkles. I used to watch him when I lived here. I used to show him to my kids. Oh, how I've longed to see that bird again. When you get back, we'll see him together."

I turned and I ran all the way back home.

13. Hobo

SAMUEL BLUE WAS SPOT ON about the timing of the train, and where it slowed down and how to pick a car, throw your sack in and jump it, all that. It made me trust him all the more, it let me sort of settle into the idea that I really did have a friend, finally, and as I sat there in the boxcar of that southbound train, I imagined coming back and telling my friend what I learned in my adventure, and how glorious it all was.

Because, let me tell you, if you haven't ever rode the rails before, there is something majestic about it. I mean, a train's not like a car or a motorcycle, because you don't control it, it controls you, and it's got this hugeness about it, the way it sways and rumbles as it goes, and the hard, unending clickety-clack sound, and the way that big horn sounds in the night. Sailor'd talk about getting the same kind of feel from ships, and I reckon he's right about that.

I had stuck a flashlight in my sack and I dug it out, but the batteries were so weak it just put out a dim orange glow that I couldn't see anything by, so I just tossed it out of the car. For a while at first I kept my switchblade in my hand, ready for any of the "buggers and brigands" Samuel said you find among the hobo crowd. His words, not mine. I didn't know what either of them was, except they liked to prey on anyone littler than them, and they wouldn't mind waiting in the shadows to pounce on a sleeping victim, so I was bound to prove up front I'd be nobody's victim.

"Anybody else in here?" I called out. No answer. I rode quiet for a while but after a bit, no answer to a question like that didn't seem like proof I was alone. So I said, and I made my voice low and grumbly, "I got me a blade and I know how to use it, and I'll sure enough kill you, you buncha buggers and brigands, you mess with me!"

Now, I can't really tell you why I used Samuel's words like that, as back in those days I cussed as bad as Sailor, though not as bad as my mother, but I guess it was lucky I did because if I had just tossed out some f-bombs, likely the others would have stayed quiet and I wouldn't have noticed them until they got me in my sleep.

But right after I yelled it out I heard a kind of hoarse wheezing in the shadows on the other side of the boxcar. At first I thought, or hoped, it was some mechanical sound from the train itself, something scraping and rubbing from the sway of the car because it almost didn't sound human. I stood there with my legs far apart to keep my balance and my blade shining in the moonlight coming in through the open car door.

The hoarse wheezing got louder and jerkier and another sound joined it, more like a grunting, but I still couldn't tell if it was human, and in fact I began to wonder if I had gotten into a livestock car with pigs or goats by mistake. But then the sound changed, kinda like a car engine that wheezes and spits a bit before it catches, and I realized it was somebody laughing.

"Show yourself!" I yelled. "I'll cut you up, I swear to God!"

Of course, that made the laughter even worse, and I was about to make the decision to either jump out of the car or go on the attack when the crackly voice sang out:

> *Buggers and brigands*
> *Brigands and bugs*
> *Any post office got*
> *Shots of our mugs*
> *Stuck on the clipboards*
> *Nailed to the walls*
> *Praise the Postmaster*
> *For bustin' our balls*

And the mocking laughter surged again before the voice said, "Whoa, Nellie, settle down, son, any friend of Singin' Sammy Blue is a friend of ours." Then into the moonlight stepped this woman, must've been six-foot tall and a good two hundred twenty pounds, and layered in one shabby garment over another and boots without laces with the tongues hanging out like panting dogs, and this worn out hat with a tiny little brim. And she stood there wheezing like a coal miner who had pounded down more coffin nails than an undertaker and she said, "Son, you wouldn't happen to have a smoke, would you?"

"No."

"Oh well. You can put away your shiv. We're just a couple of harmless old folks, one foot and four lil' piggies in the grave. Like I said, any friend of Singin' Sammy is a friend of ours. I've done rode with him going back twenty, twenty-five years." She stuck out her hand. "Bon Julia. What's your name?"

I didn't shake her hand. I tried to look into the shadows behind her to see the other person without taking my eyes off her either, but I couldn't make it out. I kept my knife at the ready.

"Uncle Pete!" she called. "Uncle Pete, come on out in the light. The boy can't see who you are, no wonder he's suspicious."

"I ain't comin' nowhere near," the voice said. "Boy's got a shiv. I get stabbed again, I could die. Huh-uh. No. No way."

"Aw, come on, Uncle Pete! This boy ain't going to hurt you. He's friends with Singin' Sammy Blue, and Singin' Sammy wouldn't hurt a flea. You like Singin' Sammy, don't you?"

"Singin' Sammy ain't here!" the man barked. He sounded stupid, maybe retarded.

"Well, any friend of Singin' Sammy's got to be peaceful, ain't that right, boy? You wouldn't hurt old Uncle Pete there, would you?"

"I might," I said.

"All right, all right," she said, drawing back her hand. "No offense, now. I tell you what. Me and Uncle Pete'll just stay on that other side and you can have this side, and we'll just ride in peace, how's that suit you?"

"Suits me fine," I said. "You first."

Bon Julia nodded and shuffled backwards into the shadows toward the far side of the car. "We're sorry about laughing at you, young feller. It's just that when you said buggers and brigands, well, it just brought to mind old Singin' Sammy, that was one of the songs he used to sing, wrote it himself, in fact. That fella must've made up a thousand songs. I used to watch him, he'd stand there just about where you are now in the moonlight at night and make up a song as we went along. He could sing real nice too. So, uh, how'd you get to know him, if you don't mind my asking."

I sat down against the boxcar wall opposite from Bon Julia and Uncle Pete. "I just met him... out of the blue, I guess."

"Out of the Blue, out of the Blue," Uncle Pete said. "I get it. Out of the Blue, cuz Sammy Blue. I get it, I get it. Dat's punny."

"How come he ain't with you?" Bon Julia said.

"He couldn't make it."

I was quiet then because I didn't get the same feeling out of these two that I got from Samuel Blue, and I didn't trust them.

Bon Julia got to talking about stuff, hobo stories I guess you could say, and pretty soon I recognized them as pretty much the same as the sea stories Sailor's crew were always telling, and I kinda tuned her out—except when she said something about how Uncle Pete got to be called Uncle Pete not because he was her uncle, but that's how he presented himself to the children he'd molest. He didn't even take up for himself when she talked like that, he just laughed along like he agreed. I couldn't tell if he was shameless or just stupid. But I kept my knife in my hand.

That train rocked like a cradle, and its clickety clack lullaby was making me drowsy. I interrupted Bon Julia, "Do you know Harlington?"

"Harlington?" she said. She sounded relieved that I finally spoke up. "Sure, been there many a time. They got a good soup kitchen there. Why?'

"That's where I get off."

"Uh-huh."

"I don't want to fall asleep and miss it."

She laughed. "You won't. There's a sharp turn there and a road crossing. Engineer slows down and blasts his horn just before that."

That squared with what Samuel told me. "OK," I said.

"We'll get there around sunup," she said. "You can get some sleep. We won't hurt you. Shoot, we're more ascared of you than you are of us, guarantee you that. I'm near seventy and Uncle Pete here's... what you got on me, Pete, two, three years?..."

She kept on yapping, but I tuned her out. Ever since I lived in the red house, and especially after she hooked me in New Nod, I learned to sleep real light and keep one eye open for my mother. I tried to convince myself I could do the same thing on the train, but I was getting really sleepy. The only other option was to throw them both off the train so I could have the car to myself, and the thought crossed my mind, but I didn't do it.

The train rhythm got too much and I fell asleep. I had a dream. It was a bad one, very tense and weird. In my dream it was night but I wasn't on the train, I was in the tall sawgrass next to the railroad tracks as the train went speeding by. And the train never slowed down like Samuel said it would so I couldn't find a way to jump aboard. Down the embankment from the tracks there was a swampy area with cattails and standing water and I could hear the slurp-thunk, slurp-thunk of the huge river cat coming my way but it was all in the darkness and no rainbow. And I couldn't move, it was like my legs were made of rubber and real weak, and I was panicking because it was getting close and I couldn't get on the train. And as the train rushed by there was a girl sticking her head out a passenger car window and yelling something, but I couldn't hear what, from the noise of the train. And then I saw the fishhook, the one my mother used on me, and it was bouncing wildly in the weeds, like it was being dragged from the running train by a fishing line I couldn't see. I looked at where the river cat was parting the weeds as it stalked me and I looked back at the train and all of a sudden, bam, the fishhook caught me in the cheek and dragged me along and it hurt so bad I woke up.

And I was awake in real life on the train and my heart pounding and the moonlight was gone but the stars were really, really bright and I saw the man's silhouette in the boxcar doorway against the night sky.

I was shrieking as I clawed my way up through nightmare alley and my voice came bellowing out as I sat up in fighting reflex, first just like a cornered dog and then yelling curses and threats as I fumbled for my knife.

Uncle Pete almost fell out of the train as I startled him and then he was crying out, "No! No! I'z just peeing! I'z just peeing! Don't hurt me! Ahhhh!" as he turned and stumbled blindly back to the other end of the car.

I was just wildly throwing out threats, "Get back! Get away from me! What are you doing! What the hell are you doing! I'll cut you to pieces, man! Get back!"

Uncle Pete was wailing and crying, "I'm sorry, don't hurt me," and Bon Julia was moaning and groaning all disoriented from being woke up and as she came to she kept begging me to "calm down, calm down, son, we wasn't doing nothing, I swear, take it easy..."

I sat back against the boxcar wall and let my breathing calm down. As I did I realized that my cheek throbbed with pain—not as bad as it did when I first got hooked, but in the same place. I couldn't taste any blood in my mouth, but when I touched the outside of my cheek my fingers felt wet and slimy, like with blood. But it was too dark to see and I didn't have a flashlight. I knew then it wasn't just a dream. Something happened.

Uncle Pete was whimpering so pitiful I was almost ashamed to accuse him of anything, but he was standing there when I woke up. I was wondering what to do about him when I realized I didn't know where my sack was, that I had been using for a pillow. "Hey!" I said, "Where's my sack? Did you steal my stuff?" I swept my right hand across the floor to feel for it and accidentally smacked my knife, which spun around and skittered

toward the open door. I lunged blindly for it and by
sheer luck slammed my hand down on it before it could
slide off the train. I nicked the side of my hand when I
did that, but I clutched it in my fist and rolled back, and
when I did I bumped into my sack in the dark. I grabbed
it and put it on my lap.

"We didn't steal your stuff, young fella, I swear, we
didn't do nothing like that," Bon Julia said. "We
wouldn't do that to a fellow 'bo, I swear."

"I didn't do nothing," Uncle Pete whimpered, "I'z just
peeing, just peeing out the door, I'm sorry, I'm sorry..."

The dawn had just started to break and a soft light
crept into the car. I think that helped me gather my wits
and bit by bit I figured out what probably happened was
the train car made a sudden jostle and my head fell off
my pillow sack and I nicked my cheek with the blade I
still had open in my hand. So I kinda felt ashamed for
scaring those people, but still I didn't trust them so I just
kept quiet. So did they.

When the horn blew it was so brassy and loud and
sudden I jerked. Bon Julia said, "This your stop.
Harlington." The red sky in the east gave way to pink
and gold when the sun finally peeked over the horizon
and came streaming in the boxcar. As the train slowed I
poked my head out the door and looked forward. I saw
the crossing road that Samuel Blue told me about.

And there was the girl, sitting on a four-wheeler. I
must confess, I had one of those anxious moments
where my guts kinda went jumbly. I never had a friend
of my own age, girl or boy, that I could remember. Oh

sure, there were a lot of females among Sailor's crew that would come around, and some customers, but they were all grown women, and even when they would flirt with me, that was different. That was all joking around. Well, not all of it, but, you know what I mean.

Anyway, I remembered how Samuel Blue had helped me contact her when I was reluctant, so I stuck my hand in my sack, just to touch the Bible he gave me, the one with the inscription, just so a bit of his confidence might rub off.

It wasn't there. I almost panicked, I swear. I rummaged hard through the sack, but no deal. It wasn't there. "Damn!" I said. I thought for sure I stuck it in my sack when I was packing. And then I looked back at Bon Julia and Uncle Pete. "Hey!" I yelled at them. "Did you steal my book?"

I clicked open my switchblade and stepped toward them. "Did you steal my book, Pete? Goddamnit you better give it back!"

They both huddled together and drew their knees up and raised their hands to defend themselves. "We didn't steal nothing of yours," Bon Julia said.

But it was Uncle Pete who had been standing near me when I woke up in the night. I leaned in on him. "Did you steal my book? Gimme back my book, right now, or I'll cut you up!"

"Waah! I just had to pee!" he cried. "I just had to pee! Please, please..."

"Come on, young fella, don't hurt him, now!" Bon Julia pleaded. "Uncle Pete can't even read! What would he want with a book?... Look, if you want to get off here, you best jump now, the train's speeding up again, ten seconds more and you won't be able to get off for another hundred miles!"

So I did. Sack in one hand, open knife in the other, I jumped off. I was almost glad for the pounding I took when I hit the ground and tumbled off the edge of the crossing street down into the drainage ditch at the bottom of the railroad embankment.

After the train passed, I heard the girl call to me from above.

14. Laura

"ARE YOU OK?" THE GIRL CALLED DOWN.

Sailor had always said to keep a switchblade out of people's sight unless you need it, since a lot of places they're against the law. I snapped the knife closed and stuffed it into my pocket before turning to face her.

"Hi, I'm Laura," she said.

"I'm Ca..." No, wait, not Cain, I thought. Dang, what was it? "I'm, uh..."

She smiled. "Richard?"

"Yeah, Richard. Richard, um,..."

"Tyler?" she laughed with a little giggle. I liked it.

"Tyler, right," I said. "Richard Tyler. Sorry. People don't call me by that name much anymore."

"What do they call you?" she said.

I humped it out of the drainage ditch and when I got to the top I said, "Cain."

"Cain?" she said with a sour look. "You're kidding... Oh." She caught herself and looked away for a moment. Then she said, "Can I call you Richard? That's how I remember you."

"Yeah," I said. "I'd like that."

Suddenly she got off the four-wheeler and threw her arms around my neck and hugged me tight. "I can't believe you're really here! Can you believe it's been ten

years since... well... Do you remember anything from
back then?"

"Some," I said. "A little."

"Do you remember me?" she said. "Oh, never mind.
We have all day to catch up on that. Are you hungry? I'll
bet you're famished. Riding all night on a train like that.
What was that like? It's seems so romantic! What would
you like to eat?"

I shrugged. "I have money," I said. "If we can stop by
a gas station, I'll..."

"Gas station! No way! You see that house over there?
That's where I live. Nobody's home right now, so we'll
just go there and I'll fix you some breakfast. Come on,
put your bag in the basket and hop on."

So I did. I had ridden on motorcycles lots of times
with Sailor and his crew, so I knew how to sit on the
back, sissy bar or not, but she reached back and took
both my wrists and then placed my hands on her sides
and she said, "hold on!" So I did that too. And let me
tell you something. It wasn't a far ride, but it was nice,
man, my hands on her hips and her hair blowing in my
face. This girl was well on her way to blossoming into a
pretty young woman. "Thank you, Samuel Blue," I said
to myself, and I grinned as I imagined telling him about
all this when I got back.

It was a big old white clapboard style farmhouse, two
stories, brick chimneys, and she had the windows open
and the breeze made the lacy white curtains billow. It
was real nice. She let me take a shower while she cooked
breakfast and I got into clean clothes I had brought with

me. She put a plate in front of me with scrambled eggs with cheese, and sausages, and grits, buttered toast and fig preserves, and set down a glass of orange juice and a cup of black coffee.

She put cream and sugar in her coffee. Just as I was about to dig in, she said, "Wait, aren't we forgetting something?" She held out both her hands. I didn't know what she wanted. "Hold my hands," she said. So I did. She closed her eyes. "Father," she said, "I thank you for delivering Richard to us safe and sound, and Father I thank you for this food, may it give us the strength to follow you this glorious day, and Father forgive us our sins and, um, lead us not into temptation, and... Father please watch over those in need. In Jesus' name we pray. Amen."

She opened her eyes to see me watching her. "You're supposed to close your eyes," she said.

"Oh. Sorry."

"And you're supposed to say Amen."

"Amen?"

"Yes. And if you want to eat, you're going to have to let go of my hands."

"Oh. Sorry." She stayed kinda quiet while I ate, even though I could tell she was itching to say something. Hungry as I was, it didn't take me long to finish, and when I pushed my plate back she kinda wiggled in her chair and said, "OK, where do you want to start?"

"Well," I said, "I'm not sure, but, uh..."

"I can't believe you're really here!" she said, slapping her hands on the table. "This is amazing! I mean, now of all times. Of all times! Oh, Richard, it's insane. It's crazy what's been going on here. And out of the blue, your letter comes. It's... Oh my God Richard you need to come down to the jail and see this guy! It's like... Oh, dang it. I promised myself I wouldn't do this. OK, OK..." She took a deep breath and let it out slowly. "OK, we don't need to go there yet. I'm sorry. I am, like, so, so sorry. OK. Let's start again. I mean, you wrote a letter looking for information about yourself and your parents. Where do you want to start?"

"Well, I guess, the main thing is..." I knew what I wanted to say, but for some reason I was freezing up and not able to get the words out of my mouth. The fishhook was acting up. I could feel it throb.

Laura reached across the table and put her hand on my arm. "Go ahead. You can say it. Say anything."

Looking at her and seeing how she was looking at me was like sweet candy in my mouth, and the throbbing went away. "I need to find out who my mother is. I remember there was this woman and I think she loved me, but this other woman, well she took me away from here and raised me up in New Nod but she never loved me like a real mother, and we don't even look anything alike, and... I think I was kidnapped when I was little. So I guess I want to find my real mother."

"You poor thing," she said. She stood and walked around the table and leaned over to hug me around the neck. "I think I can help you with this question. Wait here." She walked out of the kitchen, and when she came back she set a photograph down on the table in front of me. I couldn't help it, but my eyes got watery and I had to wipe them with my sleeve.

There were four people in the picture. A man and a woman and two little boys. The man was holding the older boy and the woman was holding the baby.

"This is a picture of your family," she said softly. "That's your mother. Is she the one who took you away?"

"Yeah," I said. "That's her."

Laura laid another picture down. It was of a woman holding a boy. "That's your Aunt Violet," she said. "And that's you she's holding. She really did love you, Richard. She still does. She worries about you, and what became of you."

I couldn't help it. I was supposed to be the strong one. But I broke down, and I started to cry like a baby. I mean, I was sobbing, like when you have to catch your breath, you know? I don't know how long it lasted. Not too long, but Laura was hugging me and crying too and saying she was sorry, maybe she shouldn't have shown me those pictures. She walked off to get some tissues and even though I kinda liked the way she was comforting me, I didn't like crying like that.

When she got back I tapped my finger on the man in the picture. "That's my dad?"

"Yes. And your Aunt Violet is his sister. Richard, we don't have to go through these if you don't want to."

"No, I'm fine. I want to. I came a long way. I want the whole truth." I picked up the family snapshot. "And that's my little brother."

"Yep. Emmanuel."

She set a third picture down. "Look, this is all of us. There's your mom and the baby, and there's your dad, and your Aunt Violet, and there's my dad, and there's you and me. We're sitting right next to each other. We were best friends, Richard."

I stared at it for a minute before it dawned on me. "This was taken..." I couldn't finish.

"It was taken the day your brother... went missing. We were all on a picnic together. At the river. This was not long before your dad took you and your brother out in the boat."

"Where's my father now?" I said.

"I don't know, Richard. Nobody knows. All we know is that he... well, he had sort of a nervous breakdown or something. He spent all his time in the river looking for 'lil Man,' that's what they called Emmanuel, and then one day he just disappeared and never came back. Nobody's seen him since."

"Is he still alive?"

"I don't know. I'm sorry, Richard. Miss Violet prays for him every day. And you too. She's never let anyone take you or your dad off the prayer list at church since that day. That's been ten years, Richard. That's more than five hundred Sunday church bulletins with your name in them! Ten years almost to the day, can you believe it?"

My feelings were all weird and jumbled. I felt like I needed to focus on something to get my bearings again, so I said, "Did you see what I saw?"

"What do you mean?"

"Out there on the boat. A river cat took my brother. A huge fish. Right out of my hands. You said you were there. Did you see it?"

"No. But I believe you, Richard! I have always believed you!"

"Did anyone else see it? Did my father see it? He was right there."

"Well, I'm pretty sure he didn't. I mean, I've read the case files—my father's the sheriff, so he knows pretty much..."

I stood up quick. "Your father's... what?"

"The sheriff. Oh, but don't worry! You're not in trouble or anything. He and your dad were best friends. He was there with us that day on the riverbank. Richard, please, don't worry. He's worried about you from the very beginning. He's just... well... he can't..."

"What?"

"Well, Daddy's an officer of the court, as they say, and he has to uphold the law. That stupid old judge issued a restraining order against your dad and your Aunt Violet, she's so sweet, Richard, I wish you could meet her! Anyway, he doesn't know you're here. But he's on your side, Richard, he really is."

"Does he believe me? About the river cat, I mean."

"Well, he..."

"He doesn't, does he?"

"Richard, Daddy's the sheriff, he has to deal with legal evidence, and, well..."

"So I'm the only one who saw it. A four year old kid."

"Yes, well, you were almost five, but it's hard to rely on the testimony of a small child, but there is at least some corroborating evidence and Daddy knows that..."

"Some what?" I said.

"Corroborating evidence. What I mean is, evidence that backs up your story."

"Like what?" I said. "Can you tell me what it is?"

She stared at me for a while before speaking. "I'll do better than that. I'll show you. Come on."

So we went back outside and she cranked up the four-wheeler and said, "Hop on," and we drove, partly on the paved roads, partly on dirt roads, across fields and on a trail in the woods until we wound up on another crumbly old paved road and a worn out gravel driveway where she stopped and pointed up at the sign.

There was a fence and a gateway through it but the gate was open and leaning to one side because of a broken hinge. Over the gateway was a wooden sign held up about ten feet high on two cedar poles. The sign said "River Cat Coliseum" and "Home of Blue Belle, Eighth Wonder of the Natural World." Below that it said, "Catfish Crouch Roop, Proprietor."

"This is where it all started," she said. "Come on, I'll show you." She drove the four wheeler along the gravel driveway past a yard filled with tall weeds, then a house that looked abandoned, and then behind the house a couple hundred yards to where there were a few ponds.

Laura stopped the engine and we got off. "OK," she said. "There was an old guy that used to live here named Crouch Roop. He called himself Catfish Crouch because he raised all kinds of catfish in these ponds. And in this pond right here he had the biggest blue catfish in the world, or that's what he said, I don't know if it was the biggest one or not, but he said it was. He named her Blue Belle."

"Did you see it?"

"No, not personally. Daddy did, and he said she was really, really huge. I read in the case file this one guy who worked here said he fed Blue Belle roadkill carcasses, like cats and raccoons and possums and stuff, and that fish would take them in one gulp.

"Anyway, Catfish Crouch wanted to turn this place into a tourist attraction, based on having these enormous fish, and he advertised and all, and there was actually something on the TV about him, and they had pictures of Crouch feeding Blue Belle. I don't think he got many customers, but what happened was this group called the Riverine Reparations Collective, which is like an animal rights terrorist group or something, they must have seen it on TV and so they came and liberated Blue Belle. They left a sign taking credit for it, and they even made a video and posted it on the Internet. Anyway, they somehow got Blue Belle into this big sling and put her in the back of a pickup truck and drove right down there to the river—you see the river? Look through the trees down there—and they released her.

"And Richard! This is only about a quarter of a mile from where we were that day. And! And, this happened only about a week before... before your brother... before a fish took your brother. It had to be Blue Belle, Richard, it had to! Some people don't believe it, but I do. I really do."

I was staring down at the river. "Can we go there?" I said.

"Where? You mean..."

"Where we were that day."

"Sure, it's easy to get there from here. Hop on." So we hit the roads and the trails again, Laura driving and me sitting behind her with my hands on her waist, taking in the view over her shoulder and feeling her hair brush my face in the wind. That felt good, but there was a knot growing in my belly that tightened up when we got there.

I got off the four-wheeler and took a few steps toward the riverbank. I stood there, staring. This was the place, for sure. It clicked in with my memory. The scene ran through my mind like I was living it again. Then I realized Laura was speaking.

"Richard? Are you OK?" she said.

"I guess so."

"Come with me, I want to show you something." She walked me up the bank toward an old fence line covered in Virginia creeper and poison ivy. In the shade of a big oak tree she stopped. There was a dark shiny stone with writing on it. "Your Aunt Violet had this put up for your brother," she said.

"You mean they found his body?" I said.

"No, it's not a gravestone, it's a memorial stone. See? It says: 'In Memory of Emmanuel Tyler' and it gives the birth and death dates, and then see that smashed place at the bottom? It used to say 'He's with Jesus now.' Your mother took a sledge hammer to it. That's what my dad told me. Miss Violet spent a lot of money on this stone, and your mother just about ruined it."

A marking on the stone caught my eye. It wasn't part of the original message. It had been scratched or chiseled in very crudely. I knelt down and brushed the dust from it.

"That's from the cult," she said.

"The cult?"

"Yeah. Remember what I told you, about the Riverine Reparations Collective? Well, after your story—I mean your testimony—about how a river catfish took your brother, when it got out in the news, they..."

"Wait. My story got in the news?"

"Well, back when it happened and there was an investigation and, oh, my dad was so angry about this, but back then the local paper published a story about how you said a fish took your brother, and I think it got picked up by other newspapers and TV stations and all, and anyway, the Collective heard about it and they were like, wow, this is exactly what should happen! Human beings were guilty of killing the river, and the river goddess demanded a sacrifice, and it was like... I mean... Richard, they think you're their prophet or something because, you know, they were just thinking of liberating Blue Belle from captivity, but it's like they think you showed them the true way by... by sacrificing your brother. I mean, that's what they think! And so that's what they chose as their cult symbol. See, it has the Christian fish, but his mouth is open and see that circle there? That's the baby's head and those 'x' eyes means he's dead. Isn't that sick?

"I mean, Daddy said for about two years after the incident they were spray painting that sign all over the place, or carving it into trees and stuff like that. But then, and it seemed to die down after a while and daddy got the county and boy scouts and all to paint over the signs, and we didn't hear much more from the cult for a long time and then all of a sudden, bam, here we go again. Because, Richard, think about it! It's the ten-year anniversary! Tomorrow!

"And guess what, Richard. Just yesterday, somebody kidnapped a baby! And guess who's in jail right now under suspicion for that? Aldo-the-Bear! His real name is Aldo Singer-Sanger. He's the cult leader! Isn't it amazing all this is happening right when you come back? Miss Violet was saying just yesterday, that as much as she hates your mama for being so mean to you, it was probably best she took you away from here. Who knows what those cult people would do if they found you."

"They did find me," I said.

She looked like I had punched her in the gut. "What?"

"About a week ago, a guy came to where I live. He painted this sign on our house, and then he tried to kidnap me."

"Oh my God, Richard! What happened?"

"I stabbed him."

"You what? You..." She hesitated, then let out a nervous laugh. "Oh. You're just teasing me."

Then I did something Sailor told me never to do. I reached into my pocket and pulled out my switchblade. She jerked when I snapped it open. I touched my side with the tip of the blade. "Right here," I said.

"Are you serious? You're really telling the truth?"

"I can't lie," I said. "My mother hates me for that."

"Oh my God, Richard! Did you kill him?"

"I don't know. I don't think so. He bled a good bit, but I don't think I nicked an organ or artery or anything."

"Well... what happened to him?"

"Somebody I know took him away. That's probably all you need to know."

"How long ago was this, did you say?"

"About a week ago. A couple of weeks after I sent my letter to the judge."

"Oh my God, Richard, this is my fault. I knew I should have kept your letter! But I had already logged it, so I... I just copied it and put it in a pile that doesn't really get checked much... I didn't think... Richard! There's a mole in the courthouse!"

"A what?"

"A mole. A spy. Someone from the cult. Oh my God! But wait... How would they know your address to get there? Didn't you use a post office box?"

"Yeah, but I was checking it every day. He could have followed me home from the post office."

"Richard! These are bad people. I mean, we think they're planning on sacrificing that baby they kidnapped. Somewhere in the river. Tomorrow. The tenth anniversary of... You know."

"I thought you said the guy was in jail."

"Aldo is, but his followers aren't. He had a bunch. Maybe ten or twelve. Or more, I don't know. I'm sure he sent that guy to your house."

"I don't get it," I said. "Why doesn't your dad just make this Aldo guy in jail tell you where they are?"

"Well, Daddy can't just make him talk," she said.

"Sailor could."

"Who?"

"Somebody I know."

"Richard, he can't, like waterboard him or anything. Daddy has to obey the law. He's been trying to interrogate him since yesterday, but the guy won't talk."

"So the kid dies."

"I don't know what else to do, Richard."

I stared at the river. Ever since we got there I had a queasy feeling in my stomach I couldn't shake. My brother's memorial stone didn't help any. The longer I stood there the worse it got.

"I don't like it here," I said.

"Are you sorry you came down?"

"No, I don't mean that. I mean here. Right here. This place."

"Oh, OK, do you want to go somewhere else?"

"Is there anything you can tell me or show me about my dad? Anything at all?"

She thought about it for a minute. "Yes, there is. Come on."

THE BOOK OF CAIN

15. Sister Ada's Shack

WE GOT ON THE FOUR-WHEELER AGAIN. In a little while she turned onto this long dirt road and drove very slowly. She kept standing up and peering over the brush as if she was looking for something or someone. Then she turned off the dirt road onto a trail into the woods and as she did I saw a little, broken-down house, not in as bad shape as Samuel Blue's, but pretty run down. There was an old station wagon parked there and some chickens in the yard.

The trail went downhill, and the queasiness in my stomach returned when I saw the river through the woods. She stopped and turned off the motor. There was a shack in the woods, if you could call it that, more of a lean-to than a shack. There was junk scattered all around it, mostly covered with years of fallen leaves and forest vines.

"Did you see that house we passed?" she said. "That's where the Potters live. They were the last ones to see your father alive."

"Can we go talk to them?"

"No, it wouldn't do any good. They're really old and they have Alzheimer's, so they won't remember anything anyway. But I heard my daddy talk about it and I read the case files. It was after you left, you and your mom, and your dad had been basically living in the river for a

long time, everybody thought he was crazy, but he never
hurt anybody. Anyway, he went to the Potters' house
and he asked them where their daughter was. Sister
Ada. She was a witch. She used to live right here in this
shack. And the Potters told him they didn't know, this
is what they told my dad, that she often went wandering
across the country, preaching, or doing voodoo if you ask
me. Anyway, they asked him why he wanted to know
and he told them he had spent the night in this shack
and he had, like a dream or a vision or something, that
his little boy that drowned had been there. In this shack,
I mean. And you know the weird thing about that, Richard?

"It could totally happen. Look at the river. See how
there's a sharp bend in it right here? And see all those
logs and stuff piled up down there? Well, lots of stuff
from upriver gets stuck here where the river turns. In
fact, that's where Sister Ada got most of her stuff to live
here. She's the Potters' daughter, the witch, people
called her Sister Ada because she was real religious, but,
you know, not like us, but weird, I mean, she spoke in
tongues and handled rattlesnakes and made potions and
healed people, supposedly. Well, after your brother
went missing, my dad and his deputies and volunteers
and all, they searched the river, and they came here to
talk to Sister Ada because this is where stuff turns up all
the time, and they thought... well, they thought maybe
your brother's body might have turned up here and
maybe Sister Ada found it.

"But she told them she didn't see it. Then some time later they went to interview her again and she was gone. Nobody's seen her since. And then your dad went looking for her. And he never came back either. Isn't that weird?"

"Yeah. I guess."

"I know people who say Sister Ada found your brother's body and took it away for, you know, like, satanic rituals or something. Some people even think she found him alive and she ran away with him to raise as her own child, because she couldn't have children of her own, because of all the rattlesnake venom in her system. Well, plus, she was crazy and didn't have a husband, but they say rattlesnake venom can make you sterile."

My stomach was feeling really sour. I was sweating and my heart was starting to race. I didn't like being near this river at all. But I didn't want to show how anxious I was. I closed my eyes and thought of my father and I heard his voice, "You're the strong one, Son." I stepped into the little lean-to and stood there in the shadows. Something glistened in the corner of my eye. There was a crack in the window. And the way the sun was coming through the forest canopy, a little ray of it fell on that window and the crack shone with the colors of the rainbow. It wasn't a real rainbow, but it made me feel better, so I stood there where I could see it.

Laura stepped in after me. "Isn't this just the spookiest place on earth?" she said, holding her arms as if she was cold. "Do you want to look around, see if we can find something your dad or Sister Ada left behind? Like a clue or something?"

"No, I don't think so," I said. I wanted to run the hell away from that river. But I stood real still and kept my eyes on the rainbow. I was afraid if I moved, if I lost sight of that rainbow in the window, I'd get sick.

Laura looked around for a few minutes, poking things with her foot and turning them over with her hands. "Look," she said. "See how she carved words in the walls? They're sayings from the Bible." She started reading them in the dim light.

She went on and on, reading those sayings. I wondered if she'd ever stop. Then she saw me staring at the window. "What do you see out there?" she said. She walked to the window and looked out. For a second, she blocked the rainbow colors, and I said, "Wait..."

When she turned to look at me, I could see the colors again. And I saw her face next to the colors, looking at me. It was... I don't know. Beautiful, I guess. Not just the rainbow, but the girl. She was my age, not quite fifteen, but you know how some girls are. They hoist their sails early in the morning, as Sailor would say. I mean, what did I know? I had only hung around with these rugged biker chicks with tramp stamps and smoker's coughs, but this girl, this Laura, well, she was all new and fresh, man, she was blossoming, big time.

As much as I wanted to get away from that river, I also wanted to stay right there, right in that exact position, with the rainbow and the girl.

Then, all of a sudden, the rainbow went dark.

Someone was outside the shack. Whoever it was had looked in the window, then ducked around the side. I could hear the footsteps. I pulled the switchblade out of my pocket with my right hand, and used my left arm to keep Laura behind me as I faced the doorway. I clicked the blade open and held it behind my back.

If I was back at New Nod I would have lunged forward right when the man with the gun came into view. Sailor always said a man with a knife could take a man with a gun as long as he jumped first. But the river had made me sick and sluggish, and I hesitated.

The man raised his gun and yelled, "Freeze!" and Laura cried out, "Daddy, no!"

"Laura!" He kept his gun pointed at me. "Come over here behind me, girl."

"But, Daddy!"

"Now! Come on, get behind me. Who are you, boy? I don't think I know you. And I know everyone around here."

"Daddy, put your gun down, please! This is Richard."

"You're sneaking around a place like this with a boyfriend? Why I oughta tan your hide. You're too young..."

"No, Daddy, this is Richard Tyler. Ty Tyler's son. He came back."

"Oh good Lord," he said. He put his gun back in its holster. As he did that he briefly looked down and I took that opportunity to close my blade and drop the knife in my back pocket.

"Come out here in the light, son. Oh my Lord you are Richard Tyler, aren't you? You got your father's look about you. So how did you... When..." He looked suspiciously from me to Laura. "Wait just a cotton picking minute. You got some explaining to do, young lady."

"Can we do it somewhere else?" I said. "I need to get away from this river."

16. You, Aunt Violet

SHERIFF MCKENZIE MADE ME RIDE back to his house with
him in his patrol car while Laura drove the four-wheeler.
Before we left, Laura told him we hadn't had any lunch
and would he mind picking up some hamburgers on the
way home. So he did, which is why we were a little bit
delayed. And when he pulled up the gravel driveway to
the old farmhouse he saw the four-wheeler and another
car parked there and he muttered, "Laura, I swear, I will
tan your hide."

I didn't like being in the patrol car so I got out as soon
as we stopped. Just then the front screen door flew open
and a woman came running out onto the porch. It was
you, Aunt Violet, remember? When you saw me you let
out a scream and fell to your knees, and held your arms
out toward me and you cried out, "Oh, Richard! Richard, sweetheart, come to Auntie Violet! Come on, baby,
come on!"

I can't even describe it. It was like I wasn't even in
control of my own body. I just found myself running,
right up the steps and jumping into your arms, and you
were hugging me and kissing my cheeks and your cheeks
were wet with tears. And I was kneeling next to you, almost in your lap, and hugging your neck so hard, like I
didn't even know what I was doing until you said, "Richard, dear, you're choking me."

And so I let go and sat down next to you and you put your arms around me and kinda rocked as you kept saying, "Oh Richard, you're home, you're finally home," and kissing my cheek.

I never felt so loved in all my life as I did right then and there, sitting on that porch with you, Aunt Violet.

"Come on, inside, everybody, inside," the sheriff said. When we got in, I sat down at the kitchen table with you, and the sheriff turned to his daughter and said, "Laura, did you call Miss Violet? You did, didn't you? You know the rules, Laura."

"But Daddy, Miss Violet should get to see Richard, if anybody should..."

I remember you looked at the sheriff like you were going to spank him. "Tonnie McKenzie!" you said, real stern and all. "How could you even think of letting this child come here and not telling me?"

"Violet, do I have to tell you, that restraining order is still in effect. We are breaking the law."

You slammed your hand down on the table. "The devil himself could not stand in the way of my seeing my brother's child, Tonnie. I will be damned—do you hear me, I say damned and excuse my French—if that horrid judge is going to stop me."

I could tell by the way Laura and her dad looked so shocked that my Aunt Violet was not in the habit of cussing.

You turned to me and said softly, "Oh, Richard. Where have you been all these years? I've been so

worried. How has your mother... been treating you?"
You started to cry again. "Oh, I just can't imagine."

I didn't know what to say, or even where to start, and
I couldn't get any words out. I looked at Laura.

Laura said, "OK, I guess I have to make a confession.
About three weeks ago I was opening and sorting mail at
the courthouse and I came upon this letter. It was from
Richard. He wanted to know some information about
his family, and who his real mother is."

"Your real mother?" you said.

I nodded. "I uh... this is going to sound stupid."

"No it's not," you said. "Say what's on your mind,
sweetie."

"Well, I thought maybe my mother wasn't really my
mother because how she treated me, and I didn't look
anything like her, and... and I remembered a woman
who was nice to me when I was little, and so I thought
maybe... maybe my mother wasn't really my mother and
she just kidnapped me or something from my real
mother, and then I found these papers in a lockbox in
her closet and I thought maybe they had to do with me,
but I didn't remember my name was Richard, so I wrote
a letter to the judge, and... I know this just sounds
dumb."

"No it's not," you said, and kissed my cheek again.
"But... you didn't remember your name was Richard?
What has she called you all these years?"

"Cain," I said.

Your eyes welled up with tears and they ran down
your cheeks again as you looked desperately from Sheriff

McKenzie to Laura and back to me. I was not prepared for how hard that name would hit you, Aunt Violet. You were trying not to sob, but it wasn't working.

"Listen to me," you said when you regained control of yourself. "What happened to your brother is not your fault. Do you understand me? It is not your fault, Richard."

"I was supposed to be the strong one," I said, starting to cry again. "But I couldn't hold on. I couldn't hold on."

"Now you listen to me, Richard Tyler!" you said. "You are the strong one. If you could survive all these years living with that evil woman, then there's no one on earth stronger than you. What happened to your brother was an accident. Do you hear me? An accident. Accidents can happen to anyone." Then you smiled. "You remember what your father used to say. You're the strong one. Oh Lord I wish he were here. He'd be so happy to see you."

You looked at Sheriff McKenzie hard. "This child is not going back to that woman. He's going to stay here with me."

"Violet, you know we can't just..."

But you weren't paying attention to him. You said to me, "Are you doing all right in school, Richard?"

"I don't go to school."

"You don't... Have you ever gone to school?"

"No. I'm home schooled." I didn't really think before I said that. Sailor had drilled it into me to say that in case anybody asked, and it just tumbled out. But it was true, in a way, and I was pretty sure I didn't want to go to school anyway, so I let it sit.

You glared at Sheriff McKenzie for a moment, then asked me, "And what curriculum does your mother use, dear?"

"Curriculum?" I had never heard the word before.

"What does she teach you? What kind of subjects?"

"She doesn't really teach me anything. Sailor does..."

"Sailor? Who's that?"

"He's... Well, he's her..." I realized I had never thought about what their relationship was called. "He's kinda like a..."

"Boyfriend?"

"Yeah, I guess so."

"Are they married?"

I just shrugged. I didn't know. I hadn't ever thought about it.

"Richard, this Sailor. How does he treat you?"

"OK, I guess. He's taught me a lot of stuff."

"Like what?"

"Well, reading and writing and doing numbers, especially for business, and how to handle the mail and the bank accounts, and working with tools, you know, fixing things, machine shop stuff, and I've done some welding, I'm pretty good at that, I work on motorcycles and cars, and he taught me how to use a kn... uh, how to fight, I guess, you know, punches and kicks and some submission holds, I can work a heavy bag and a speed bag pretty good. I can cook and clean too, I've pretty much done all of those chores for my mother since I was little."

"Well, that's nice, dear. What about history, and civics, and literature? Do you know who Shakespeare is?"

"I can take care of myself."

"Oh, I know you can, dear. You are a very capable young man. I just want to understand how broad your education is. You said Sailor taught you to read. What have you read? Can you give me an example?"

I started to feel a little anxious, like I was being interrogated. "Well, I read all the mail we get, like bills and stuff, and I can write checks."

"What about the Bible? Have you read the Bible?"

Suddenly I remembered Samuel Blue. "I got a Bible just yesterday! From a friend of mine. He's an old guy, but he's really nice. But I think I lost it on the train. Or somebody stole it. I don't know, maybe I left it home, I'm not sure, but I meant to bring it. He wrote something in it for me. I was going to read it."

"Don't you worry, dear. I'll give you another one." You kissed me on the cheek. And then you brushed my cheek with the back of your fingers and you said, "What happened here? How did you get this scar?"

"I've had that since I was little," I said.

"You did not have this scar when you lived here," you said. "You got this after you left. Richard, sweetheart, don't be afraid. You can tell me anything, anything at all. Do you remember how you got it?"

Of course I did. Like it happened yesterday. And as I drifted into the memory, it was like I was reliving it in my head. I could feel the pain and the sickness all over again. I wanted to tell you but I just couldn't, I don't know why. I just sat there and shook my head and looked dumb.

I remember how you reached out and touched my cheek again, Aunt Violet. And your voice was soft. You said, "It's all right, dear. Take your time."

And I could only shake my head "no" and you said, "That's all right. Don't talk now." And we just sat there for a little while til I calmed down and you said, "Just promise me one thing, dear. Whenever you're ready, and I don't care how long it takes because I'll always love you, one day, you tell your Aunt Violet the whole story— of how you got that scar, and how you got the name 'Cain,' and how your mother has treated you, and... everything. OK? Promise?"

I looked at you and I nodded, Aunt Violet. So that's what I'm doing now. This is the whole story. I promise.

I let you rub my neck for a minute. It felt good. Kinda gave me strength. Then I said, "Did my mother ever love me? Just tell me the truth about it."

"All right," you said. "I'll tell you the truth. You deserve to know about your past. I cannot to this day understand what your father saw in that woman. The first time he mentioned her, I thought he called her 'Heiress,' with an 'H' which I thought was an odd way of referring to a lover, but then I learned it was 'Eris' with an 'E' and so I looked it up and found it referred to the goddess of strife and discord, or something like that. Lord, if her parents named her that, they sure knew what was coming.

"They were nothing alike. Nothing. Ty was an accountant. Well, he was also very physically fit—he and Tonnie played on sports teams together, didn't you, Tonnie?"

"That's right," he said, "Football, baseball, wrestling, all of it. We were tight."

"But Ty was good with numbers and organizing things, and paying bills, just like you are, sweetheart, and he became an accountant. But I guess he had a time, like most men do, of sowing his wild oats, so to speak, and suddenly out of nowhere, he brings this woman home. He is totally smitten with her, and they are married. Married! I could not believe it. Ty, have you gone crazy?

"Well, she was an artist, and quite talented, although I never grasped the things she drew until she got pregnant with Emmanuel. But you know the first clue I got that this marriage might not be the best thing for Ty? She referred to her wedding as an installation. That's some kind of artistic term. And performance art. Walking down the aisle was performance art. My Lord, what kind of woman thinks that way?

"Well, pretty soon she got pregnant. With you. I did not think she was the type, but there it was. And at first the pregnancy seemed to be going along just fine, but then something happened. I was there, and I saw it. You kicked. Now, usually when a young mother first feels her baby kick inside her it is a beautiful, wonderful thing.

"But Eris? Oh my Lord, it was as if someone had just stabbed her. She absolutely doubled over with this... this look of absolute horror and sickness on her face, and she just went pale and shaky and she actually fell to her knees and vomited. Well, we took her to the doctor, and he thought it was just some hormonal thing, but my word, she was acting like a woman possessed.

"And she... Oh Lord, Richard, you don't have to hear this..."

"Go on," I said. "I can take it. I'm strong."

You smiled through your tears. "Yes, you are the strong one, aren't you?" You took a deep breath to calm down. "She kept demanding that we take her to... to get an abortion. I mean, she couldn't even walk on her own power, much less drive, so she would have needed someone to help her, but even if we were disposed to do that, she was too far along in her pregnancy, it would not even have been legal.

"And Ty, he just couldn't abide it. He had always been a church-going man, but it wasn't even just that. He loved his wife, but he had absolutely fallen in love with the baby growing inside her. He was by her side all day and night, trying to comfort her as much as he could.

"And then she went into labor, and my oh my, it was horrible. Thirty-six hours. We tried to convince her to have a C-section, but she refused. She would have an abortion, but not a C-section. I'm telling you, the woman did not make any sense.

"Finally, you were born, Richard. The nurse said you were absolutely the strongest newborn she had ever seen. She said you nearly broke her finger you squeezed it so hard. And you had the loudest cry! I mean the windows just about shook when you cried. But then when the nurse brought you to your mother, she just... well, she just rejected you. She wouldn't even touch you. She just turned away. It was so sad. But I held you, Richard. I held you every day. I can't have children, Richard, but it was like you were my own from the very beginning.

"They said your mother had severe postpartum depression. And drugs could not seem to fix it. Therapy could not fix it. Nothing fixed it. She couldn't do her art, she had not done any art since that first kick, and she was just a mess. I mean, in a way I felt sorry for her because she was suffering, she really was, but to just show absolutely no love for her own baby, I just couldn't forgive her for that. That wasn't very Christian of me, was it?

"She stayed in her room, lying in bed all day with these eye shades on. And then one day it all changed. It was as if she had gotten an injection of pure happiness, and she was up and walking and talking, and do you know what she said? 'I'm pregnant!' Pregnant! Can you believe it? We were stunned! Flabbergasted!

"And I thought, I cannot believe she's going through with this again. Oh, we all held our breaths, just waiting for that day when that first kick came, to see if she fell into that black hole again.

"But no. The baby kicked, granted it was a much weaker kick than yours, dear, and she just smiled! She laughed, in fact. And day after day we would watch and worry, but she just stayed as bright and happy as you could imagine.

"She had started doing her art again soon after she got pregnant, in fact I believe it was the very same day, and it was beautiful. It wasn't this weird modern art stuff she used to do. She drew from life, and it was just absolutely stunning. She was by far the best artist anyone around here had ever known.

"And do you know what else? She even came to church. Now, I thought she was a dyed-in-the-wool atheist if there ever was one—oh, you should have heard how she condemned Christianity and everything holy when she was sick—but there she was, always dressed in white, sitting in the pew just staring at her baby, and him staring back at her with his sparkling little blue eyes.

"And the pastor preached a sermon about how our Lord was called Emmanuel, which meant 'God with us,' and that's what she named her child. And I thought she may be taking this a little too literally, in that she really thought that her child was... well, was God.

"And that year little Manny lived, that's what your father called him, little Manny, or lil Man, she was just in heaven and everything was beautiful, except for one thing. She still would not accept you, Richard. She wouldn't touch you, she would hardly look at you, and she certainly didn't want you getting near her baby.

"But you were there," I said.

"Yes, I was there. I was there for you. And I still am, Richard. I still am."

"What about my dad?"

"Oh, Ty thought the world of you. Eris would hardly let him near lil Man either, so he spent a lot of time with you. You were both a lot alike. Strong, rough and tumble, you know. Do you know why he named you Richard?"

"No."

"After Richard the Lionheart. King of England. You were strong and brave, and he thought that name was perfect for you. You have the heart of a lion, Richard. I remember how desperately you wanted your mother to love you. Over and over again you tried to prove yourself to her, and... nothing. I felt so sorry for you. But you never gave up. You never lost your spirit, your lion heart. And you never will."

"So what happened to my dad? Why didn't he ever come for me?"

"Oh, Richard. That day, the day your brother disappeared, he..."

"He didn't just disappear. A fish took him. A river cat."

You rubbed my cheek again. "I believe you, Richard. I believe you. Well, that day something was different, I'm not sure I can put my finger on it..."

"The cicadas," I said.

You looked at me as if you remembered something long forgotten. "The cicadas. Yes. You remember. Well, your mother would normally not let lil Man out of her sight, but that day she let your father take him while she drew. And it was. It was the cicadas and the noise they were making, that whole spectacle, that seemed to change her to where she would let it happen. And Ty, he had been so wanting to do things with lil Man. He was afraid he'd grow up, I don't know, a sissy or something if he never got away from his mother. So he decided to take you and your brother out in the boat fishing. He didn't tell Eris. She never, ever, would have let him do that.

"He was in love with her, deeply, but he was a man, too, and he had his pride. So he took the chance. Well, after... after the fish took your brother he dove into the river to try to find him. He was in that river all day. Long after the rest of us realized that that poor baby was gone, he just kept at it. We tried to get him to come out, but he wouldn't.

"He became totally obsessed. He never went back to work. Every day he would go to the river. His hair grew long and wild. His beard. He looked like the wild man of Borneo. Except with red hair. He learned to, what do they call it?"

"Noodle," Laura said.

"Yes, noodle. He learned to noodle for catfish..."

Laura jumped in. "That's when these guys go into the water and they go up to these mudholes on the bank and they stick their hands in and wiggle their fingers like it's a worm, and that's how they catch these huge catfish—with their hands."

"Did he catch... uhh... what was the name of that catfish you told me about?" I said.

"Blue Belle. I told him about Blue Belle," Laura said, looking at her father.

"Well, no," the sheriff said. "He didn't catch her. Caught some big ones, but none of a size that could have... well, that could have done what you said."

"It's true," I said.

You squeezed my arm. "We believe you, honey."

"Tell him about Sister Ada, Daddy," Laura said.

"Sister Ada the witch?" I said.

"Laura!" the Sheriff said. "What did you tell this boy? How many times do I have to tell you, Sister Ada Potter was not a witch. She was a good Christian woman. A little odd, maybe, perhaps even autistic to some degree, but she was not a witch. Look, we talked to her. She testified she did not see the child's body. It did not wash up in the crook of the river."

Laura wasn't quite ready to give up. "OK, well then, where did she go? Didn't she disappear right after that? How do you know she didn't find him after you questioned her, and then ran off with him?"

"I will not tolerate that tone of voice from you, young lady. And no, Sister Ada would not have taken lil Man's body away somewhere. You kids need to stop telling tall tales. In fact, there was one time, this was some years before lil Man... well... there was a flood, and a little lamb got swept away and wound up down by her shack with all that debris. Well, she fished that little lamb out of the water and she carried it—carried it in her arms, mind you, and it was still alive—all the way to my office, just so I could return it to whoever lost it. That's more than two miles she carried that lamb. She was sweet and kind, she knew the Bible backwards and forwards, and couldn't tell a lie to save her life. If she found that child's body, you can bet your bottom dollar she would have done the right thing.

"Look," he went on, "Things disappear into the river. Happens all the time. They go down, they never come back up. That's what happened to lil Man. As for Sister Ada, well she had a habit of taking off for months, trekking through the countryside preaching to these little backwoods congregations. And yes, she was one of those who used to handle rattlesnakes, and who knows? She could have been bitten, she could have died, anything could have happened. She might have just moved away. She didn't have a social security number, she was totally off-grid, but I am telling you this. If she had found the child, she would have done the right thing."

"What about my father?" I said. "Didn't you say he followed her?"

"Yeah, daddy, what about Mr. Tyler?"

He let out a tired sigh and rubbed his eyes. "All right. Yes, he did. Or that's how it appears. But that was a good long time after Sister Ada was already gone. Look, Richard, I hate to tell it like this. Your father and I were best friends from boyhood, but he went nuts. That's all there is to it. The man went crazy. We searched for him for a long time. Now he was definitely not off-grid like Sister Ada was. I mean, he had a social security number, work history, people knew him from church and business, and I sent his picture and information out to every single police jurisdiction in the country, and nothing. Nothing. It was like he disappeared from the face of the earth. Now I suspect he drowned in the river. The Prevene is a big river, y'all, and it flows directly into a very large lake not five miles downstream. He hardly wore any clothes when he dived and it is my professional opinion that he drowned and was subsequently eaten by crawfish and whatnot."

"Tonnie!" you barked. "That is no way to talk. And in front of his son."

"That's OK," I said. "Last time I saw him, he looked crazy. Or I think it was him. Maybe not, I don't know. That was when we lived in the red house."

"Red house?" the sheriff said.

"What red house?" Laura said. "That house they lived in was white, wasn't it?"

"Yes it was, it was white with a kind of blue color metal roof," the sheriff said. "Are you... sure about that, son?"

"You two hush!" you said. "Stop doubting him. It was red, just like Richard says. Inside, not outside. After... after what happened, that wicked woman painted the interior red. Blood red. Red curtains and everything. And she kept Richard in it, all day, every day. And that horrible Judge Witt wouldn't let us rescue him. Just more child abuse if you ask me. Remember? Eris lived there about a year after the incident. After she left—with Richard—we had to paint it because nobody in his right mind would buy a house like that, even at auction."

I was tired of talking about this family stuff. Nothing was being answered the way I had hoped. My mother was still my mother. Nobody kidnapped me. My father was still gone, nobody knew where. And I was pretty sure nobody really believed me about the river cat taking my brother. So I changed the subject.

"What about the cult?" I said.

17. The Cult

LAURA GASPED. "Daddy, there's a mole in the court-house!"

He frowned, like, what kind of nonsense are you talking about now?

"I am so sorry, I am so sorry!" she said, as if talking fast would keep her out of trouble. "But the cult has a spy working in the courthouse! When Richard sent his letter to the judge, I opened it and I copied it so I could reply to him personally, but I should have kept the letter because somebody, I don't know who, somebody saw the letter and gave that information to somebody in the cult, and then, and then they sent one of the cult members up to Richard's house and he tried to kidnap him, didn't he, Richard? And..."

"All right, stop!" the sheriff said and put his hands up like a traffic cop. He pointed to Laura. "Now you be quiet. I'll deal with you later. Son, I believe you said you found some papers in your mother's closet, then you wrote to Judge Witt to find more information? And other than getting a reply from a certain young lady who should have told me about it back when it was all going on..."

"I'm sorry Daddy, but I..."

"What happened, Richard? You can tell me, son. This could be important. There's some very serious sh... stuff happening around here."

I knew I had gotten myself into a fix. I didn't want the cops poking around in New Nod—I should have, I know that now, but back then my instincts told me to keep the cops away.

So I gave Laura a look like, keep your mouth shut for a minute, girl, and then I said to the sheriff, "I might have seen something that kinda looked like that cult symbol. The one on my brother's memorial stone. I'm not sure, though. But I think I know how I can find out for sure."

The sheriff didn't look convinced. "Richard," he said, "why don't you just tell me the whole story?"

"Because it may be nothing. I don't want to get anybody in trouble who doesn't need to be in trouble. That's all."

"You know, son, I will ask Laura about it. And she will tell me what you told her."

I looked at him deadly serious. "That cult of yours isn't the only dangerous group of people in the world," I said. "Where I come from, well... it's best not to stir them up if you can help it. They like to live off-grid too. You don't want to go to war with them, you really don't, Sheriff. If you send somebody up there, they'll send somebody down here. They have ways of finding stuff out, too. I don't want Laura to get in trouble, I really don't."

"Is that a threat, son?"

"No, Sheriff, it's not," I said. "It's just the way they are. They like to protect their privacy, I guess you could say. Anyway, I don't even know for sure if what I saw has any connection to all of this."

"Well, son, if I could just come up there and take a look, I could tell you if it's the same symbol."

"No. I scraped it off and painted over it. There's nothing left to see. But I might be able to help out with this cult thing of yours."

He sighed and rubbed his forehead. "All right," he said, "I'll bite. How?"

"Well, this is all because of me, isn't it?"

"No, Richard," you said. "Never, ever think such a thing."

"What I mean is, these people in this cult, if I understand what Laura told me, they freed this big catfish..."

"Blue Belle," Laura said.

"Yeah, Blue Belle. But then they heard, or read in the news or something, that I said a river cat took my brother, right?"

"Go on," the Sheriff said.

"And so they, like, jacked up the crazy a notch and they thought I was some kind of prophet for saving the river or something, and they got this idea that I sacrificed my brother to, I don't know, like..."

"To punish humanity for desecrating the river!" Laura said. "That's right! Isn't that right, Daddy?"

"Yes it is."

"Well," I said, "so now they want to sacrifice this baby they kidnapped, to do what they think I did, now that it's, what, the tenth anniversary? And you have this guy in jail, but he won't tell you anything about where they have the kid, or where they're going to sacrifice it? And if you don't find out by tomorrow, the kid dies, right?"

"Where are you going with this, son?"

"Let me talk to him."

"Let you talk to who?"

"The guy you got in jail. The cult leader, what's his name."

"Aldo-the-Bear," Laura said. "Aldo Singer-Sanger. Oh, this is so exciting!"

"Son, even if I could do that, from an ethical standpoint, which I can't, what on earth do you think you could accomplish by talking to him?"

"I could get him to tell me where the kid is."

"Richard. This man is a freak. Half the time he speaks in this ridiculous gibberish, and the rest of the time he just tries to bait you into beating him up so he can file a brutality complaint. Unfortunately, none of us have obliged him yet. We have had professional interrogators interview this man, and they have gotten nothing out of him. What could you bring to the table that they don't have?"

"A prophet."

The sheriff scratched his chin and just stared at me.

"I mean, I don't know much about cults and religion and stuff, but prophet's a pretty important position, isn't it?"

"Yes it is, Richard," you said, "it most certainly is."

"So I just think, if he's going to talk to anyone, it'll be his own prophet, right? So... That's me."

The sheriff was rubbing his temples with his eyes closed and gently shaking his head like now he was in a corner he couldn't figure his way out of. "The FBI is sending someone down tomorrow," he said.

"Tomorrow will be too late, Daddy," Laura said. "You remember the last time you had to work with the FBI? Weren't they late? And didn't their lab mess everything up? Didn't that evidence get thrown out?"

"Federal Bureau of Incompetence," he muttered.

I remember what you said, Aunt Violet. "Surely you can let the boy try. What can it hurt? I mean, you don't have to let him into the same cell, do you?"

"Yes I do," I said, "I have to be in there with him. Right next to him."

"But Richard, dear, that man is dangerous. He could hurt you."

"I can take care of myself," I said. "If he's anything like..." I almost blurted out 'like the other guy,' but I caught myself just in time. "I can take care of myself. Really."

"He'd be shackled," the sheriff said.

"Then you'll do it, Daddy?" Laura said.

"Well, the FBI sure as hell won't like it," he said. "But a child's life is at stake. I don't guess I have much other choice. Besides, there's one thing I haven't told y'all."

"What?"

The Sheriff looked at me. "Mr. Aldo Singer-Sanger, aka Aldo-the-Bear, well, he's been asking for you."

18. Prophet

THEY DIDN'T FIND THE SWITCHBLADE in my pocket when they let me into the interrogation room. In fact they didn't even pat me down, and I figured they wouldn't. I was Laura's age, going on fifteen, and I guess they lumped us into the same pot of "kids," but we two couldn't have been raised more different. But the way I figured it, I was a lot more dangerous to Aldo than he was to me.

The idea that these freaks would take what happened to me and turn it into some kind of deal where they were killing babies on purpose, as if that's what I did, like I was showing them the way or something, well, that really ticked me off, I guess you could say. The more I thought about it, the angrier I got. This Aldo-the-Bear guy was worse than my mother, for crying out loud.

All my life I hated myself for not being strong enough to protect my little brother when he needed me the most. Well, you know what? I was bigger now. Stronger. I knew how to fight. I knew how to use a knife. I had already taken one of this bunch out. When I first saw Aldo I thought, I don't even need my blade, I can take this dude with my hands. I suppose you could say I was getting myself worked up for a fight that I couldn't let happen.

That's because I really did want this to work. Just taking my anger out on this guy wouldn't save the baby, that much I knew. But I'm not all that smart, you know, I'm not tricky and clever like some of the scam artists Sailor knew. They'd do it one way. Sailor'd do it another. Honest to God I did not know what I was going to do or say when I stepped in there.

When the Sheriff opened the door of the interrogation room and let me in he said, "All right, Aldo, I brought you what you asked for. Richard Tyler, in the flesh."

"How do I know you're really the One... Richard Tyler?" Aldo said.

He was twitching and moving around all nervous in his seat like a dog that didn't know whether to pee himself or bite me. One thing about dogs I learned over the years, they really can smell fear. And they can smell other things, too, especially when they're desperate and anxious, like Aldo was. They can smell when you're a threat, no matter how you try to fake it. And I was a threat to him, honest to God I was, and he sure enough would have clammed up had I not done what I did.

I carried my memory of the incident, and the feeling of grace, in there with me. There was a chair for me on the opposite side of the table from Aldo. Real calm, I dragged the chair around the table and sat right next to him. And I looked him right in the eyes and I just told him my story of how the river cat took my brother. Straight up and honest. It was something I could never lie about, and I could never fake.

I told him how, as terrifying as it was, there was something beautiful and smooth about it, and I told him how Samuel Blue taught me the word for it and the word was grace.

It was almost like I had hypnotized him right out of his fear and suspicion. He said, "You really are him. You are Richard Tyler."

"That's just my despoiler name," I said. Sheriff McKenzie had told me about the cult on the drive over, and words they liked to use. Despoiler was one.

"My true name is something else," I said.

"What is it?" he said. "What's your true name?"

I waited a bit and I locked on his eyes and I said, "I am Cain."

Man, you should have seen him. His eyes darted about like he was looking for something for a second or two, and then his body jerked and he suddenly locked his eyes on me and whispered, "Cain" and this weird little laugh came out. And then it was words. And words and words and more words like a dam broke, and he was all like:

"Cain! Cain, who slew his brother Abel. Cain, who made his offering of fruits and vegetables and grain, and was rejected and condemned by the god of the West, the patriarchal god of violence and oppression. And the god of the West favored Abel, who offered the bodies of murdered animals. Cain! Cain, the first one who knew that meat was murder, and who took righteous vengeance on Abel the murderer of innocent lambs and calves and fish. Cain, who was punished for his righteousness, as all the righteous are punished by the despoilers. Cain, the fugitive, has returned. You have come to show us the way. The way to end the disease of humanity. The septic infection that has given Gaia a fever from which she may never recover. Humanity must be stopped. It must be stopped, and you, Cain, have come to show us the way.

"Cain, my prophet Cain I have tried to follow your way. I confess when I started, my heart was in the right place but I knew not the way. Yes, I wanted to bust the dams that were killing the river, and yes I wanted to destroy the factory farms and the power grid, but we were just a small collective and we thought that liberating that beautiful catfish from its enslavement was a righteous act, and it was, but it wasn't enough and we didn't see that until you, Cain, showed us the way. Because liberation and freedom, these are just Western concepts, and the very ones that have been at the root of the human infection from the beginning. It was not liberation we should be working for but submission. Humans must submit to the will of Gaia. They must be made to submit."

Man, how this dude jabbered on. All this crap about dams and factory farms and the human infection and whatnot. But I figured I oughta let it play out and so I sat there all calm and listening, you know, with a real even keel, as Sailor would say. Finally he got to where I hoped he'd go.

"Cain, what you showed us was something vastly older and more profound than the illusion of liberation. Human sacrifice. The purest form of submission. We had been seeking reparations in the form of monkey-wrenching and vandalism when we should have been seeking it in human blood. Extinction is never voluntary, Cain, we know that now.

"We wanted to follow your next move, O my prophet, but you disappeared. We went looking for you, but like your namesake you had vanished to an unknown land. And so we too went elsewhere." He leaned toward me and lowered his voice to a hoarse, excited whisper. "Every year at this time, one river after another, we sacrificed a human baby, just as you did here. The Alabama, the Mississippi, the Rio Grande, the Colorado, the Columbia, the Saint Lawrence, the Hudson, the Delaware, the Potomac. And now, exactly ten years after the original sacrifice, you're back. And so are we. Are you not pleased, O my Prophet?"

I felt sick. It was all I could do to keep from snapping out my blade and cutting his tongue right out of his mouth and feeding it to him. But I figured I only had one hand to play if I was going to save that baby and I played it.

His hands were shackled in front of him to a chain around his waist so he couldn't reach out. I put my hands down under the table where his were, where the sheriff couldn't see them through the two-way mirror. I whispered, "Aldo, put your hands in mine."

As he did I grabbed his fingers in a submission hold that Sailor taught me and I twisted just enough to make it hurt. I could see the pain flash across his face.

"River cat is not pleased," I said.

"What?" he said.

"All those babies in all those rivers, how many did you give directly to river cat?"

"Well..."

"That's what I thought. You just drowned them, didn't you? Left them there for the turtles and the crawdads. That insults river cat. You can't just throw a baby in the river. That ain't no sacrifice. River cat has to take it directly from your hands."

"Tomorrow river cat will be there," he said. "She's still in this river. I know it. All the signs are in alignment. It's been ten years exactly. Ten. And... and you're here! It's going to happen. It's going to happen and it will be righteous. All the signs are in alignment. Nothing can stop it now, nothing!"

"River cat thinks you're a damn retard."

He blinked. "What? Why do you scorn me like this? I have been faithful!"

"River cat don't give a flip about ten years. River cat can't even count to ten. River cat don't have ten fingers, Aldo. River cat don't need to count to ten. That's... that's the Western way. Ten! Crap. That sounds like a Western number to me. River cat don't count at all. River cat listens."

"Listens? Listens for what?"

"Cicadas. When the cicadas come out all at once, after they been sleeping all these years, they call river cat and river cat comes, and that's when you do it. Don't you remember the cicadas ten years ago?"

"That's right... there were cicadas... I remember now."

"Well they ain't out this year. And there's another thing, even more important."

"What?"

"That baby you're going to sacrifice tomorrow. Is it kin to you? Blood relation?"

"No, it's just some capitalist piglet we took from a despoiler."

I twisted his fingers and he winced. "You insult river cat. It has to be your blood kin. That's how river cat knows you mean business. That's how river cat knows you got the right faith and dedication. That's the only way you get the grace. Like it was with my brother."

His eyes darted around with that look of desperation again. "My brother is grown. He's too big. How can I..."

"Just get your mother to have another kid," I said.

"I can't!" he wailed. "I had to... I had to silence her... She was going to turn us in. She's gone." Man, he started carrying on wailing and crying out how all was lost, and he kinda went limp so twisting his fingers didn't do any good any more. I know how stubborn people can get when they give up hope like that, so I threw him a bone.

"It doesn't have to be a brother, Aldo, you could just have kid of your own. It just has to be a baby, and a blood relation. Isn't there some chick in the cult or collective or whatever it is you could knock up?"

He stopped wailing and latched on to the idea. "My own child, yes, yes, I can do that. Jackie-the-Swallow, maybe, or Emma-the-Mouse, that would be even better. We had all pledged not to have any children because of the human infection, but this... this I can see is right-eous, and I can make them see it too. Yes, Cain, yes, I can do that. I can make my own blood relation for a proper sacrifice."

"You have got to stop tomorrow's sacrifice," I said.

His face twitched and he started to look suspicious again. I realized I had probably used the same words the sheriff already said to him and I was afraid he might start sniffing out my fakery.

"River cat's wise," I said. "River cat knows what's go-ing on. River cat can smell a fake sacrifice a mile off. If one foot of a baby that's not a blood relative touches the water, river cat will be insulted. Really insulted. And river cat'll get angry. Really angry. And you know what angry river cat does? Splashes. Makes a big scene. And then you know what happens? People hear it. Despoil-ers. Fishermen. Abel's people. And then they come and they capture river cat, and it's back into slavery for river cat in some stinking zoo. Or worse yet, river cat gets cut up and fried and served up with hush puppies and cole-slaw to a bunch of fat despoilers. And it'll be your fault, Aldo.

"Aldo!" I said, and I grabbed his chin and peered real close into his eyes. "You can still be redeemed for all the wrongs you've done. Next time the cicadas are out, if you do it right, river cat will come and then you'll know what grace is. That's the key to ridding the earth of the human infection. But til then you have to suffer for your faith. You got to show your devotion. River cat demands your total devotion. Can you show your devotion, Aldo?"

Aldo-the-Bear smiled at me and he pushed his hair back with his hand. There on his forehead was the cult symbol of the fish with the dead baby in its mouth. It had been crudely carved into his skin with a knife and scarred over.

"Well, that settles that," I said. "Now. We need to get that baby back in its mother's arms by sundown, or Abel's people win. So tell me where I have to go."

19. The Hero of Harlington

IT WASN'T HEROIC, AUNT VIOLET. It wasn't even very hard. Aldo told me where the hideout was and what the secret knock was, and so we went there. I told the Sheriff he ought to hold his men back because these freaks could kill the kid on the spot if they sniffed cops. So I went up and did the secret knock, and some guy inside said, "Who is it?"

"Richard Tyler." Man, that was like an abracadabra word if there ever was one with them. They opened the door and it was all, "Oh, my goddess, is it really you? Oh my goddess, it's really you! It's Richard Tyler! Everything is falling into place, just like Aldo-the-Bear said." On and on they went, if they had tails they'd be wagging them like puppies.

I said, "Give me the baby, I have to prepare it," and they led me to the back of the room. There was a young woman sitting cross-legged on the floor and she had the baby on her lap. She was rocking gently. This dude with long dreadlocks and a scraggly beard said, "Brenda-the-Dove, this is Richard Tyler, the Prophet. Give him the baby."

But Brenda didn't even look up. She just kept gently rocking the baby and looking into the kid's eyes. "Come on, bitch, give it up!" Dreadlocks dude kicked her in the thigh and she cried, but I knew it wasn't from the kick. I pushed my forearm against the guy—man, it was all I could do to keep from snapping my blade out and peeling his Adam's apple—and I said, "Let me handle this."

I squatted down and whispered in Brenda's ear, "Come with me, the baby will be safe, I promise. Come on."

Well, she got up and followed me as I headed toward the door. A couple of the people said, "Wait, what are you doing? We can't go outside. They'll see us."

"Are you questioning your prophet?" I said, real serious. They looked at each other. "The sun has to set on the child the day before sacrifice. That's the rules."

"Rules?" one of them said.

"Look smart-ass. It's river cat's river. It's river cat's rules. How many of you have ever had river cat take a child right out of your hands like I have? Yeah, that's what I thought. Any idiot can drown a kid. But you can't win river cat's favor that way. That's not a proper sacrifice. You got to do it right. You got to follow the rules. Now open the damn door."

They did. I nudged Brenda out the door ahead of me and I told her to keep walking across the lot and keep the setting sun on the baby's face. I figured she'd run off with the baby. Then I'd go back in and show dreadlock dude some pain. But when she was about halfway across the lot, Sheriff McKenzie and his men ran out from behind a tin shed where they were hiding. Two of them hustled Brenda and the baby away while the sheriff and his other deputies drew their weapons and captured the rest of the cult. The cult freaks didn't run. They didn't pull guns and shoot. They didn't commit, like, mass cult suicide. They just kinda put up their hands and surrendered. And that was that.

Later that night there was a gathering at the sheriff's house, remember, Aunt Violet? He had kept the radio chatter down during the rescue operation, which was a good thing because the cult was using a police scanner, but word gets out anyway, once it's all said and done. Lots of people came. The mom and dad and a bunch of the family members of the kidnapped kid came, and they were all teary eyed and laughing and crying and wanting to hug me and shake my hand. There were some deputies, of course, and I think the mayor of Harlington and some other busybodies and then some people just started coming with pots and plates of food and pitchers of sweet tea and whatnot.

And then some reporter from the local paper showed up and Sheriff McKenzie told her there would be a press conference tomorrow in town and she'd have to wait til then to get a statement. She kinda wouldn't take no for an answer, so he told her this was private property and she'd have to leave, but she just went back to the road and kept shouting questions at people she saw and taking pictures and everything.

People were making me out to be some kind of hero, and wanting to take pictures with me, but I didn't want to be in anybody's picture and I got fed up with all the rest of it pretty quick and I hid in the bathroom and locked the door.

The sheriff's house has a porch that wraps all the way around it and while I was sitting there in the bathroom with the window open I heard Sheriff McKenzie and you, Aunt Violet, talking outside on the porch.

You were saying, "Now, Tonnie, we're just going to have to do whatever it takes. That child is not going back to his mother, and that's final. I don't care how much it costs, we'll get the finest lawyer, one who can help Richard sue for his emancipation from that evil woman once and for all. I'll be his guardian, he can live with me. I'll get him into school, and..."

"Now, Violet, don't get ahead of yourself," the sheriff said.

"I'm not getting ahead of myself, Tonnie, he's staying here. And if you have to go up there and arrest her on charges of child abuse, then you just go do it!"

"It's not my jurisdiction, Violet, you know that. I can't just go do it. You have to have evidence. And Richard would have to testify against his mother. Very likely before the same judge who granted her divorce and her restraining order. Against you, I might add."

"Judge Jurlean Witt," you said. "More like half-wit. We would have to get her to recuse herself, Tonnie. She cannot be impartial. She wasn't then, she won't be now. She should be impeached, that corrupt..." I could tell you were trying to find a word that wasn't a cussword, but couldn't manage it.

"Well, we'll see what we can do, but it's not easy to force a judge to recuse herself."

"Tonnie, Jurlean Witt absolutely worshipped Eris. She was totally biased as a judge. It was unhealthy from a character standpoint, and unacceptable in a court of law. Why, the portrait of herself she has hanging in her office was drawn by whom?"

"Yeah, I know."

"And the portraits of Judge Witt's despicable children, who drew them?"

"Violet, I'm not saying you're wrong, and I'm not saying it can't be done. But courts work in a certain way. Judges have a lot of power and a lot of leeway in their own courtrooms."

"Well, he's not going back there. I have prayed for that boy every day since before he was born. And twice a day since his mother took him away from us. Well, God has answered my prayers, Tonnie. He has delivered Richard back to us, back to where he belongs, and to the people who love him. And there's nothing that Eris or Jurlean can do to oppose it because it is God's will.

"That poor boy has not been to a day of school or church since she took him. Well, he's going to go to school like a normal child, and he'll have normal friends, and I'll buy him a whole new wardrobe, and he'll sit right next to me in church, and... and..." You started to cry.

"It'll be all right, Violet."

"His mother has not let him forget what happened to his brother. She has just tortured him with it. Oh my God, Tonnie, she calls him Cain! The poor child still believes that a giant fish took his brother from him. Can you imagine? Living day after day, year after year, with that horrible image? He'll need therapy, and a lot of it, if he's ever to be normal."

"From what I hear, these invented memories can be impossible to break, Violet. That can make it really hard to raise a kid like Richard. It happens to foster parents and adoptive parents all the time. They get some kid who's had a hard life, who has suffered abuse or neglect, and they have all the best intentions to help him, but the kid's broken, and he acts out, and they end up regretting..."

"Tonnie McKenzie! You hush that kind of talk. I will regret nothing. Richard is not just some kid from an orphanage. I raised him from birth. When she wouldn't even touch him, I was... I was... his mother." More crying.

So that's how I found out you didn't believe me, Aunt Violet. Nobody did. I couldn't take it anymore. I snuck out of the house and walked across the yard into the darkness and just kept walking. I was walking blindly—across fields, through gullies, over barbed wire fences. When I finally stopped, I looked around me and I couldn't believe where I was.

My little brother's memorial stone. There was a security light on a pole nearby so I could see. I stared at the stone for a while. Down the hill was the grassy area by the riverbank where we had our picnic ten years before. I thought I could hear the river. Maybe it was my imagination. I could smell it, though. My stomach got queasy, but I didn't want to leave my brother, so I just stood there.

A thousand times in my life I regretted losing my grip on my brother. Not being strong enough to hold on, to protect him. But never more than when I was standing at his memorial stone that night. If ever anybody didn't deserve what happened to him, it was lil Man. My brother, Emmanuel. Fed to a fish by his jealous brother. When I held him over the edge of the boat, he smiled at me. He trusted me.

"I'm sorry, lil Man," I whispered.

And then I heard a sound that gave me a chill. It sounded like slurp-thunk, slurp-thunk. I jerked around and reached into my pocket for my knife.

"Well, if it isn't Richard the Lionheart, hero of Harlington." It was Laura. "Hey, why'd you run off?"

"I don't know," I said. "Just wanted to get away from all that, I guess."

She took a step closer to me. "All of it?" she said.

I looked at her in the dim blue light. I'm not going to lie, Aunt Violet. Laura looked nice. Beautiful, in fact. I don't know. Maybe for a young guy like me there was nothing that could burn through a bad mood and a queasy stomach like hormones. Maybe that's all there was to it. But I desired her. I thought of how good it felt, sitting behind her on that four-wheeler, my hands on her hips, her hair blowing in my face, the view over her shoulder and down her swelling chest.

I stepped to her. I put my arms around her waist and I pulled her against my body and I made to kiss her.

"Richard, don't!" she said, and she slapped my face as she pushed away from me. "I'm a good Christian girl! I don't... I'm too young for that!" and she turned and ran into the darkness back toward the house.

Her slap caught me right on my fishhook scar and it started to throb like mad. It felt like she had just jabbed it through my cheek again. I almost doubled over with pain. Just then I heard the northbound train horn sound, and I took off running toward it.

20. Indigo Bunting

WHEN I JUMPED THE TRAIN THAT NIGHT I let out a howl that must have sounded like a wildcat caught in a trap. Two people immediately jumped out the other side of the boxcar. I'm pretty sure it was Bon Julia and Uncle Pete, but I didn't bother to look to make sure. I didn't want any company anyway.

I didn't have my bag with me but I didn't care. The one thing I treasured, the Bible that Samuel Blue gave me, was already gone. I had the clothes on my back and the switchblade in my pocket and that's all I needed.

Yeah, I know what you're thinking, Aunt Violet. What are you doing, going back to New Nod where you're hated when you could have just stayed in Harlington where you're loved? What kind of idiot would choose my mother over my Aunt Violet?

I was a hero in Harlington. In New Nod I was Cain.

But too many things were bothering me about Harlington. Getting slapped by Laura hurt, I won't lie to you. But why? Back in the pain pit I had been hit a hundred times harder than that. It's like, when she slapped me and gave me that line about her being a Christian and all, I felt that hook go right through my cheek again. I thought my mother was right. Fishers of men. Hit you up with phony sweets and then bam, you're hooked, and like any hooked fish I bolted.

And nobody there believed me. About the river cat taking my brother, I mean. Well, nobody except the cult freaks. Sheriff McKenzie was a nice guy, but he didn't believe me. I know you loved me like the truest mother on earth, Aunt Violet, but you didn't believe me, either. You and I both know that. And Laura? She's just a kid that believes in witches and stuff, so, whatever.

My mother, on the other hand, she believed me. That's why she hated me. I put the truth in her head and she knew it and it tortured her, so she tortured me back. Art was about truth, Sailor always said, so maybe that's why she kept me around.

You know what else? There was no rainbow in Harlington. I mean, in the sky, not from a cracked window. I expected to see one. I needed to see one. I didn't. You know what I saw instead? A stone with my brother's name on it. And that little sign scratched into it, the cult sign of the fish with the dead baby's head in its mouth. It was disgusting. It should have driven me into a crazy rage. I should have done what my mother did and taken a sledgehammer to it. But I didn't. You know why? It was the truth, that's why. It was my mark. The mark of Cain.

And that's just it, Aunt Violet, don't you see? All my life my mother wanted me to lie about what happened to my brother, and even when I tried to lie about it, I couldn't. I still can't. And you know what that means, don't you? It means all that stuff I made up to tell Aldo and those cult freaks, about the proper sacrifice and all... well, it had to be true, you know? It had to be true, else

I couldn't have said it, right? And that could only mean one thing. I was Cain. I am Cain.

And all those people there that evening. All that love and kindness and concern, I'm sorry, but it was sickening. All that talk about going to school and having friends and getting some damn therapist to shrink the truth out of my head so I can be normal, I just couldn't stand it. Saving that baby didn't bring back my brother. All that was left of my little brother was a stone, and it was my fault, I wasn't strong when he needed me to be strong and I was so damn ashamed of myself and I deserved that shame, I needed it, Aunt Violet, so I was all, like, leave me the hell alone, I'm going back to my real mother, the one who hates my guts but knows the truth.

And if you talk to my dad in your prayers, Aunt Violet, you can ask him this for me: Where the hell were you, you sonofabitch? Pretty convenient to go nuts chasing a ghost when you could have been father to the son you left behind, huh? Pretty convenient to drown in a river noodling for a catfish that had turned your baby into catfish poop, huh?

Poop.

Damn, lil Man. Why'd you have to say that?

Nah, Aunt Violet, I couldn't have stayed in Harlington. Damn river made me sick to my stomach. I think that's why my mother went up to New Nod. No river.

All these thoughts tussled in my mind as I rode the train that night. I hated myself. I hated the world. I know, typical teenager, right? I see plenty of them at the Laz. I tell you what, though. I had one thing to look forward to. One hope that would make me get off the train at New Nod, and it wasn't my mother.

It was Samuel Blue. If there was one person in the world who got me, it was Singin' Sammy. He had been a prisoner and a fugitive and a wanderer, like me. Maybe it wasn't a walking river cat, but he had his own dark mystery stalk him, and he got past it and he found grace. He taught that word to me. Samuel Blue was wise. And he wasn't phony about believing my story. He was my friend.

And the longer I held onto the hope of seeing Samuel Blue, the more I thought, hey, maybe I left that Bible he gave me at home. Maybe Uncle Pete didn't steal it out of my bag after all. And I tried to go over in my head everything I did when I was packing my bag for the trip.

I was pretty sure that I had put the Bible in my bag, but I also might have taken it out again because I wanted to put it in a plastic bag so it wouldn't get wet. I might have accidentally left it out. I was distracted for a while by my mother, carping at me to tell her what I was doing, and how she needed me to go round up a customer because she needed to work, and threatening to snitch on me to Sailor for not doing my job, and all that. And if she found it, there's no telling what my mother would have done with it. I took a quick shower before I left, so she had the chance, I guess.

And just before I ran out the door, and I don't know why I said this, maybe I was just "feeling my oats" as they say, but I said to her, "You know, Mom, you always said I couldn't have friends, but guess what? I've got one now."

And she said, "Imaginary friends don't count, Cain."

That ticked me off. "He's not imaginary," I said. "He's real. He's got a name. Samuel Blue, and he lives right back that way through the woods. And guess what? I've got a name too. Richard Tyler. Not Cain. Richard Tyler. So there." I didn't even know for sure if that was my name at that time, but I guess I just wanted to throw something in her face. And then I ran right out of the house with my bag. I was pretty excited. You know how you can overlook things when you're excited. I might have left the Bible behind.

That's what I was thinking when I jumped off the train as it slowed down sometime around sunrise. I went to the trailer first. If I left my Bible out, there was still a chance I could get to it before she did, since she never cleaned house, that was always my job.

Her bedroom door was open. She was lying on her back on her bed with her sleeping shades on and the window open wide. I looked in my room, I looked in the garbage, I even poked around in her room while she was sleeping. No Bible. I searched the same places over and over again. Nothing.

I almost woke her up to ask her, but I figured then she'd just have that to hold over me, whether she had found it or not. So I didn't. I began to think maybe Uncle Pete or Bon Julia really did steal it. That was just as likely. And if they did, there was still a chance I could get it back, or maybe Samuel could, since they knew each other.

I hated that I lost what Samuel Blue had given me, but the more I thought about it, the more I figured he'd forgive me. That's just how he was. I'd known him for all of one day, but it was like I'd known him forever, that's how I knew he was a friend. So I said heck with it and I ran out of the house and through the woods to see him.

But he wasn't there. The pot we cooked our roadkill stew in was there, but the coals and everything were cold. I called his name. I searched through the broken down house and the yard and a little ways into the woods, but no Samuel. I waited around for a couple of hours, but he didn't turn up.

He said he'd be there when I got back. He said he'd be there. I was crushed, man. There was so much I wanted to discuss with him. All the stuff that happened in Harlington, everything I heard down there, I couldn't figure it out, and I was counting on Samuel Blue to help me. I was counting on him. And he was gone.

I went back there every day for the next week or so. No Samuel. The last time I went there, though, I saw something.

The indigo bunting.

It flitted about from one slender tree branch to another, not ten yards from me. That color just gleamed and glittered in the low afternoon sun. It was beautiful, just like he said it would be.

"My luck, next time he comes, I'll be passed on." That's what he said. Passed on. At first I thought he meant he'd be dead. Well, if that was true, if he had died, sure enough there'd be buzzards circling above where his body was, and there weren't any. I would have found his body. I would have smelled it.

I picked up a rock and I threw it at indigo bunting, but I missed. I turned back and walked home. Indigo bunting followed me. A couple of times I stopped and threw a rock and a stick at him, but he just flitted out of the way and kept following me. I yelled at him, I cussed him out something fierce, but he just kept following me.

Sonofabitch Samuel Blue had just abandoned me, and sent indigo bunting to laugh at me for being a sucker. I'm sorry, Aunt Violet, I don't mean to cuss. It's not at you.

My mother seemed to sense what was going on, though I never told her. She only said one thing about it. She said, "The fact that Cain can't have any friends isn't something I just made up. It's like your fish story. If one's true, the other's true. Think about that, boy."

That hurt, but as my mother said a million times: pain is truth.

I got a couple letters from Laura and you, Aunt Violet, and a package from you—I don't know what was in it, I didn't open it, I just wrote "Return to Sender" on them and had the lady at the post office send them back. And I wrote one letter. It was to Sheriff McKenzie. The lady at the post office found his address for me. I told him that I was home with my mother and I didn't want anybody from Harlington to contact me anymore. Including you and Laura. I said if anybody from down there contacted me about anything, I'd complain to Judge Jurlean Witt. I also told him he could put out all the warrants he wanted to for me but I wasn't about to testify in any kind of trial, either. I'd run if I had to, and no way could they ever catch me.

The lady at the post office kinda liked me, so I got her to write the address on the envelope and we didn't put a return address on it. That way I knew the sheriff would get it without Laura getting to it first. Anyway, it seemed to work. I only got one more letter from Laura, which I sent back without reading, and then I was free and clear of the Harlington crowd.

I tell you what I wasn't free and clear of, though, and that was indigo bunting. He nested not far from my window. Every once in a while I threw a rock at him, but I guess my heart wasn't in it. I never hit him, and he never got the message.

Sometimes he'd even fly into the glass in my bedroom window. The first time, he hit it pretty hard and knocked himself silly. I could have gotten him while he was sitting woozy on the ground, or even after he got to his feet and wobbled around a bit before flying. But I didn't. As much as I wanted to hate him, I couldn't help but feel like there was some grace in that bird, as Samuel Blue would have said. And maybe something prophetic, like it was a message the old man left me. For a prophet, I was pretty illiterate in signs, though. You know that saying "a little bird told me"? Well, I tried to hear what indigo bunting was telling me, but for the life of me I couldn't, and I gave up trying.

Indigo bunting didn't give up, though. I can tell you that.

21. Slave Girls

I GOT BACK INTO MY ROUTINE, only ratcheted up a few notches over what it was before my Harlington trip. I still kept the books and paid the bills, I cooked and cleaned, I worked on cars and motorcycles and whatnot.

But I was determined not to go back to the pain pit, and not to give my mother any more bloody inspiration than I had to. So she'd go into the kitchen and sit there and stare at the bloody refrigerator art. There were two pieces then, the one with the fishhook she jabbed through my cheek, and the other one with the knife I used to stab the cult stalker. Sailor said it was called a "triptych," which meant there was a third panel yet to come. I asked him what it would be. He said it wasn't for us "mere mortals" to know when it would come or what it would be, but when it did it would "rock our world." His words, not mine. But he was always talking big, so I ignored him. Maybe I shouldn't have.

Sometime after I got back from Harlington the danger alarms started to sound on my mother's tattoo business. When Sailor came back from sea he looked worried, and I had never seen that look on him before. He said that one of my mother's early customers, a seaman friend of his called Johann "Whitey" Snowden got kidnapped when he was ashore in some overseas hellhole, and he was murdered. He said some drug lord named

El Cholo saw Whitey's tattoo, but Whitey refused to tell him who did it or where he got it, so El Cholo kidnapped him and took a knife to him and peeled the skin with the tattoo right off Whitey's body while he was still alive.

I remembered Whitey. That tattoo went from his right shoulder down across his chest and belly and wrapped around his lower back. Scuttlebutt was that drug lord put that skin on his wall and shows it to his friends at parties.

Whitey was one of the early ones, the known friends, who didn't have the blindfold treatment. But the lucky thing was, he was drunk coming here and drunk leaving and he didn't have much of a memory anyway, and Sailor never used my mother's real name, and even if Whitey remembered "New Nod," like I said, it wasn't on any map.

He did, however, know Sailor's real name. And Sailor knew from scuttlebutt that El Cholo had sent people to find him, and it would only be a matter of time before he did.

The first thing Sailor did was try to convince my mother to move, but she wouldn't.

And while he was worrying over what to do about El Cholo, Sailor got another piece of bad news. Estelle, the girl I wailed over so bad in the pain pit, well, she committed suicide.

Like I said before, I can't really describe that tattoo, but I can say this. My mother turned my fish story inside out. Where I saw something that was terrifying on the surface but had what Samuel Blue called a sanctifying grace underneath it, my mother made art that had beauty on the surface and hell underneath.

That's what got to Estelle, just as I feared it would. I don't know what she went through in the time after she left New Nod, but in the end she went into some big art gallery or museum in New York and she took all her clothes off, and then she tried to take her skin off with a box cutter. That tattoo went up her neck and she cut her jugular.

At first they thought she must have been on angel dust or bath salts or acid or something, but there were no drugs in her system. Just my mother's art.

Her parents wanted to sue, but they had no idea where to find whoever did it, so they hired a private investigator. What with the magazine stories and all the stuff on the Internet, the private dick (as Sailor called him) was able to find a couple of customers, and so Sailor suddenly had people hunting us from both sides of the tracks.

When Sailor couldn't convince my mother to move he told her that El Cholo wanted her to ink all his foot soldiers, and if she could just agree to do that, they could get the cartel off their back, and they could use cartel money and muscle to keep Estelle's rich parents at bay.

But she refused, because the cartel's foot soldiers were all dark skinned. Well, dark for her purposes, anyway. She only worked on white canvases, as she put it, and the whiter the better. She wouldn't work on a white person who had even a little tan. At least, she wouldn't work on the tan part. Gerald and Whitey and Estelle were all really pale like that. And so she rejected Sailor's idea.

I remember my mother scoffing at him. "Those idiots sell smack and securities. We sell art. Art! If you don't know by now which is more dangerous, then maybe I ought to find another patron, Sailor." The screen door slammed and she went inside, but then she turned around and flung it open again. "And besides," she said, "This is New Nod. This is where Cain lives. And Cain has the mark. Look at him. You can see it best when he smiles. Smile for us, Cain! Nobody can kill Cain. Nobody. He is protected. And not by some puny drug dealer or Wall Street lawyer. But by God himself! And as long as Cain's here, we're protected too. And he's not going anywhere. Are you, Cain?"

By that time I had stopped giving my mother the satisfaction of answering her. I was building a motorcycle out of farm equipment scrap and spare parts, and I just went on welding and grinding.

But Sailor took it to heart. Thing you have to understand about Sailor is, the man worshipped my mother. She was a goddess to him, and he would do anything for her. To this day I don't understand how she could have that effect on men, but she did. Some men, anyway. Sailor was a tough guy, not phony tough like some guys but real tough. And after she laid into him like that, I saw him settle into that toughness like a boxer wrapping his fists about to go into a fight with a guy three weight classes above him.

He wanted me to be ready too, so he worked me real hard on fighting. He also got me into actual fights so I could hone my skills and my attitude. A lot of fights. We never fought around New Nod because Sailor wanted to keep the place private, so we'd travel a good distance. My fights were all in alleys and warehouses, biker bars, docks and out of the way places, illegal as hell, but I got really good. I suppose you could say I was a natural. By the time I was sixteen they had a hard time finding anybody I couldn't knock out or submit pretty quick. Didn't matter how old or how big or how experienced, or anything. Couple of knife fights, too. Well, more than a couple. Got some minor nicks, myself, nothing serious. Gave better than I got. Pretty sure I didn't kill anybody, though. Mostly, I just cut to disarm, not to kill. Not that I wasn't willing to, though. I was pretty angry in those days. Twice I even fought dogs—a pit bull and a Rottweiler, I think. Once with a knife, once without. Killed them both. Well. I don't suppose you need to hear about that, Aunt Violet.

But my mother needed tending to. She needed customers. All she required was that they were white skinned and could feel pain. When she didn't have someone to work her art on she got ill. It was like back before I saw her at the Sour Lemon, where I met Sailor. She'd get real yellow looking and depressed, and Sailor'd get all antsy about finding fresh meat to feed the beast. Belle of the Baal, he called her.

But with the news of Estelle's suicide getting out, and then El Cholo posting pictures of Whitey's peeled skin on the Internet as bait for information about the tattoo artist, the supply of rich, willing customers started to dry up. My mother didn't really care about the money, so Sailor decided to buy a little time by picking up a runaway and offering her cash to get a tattoo.

Her name was Svetlana, or that's what she said. She was Russian, and what little English she spoke was with a heavy accent. She really was pretty, and had very light skin—perfect for my mother. She apparently answered some ad from a modeling agency promising big success in America, but it turned out to be one of those sex slave prostitution rings.

She was working a street corner when Sailor found her. He actually spoke a little Russian that he learned from some shipmate somewhere, and he got her to trust him. I guess some people are just gullible. And desperate. That's a dangerous combination. She just wanted some money to get back home. He told her he knew an artist who was trying to break into the tattoo business, but needed a practice model—it wouldn't be much, just a simple little design or two, and she could pick it out, and for that he'd pay her two thousand dollars, more than enough to get a flight back to Russia and have some left over to start again.

Like I said, gullible and desperate. Well, when Svetlana's pimp saw them talking and ran up to get her back, Sailor crushed him and this other goon he had working for him. When they woke up, their teeth, their wallets, and their girl were all gone.

I could just see it. He knocks the dudes out, and then he dusts himself off, looks at the girl with those sea green eyes, gives her that famous Sailor smile, holds out his arm for her to take and says, "Shall we?" like he had just swatted a fly and they were stepping out on the town. How he convinced her to put on the blindfold, I'll never know, but she had it on when they pulled up. He can be pretty charming when he wants to be.

It took my mother four days. Even though Sailor had long ago insulated the studio so you couldn't hear the crying and screaming from the road, I could hear Svetlana from where I worked on my bike in the yard. It made me sick to my stomach.

Even indigo bunting was upset. He was nesting in a black cherry tree near my bedroom window and he and his mate had just hatched chicks not long before Svetlana came. I'd watch them constantly come and go, bringing food to the chicks and removing poop from the nest. Well, with all the wailing coming from the studio, indigo bunting seemed frantic and anxious, and then on the last day of Svetlana's session, the bird flew out of the nest with something bigger than its usual cargo of poop and dropped it on the ground close by me.

It was one of his chicks. Dead. It was weird, because it seemed like Svetlana quieted down right about then and indigo bunting went right back to gathering food for its other chicks like nothing had happened.

For a minute I got real worried about Svetlana, and I went to the studio window and looked in. She was lying there naked with her face turned toward the window and her eyes partly open. For just a second I thought she was dead, but then she took a deep catching breath so I knew she was alive and our eyes made contact. If anybody ever said "help me" without words, it was that girl, and what did I do?

I turned away. I felt bad about it, but I didn't know what I could do. The deed was already done. I couldn't take that tattoo off. I couldn't take away four days of pain. I couldn't remove from her memory that horrible look my mother has when she works. Besides, Svetlana wasn't some baby I had to save from a cult, was she? She was older than I was. She made the decision to put on the blindfold, to be brought, blind, to a place she had never been before by somebody she had never even met. And to do this after some other gang had already scammed her into sexual slavery.

It was during the four days of Svetlana's session that Sailor had his, what do you call it, his "aha!" moment. He was real nervous too, pacing the yard, muttering to himself, flicking his switchblade again and again and again. He was having this long running conversation with himself—or I guess you could say he was having it with me even though I wasn't responding to him and he wouldn't have listened to me even if I did—and it went something like this:

"We need customers, Cain, customers. People with money who appreciate art, man, real art, unique art. They're out there, I know they are, you and I both know they are, Cain. They're out there. Freaking art world's flush with money, man, and they're always looking for something special, something unique. Your mama does something no one else in the world does, no one else in the world. And it's a proven product, you know, it's totally proven, we both know that. The market's just been spooked, is all. Buncha cowards. That Estelle thing, that was... That was just... Cain, man, she walked into a gallery, a high-end art gallery in New freaking York and she takes out a freaking box cutter and she starts to cut off her own skin, just like that damn El Cholo did to poor Whitey, like she's going to hang your mom's art on the gallery wall herself just to show them what real art is! I mean, this is a gallery that'll sell some chick's rumpled bed, or some garbage strewn on the floor, or some stupid inflatable rabbit for a million bucks, and she goes in there and it's like she's telling them, hey, that's all just scam art, fools, this is real art. Art's about the truth and the truth's about pain, and this is the truth, here, take it! And those people can't even see it, because it's not just visual art, people, don't you get it? It's performance art, and it's visual art, and it's living sculpture, and it's life and death and pain. That's art. And your mother is orchestrating it from a thousand miles away, sight unseen, now is that genius or what?

"I tell you what, Cain, if people in this world had the balls to appreciate real art, there would be no better marketing than Estelle and Whitey. People would look at it and say, now this is art. Great art! I think she knew, Cain. Your mama knew. From the second she set needle to skin, she knew it would turn out this way. Freaking genius, Cain. But we can't carry on without money,

Cain. You know me, I'm all about the green. It's out there, I know it. You and I both know it. But people are cowards, man, especially rich people. Damn. It looks like we're running out of willing customers. Yeah, sure, they'll gawk at it if it's on someone else, but when it comes to paying top dollar to having it done to yourself, I tell you, that market's really not all that big, and it's shrinking. It's been shrinking ever since Estelle's parents got all riled. I mean, come on. Your daughter was part of the greatest art piece of all time, you oughta be proud. Instead you want to sue the artist. Freaking Philistines.

"Cowards. So where are we going to find willing customers now, Cain? Huh? Come on, Cain, you're the one who came up with the idea for your mama to do tattoos, remember? Come on, what's our next move? How are we going to get customers? We can't keep on buying slaves like this Svetlana chick. We can't..."

Suddenly he stopped talking and pacing and he stood there for a minute, thinking. Then he started pacing again, only slower.

"Slaves. Yeah... Only we wouldn't need to buy them. That's right. Remember that guy in, where was it, Saudi Arabia? Kuwait? Maybe Yemen, one of those hellholes. He had slaves. White girls, all of them. Human trafficking market, man, that's a thing, isn't it? It doesn't always have to be for sex, does it? Or not just for sex... Those rich bastards over there, they collect art, too, don't they? Those sheiks and sultans and everything, oil barons, rich Russkie tycoons, African warlords, Mexican drug lords.

They all like to show off. What better way to show off than with a bunch of living canvases? A bunch of beautiful white girls, walking around the biggest mansions and yachts in the world, naked, with the greatest art in the world inked on their bodies. Man, what would a rich sultan not pay for that? I can see it now..."

He stared into the studio window at Svetlana for a minute.

"Yeah, man, I can just see it. Yeah... There's money there, Cain. Big money. I'm talking millions, not this penny ante stuff we've had up til now. Damn, Cain, we've been giving it away. Are you kidding? These are people who'll pay millions for a stolen Van Gogh. Stolen! They don't give a damn about the law. Hell, that just makes it more attractive. They're above the law, they make the freaking law!

"What couldn't we do with that kind of money, Cain? Shoot. What's El Cholo got that we ain't got, Cain? Money. He's not tougher than we are. He's not more willing to do violence. He just has more money, he can buy more goons. He's got a product. But it's a cheap mass market product, man, a high volume product. Damn, Cain, your mother's right. Again. What'd she say, Cain? What'd she say? She said they sell smack, we sell art. Art! Fine art, high end art. Top dollar art...

"This is perfect, man, perfect. And no two-bit, mouth-breathing drug dealer's going to stop us. You think you're tough, Cholo? I'll show you tough. I'm going to get you back for what you did to Whitey. I'll teach you to steal art. Damn art thief."

And with that he threw his knife down into a block of wood, and it stuck there, impaled on its point, quivering, and he said, "Come on, Cain, let's play us some mumbleypeg."

But I wasn't looking at that. I was looking at my back bedroom window, where indigo bunting was flitting about and I thought, "What are you trying to tell me, Samuel Blue?"

22. Muse

MAYBE MY MOTHER WAS RIGHT. Nobody could do us harm in New Nod as long as I was there. Now, I don't know if it was the mark of Cain I carried on my cheek or not, but the fact is, nobody found us there. Sailor kept talking about it, how my mark of Cain would protect us, until I guess he felt charmed enough to go back to sea.

Without customers, my mother was like a plane in a death spiral. No canvases, no art, just a creeping jaundice. Sometimes she'd beg me to go out and bring her a customer, but I'd just ignore her and go on building my motorcycle.

Man, that bike was coming along real nice. Sailor called it my frankenfarmer contraption, what with the fact I had cannibalized this old 1940s era tractor that I found rusting near Samuel Blue's house for a lot of the parts, including the metal tractor seat, the fork springs, the muffler, steel tubes for the frame and handlebars, sheet metal from the body for my fenders. I used an old five-gallon jerry can for a fuel tank. I even welded pitchfork tines onto my front forks so they pointed forward and swept out. If I ever hit a dog I'd spear him and drag him home.

Anyway, it kept me busy when I wasn't fighting or training to fight or doing chores. And I enjoyed working on the bike, which drove my mother up a wall. New Nod was supposed to be a place of punishment for Cain. Cain wasn't supposed to have friends or nice things. Well, I didn't have friends. But I did fantasize about showing my bike off to Samuel Blue, or riding down to Harlington and taking Laura McKenzie for a ride.

None of that good feeling lasted, though. I didn't have Samuel Blue. I didn't have Laura McKenzie. I had my mother. And her death spiral was like a whirlpool and I was sure enough caught in it. Wherever she was going, I reckon I was going too.

You think I could have just walked away? Yeah, that makes sense. I was old enough. I was capable. Plenty of guys in my shoes and younger have left home and gone out on their own. I could have too. But I didn't. I can't really tell you why. I just didn't.

And that's something Sailor didn't understand. It wasn't about him, it wasn't about his love for her art, it wasn't about drug lords or sultans or slave girls or money.

It was about me and my mother and a fish story. And it was about how that story wasn't over yet. That's the part I didn't really understand, I only had some inkling of, way in the back of my mind.

I hate that so many people had to get hurt in the telling of this story, but I can't do anything about that now.

So here's what happened. One day my mother went through one of her mysterious stranger episodes. She usually started it with a migraine, stumbling around moaning and rubbing her temples for a day or so. And then she'd get real kinda quiet and soft and she'd shuffle into her room and put on her nightgown, and she would open her window wide and kinda whisper or moan, "O my love. Holy spirit. Come and take me, please come, I'm ready for you..." And then she'd put her sleeping mask on to cover her eyes and she'd lie down on her back on her bed and she'd be real calm for a long while.

Well, I had seen it a lot of times since I was little, but I had never, not once, uttered a word about it or asked her about it. Until that day. I walked into her room, I stood next to her bed, I took out my switchblade, I snapped it open, I jabbed the point into the fabric of her sleeping shades, I slowly removed them from her head, and I said, "What is the matter with you? Who the hell are you calling out to? Why are you calling him? What is wrong with you?" And then I walked back out of the room and sat down on the sofa with her sleeping shades still stuck on the tip of my knife.

She got up and came out of her bedroom. She was still wobbly, but she had a different kind of look about her. There was only one other time I remember seeing that look: Back when she fishhooked me, when she made me close my eyes and gave me those candies and talked in a voice that was soft and sweet and kinda slurred. That's how it was this time, too. Only I wasn't about to close my eyes this time.

She sat on the other end of the sofa. That was about as close as she would ever allow herself to get to me physically. She lay her head back and folded her hands on her lap and she talked.

"You were poison to me when you were born," she said. "Pregnancy, birth, after. It was just sickness and darkness I couldn't get away from. And then one day, it was a day like this, I gave up. I put on this nightgown. I opened the windows. There was a soft breeze that blew the curtains. I put that mask on. I lay down on my back on the bed. I crossed my hands over my heart like they do for corpses in a funeral home. And I thought, here I am, God, or whoever or whatever you are. Heal me or let me die. Please. And I was not going to move before one of those two things happened.

"And then I heard something. Someone coming into the room. Soft footsteps. He came to me. He lay with me. It was not your father. It was... a mysterious stranger. A holy spirit. He made love to me. I could feel the spark of life ignite in my womb. From that moment on I was healed. Everything was beautiful. Everything was light. I knew happiness. Joy. Love. True and pure. Emmanuel. God with us. Life was perfect. Through pregnancy, birth, after. And then... you know what happened then."

I said, "So you think you can get this holy spirit to come back? That's why you do it?"

"It's not something I think about. It just happens. You wouldn't understand."

I wouldn't understand. For some reason that really jagged me. And she sensed it. Because then she said, "Why don't you just take that knife and kill me? It would put us both out of our misery."

"Because I'm not a murderer!" I yelled.

"Then explain to me again, Cain, what happened to your brother."

Oh, man, she almost hooked me again, but I spit out the hook before it caught. I wasn't about to give her the satisfaction of turning me into a real murderer, and I wasn't about to waste any grace telling my story to her again. So I said, "There's only one way you can heal, you know."

"Oh yeah? What do you know, little Cain?"

"I was there."

She kinda jerked a little and went pale.

"I was there," I said again. "I saw it."

She stared at me. She stared at me like she had never seen me before. "You're a liar," she whispered.

I stared back at her. "You want to know what I saw?"

She looked away from me and stared at the wall without blinking.

I said, "It wasn't a spirit."

I could tell I struck a nerve. There was a little catch in her breathing and I saw her clench her jaw muscles and swallow. It was like she was trying hard to be calm, to stay in control. When I didn't say any more, she asked, "Who was it?"

"I don't know. All I know is it wasn't a spirit that knocked you up before. And it's not going to be a spirit that does it again. But that's the only way you're going to heal. So just forget the mask, and the open window, and calling out into the night like a fool. Just let Sailor get you pregnant."

"Sailor," she said with a hopeless little laugh. "Sailor's not my mysterious stranger."

"You don't know that," I said. "All you know is my father wasn't. He made you sick. Somebody else healed you. In fact I think you're looking at it upside down. It could be that Dad was the only man in the world who could make you sick. He was the only one who could give you me. Maybe anybody could give you a miracle baby, as long as it's not Dad. And Sailor's not Dad. He's nothing like him. That much you know, or you wouldn't have stayed with him so long."

"That's ridiculous," she said.

I got up and leaned over her. "You're an artist," I said. "Listen to your muse." And then I walked out.

As soon as I got out the door, indigo bunting fluttered right in front of my face and startled me. He dropped something on the ground and swooped away. I stepped to it and looked down.

Another dead chick.

23. The Mark of Cain

WHEN SAILOR CAME BACK FROM SEA he was in a feisty mood. "Things are rolling, Cain my boy, things are rolling. Where's your mom?"

"Sleeping," I said.

"In the middle of the day? What is it, another migraine?"

"I guess so."

"And no customers?"

"Nope."

"Well, that's all right, buddy, because old Sailor's got it rigged now. The deal's done. We got three beautiful young ladies—white as snow, man white as snow!—coming up here tomorrow. How you doing on supplies? Got enough ink? Needles? Never mind, I'm getting new stock in this afternoon. And guess what? Fifty thousand dollars per canvas. Fifty. Thousand. Dollars. Per. And if he likes that, let me tell you, the price is going up. Way up.

"What happened to Svetlana?" I said.

He grinned and pulled a thick envelope from his pocket. There were a bunch of hundred dollar bills inside. "Huh? Ha ha! You like that? Twenty-five grand, Cain. Svetlana was the seed from which an entire freaking orchard is going to grow."

"So she's a slave again."

"Slave nothing, man. She was a whore before. You know what she is now? Art. So put a stitch in that bleeding little heart of yours, my boy, because that sheik is an art lover, and he is going to protect his investment. She's going to live like a queen.

"Oh, and let me tell you this, Cain my boy, you'll love this. The New Nod crew has some new members, and they are tough, tough, tough." He pulled something out of a bag. "See this, Cain? You know what this is?"

"No."

"It's called a brand, Cain. A brand. You heat it up in a fire til it's red hot, then you shove it into a man's skin. Hurts like holy hell, a million times more pain than a tattoo needle. Takes four or five other guys to hold a man down so you can brand him proper. There's guys that have died because of the pain, man, had a heart attack or stroke. But let me tell you this. A man who's willing to get branded for the crew is a man you can count on. Brand brothers, man, that's deeper than blood brothers, even. Look here, Cain. This kind of brand, look here at the edge, is sharp enough where it can cut the skin, and hot enough that it cauterizes the cut and creates a great burn scar. You can get some real detail with this kind of brand. Our gang's going to wear the brand. What do you think of that?"

"I'm not doing that."

"Hey. Don't get me wrong. If you want to, fine, if not, fine. You're Cain, man. Freaking Cain! You don't need a brand. You have the mark. The truest mark of all. The mark of Cain." And then he pinched the fishhook scar on

THE BOOK OF CAIN

my face like he was dealing with some little kid. His mistake. I grabbed his wrist and put him in an armbar so fast he could do nothing but laugh and tap out. I would have broken his arm otherwise.

He must have really been feeling good because it didn't break his mood. "I guess I taught you right, man," he said rubbing his elbow. "That was one slick move. But seriously, Cain, you are the one indispensable man in this crew. You are her muse. You get to break the rules. But only you. Well, you and your mother, of course. But the rest of us? Branded. People are going to know not to mess with us. I'm going to get Whitey's skin back from El Cholo. That grease-ball is going to pay for what he did to Whitey. I promise you that. I guarantee you that."

About then my mother opened her bedroom window. "Sailor, is that you?" she called. Her voice was creaky and slurred.

"It's me, sweetheart. I'm home. What can I do you for?"

"Come in here."

He looked at me and winked. "Time for ol' Sailor to put on his land legs and do his duty as master of this rustbucket." He clapped me on the shoulder and disappeared into the house. Indigo bunting seemed nervous. My stomach turned sour.

The next morning one of Sailor's crew, a guy named Roscoe who taught me a lot of boxing techniques, drove up in a box truck. When he opened the back door this big tan-skinned dude in a light colored sport jacket got out. He held a big black pistol in his hand and he wasn't trying to hide it. He looked around for a minute, then motioned for the girls to come out.

None of them were wearing blindfolds, but the storage compartment of the box truck didn't have any windows, so they couldn't have seen how they got there. The girls stood there, sort of hugging themselves even though it wasn't cold and blinking in the bright sunlight. They looked pretty scared. Two of them reminded me of Svetlana, just accepting their fate. The third one, though, reminded me of someone else I had met somewhere, and then I saw how much she resembled the girl in the cult who was holding the kidnapped baby and didn't want to give her up.

Sailor hustled them all into the trailer. If I had a sense of humor then, which I didn't, what happened over the next several days would have seemed funny. You see, my mother just ignored all of them. Sailor tried prodding her gently to do her work, but all she wanted to do was get him in the sack, then kick him out and kinda wander around in her bare feet, not talking, and certainly not picking up any tattoo equipment.

Sailor paraded the girls in front of her, saying "Look, Sweetie, look at this skin. White as snow. Best canvas you ever saw, right? And tender. Oooh, are they going to feel that needle. What do you say? Come on, how about we get started now?"

She ignored him. Pretty soon he was getting into arguments with the girls' handler. The guy had a thick accent, maybe Arabic or something, half the time he sounded like he was clearing this throat. Sailor called him Moe, but I don't know if that was his real name.

After a couple of days Sailor started coming to me. "Cain! Brother! We've got to get her moving, man. I've got a delivery date in two weeks and at four days a canvas, that's really pushing it. I mean really pushing it. This sheik, he's got a big party planned and he wants to roll out his artwork for all his rich friends. We can't afford to be late and we can't afford delivering an inferior product. Cain, what the hell? What's wrong with her? I've never seen her like this. She's usually itching to put the needle to a customer."

I ignored him and kept working on my bike. He just got more flustered.

"Cain. Come on. Hey, you're her muse, do something."

"Like what?"

"I don't know. Whatever it is muses do. Just... Man, we have product to deliver. We can't fail when we're just getting this operation on its feet. Do something."

"I don't think she's going to be doing any tattoos for a while," I said.

"What? What the hell! Why not?"

"She's pregnant."

For a minute he looked like an old engine that was in the process of losing its flywheel. He shook as he tried to get the words out. "Wh... wh... Are you kidding me... That's... What the hell did you just say?"

"Break out the Cubans, Sailor, you're about to be a dad."

"What! Me? Hey... It couldn't be... I just got here."

"Well, I'm not a doctor, but I'm pretty sure it only takes one time. Oh, and she flushed her birth control pills a long time ago. Oh, and there haven't been any other men here. Oh, and she's in heat. Well, that's what she said. I don't know about that stuff."

"Aw, come on! You don't know she's pregnant. Has she... has she done a test?"

I shrugged. "I don't know about that."

"Well then how the hell do you know?"

I looked up and saw indigo bunting perched on a slender branch that swayed under its delicate weight. "A little bird told me," I said.

"You stay here," he said. "Watch these people. Don't let them go anywhere. I'm going to get one of those test kits. You better be lying to me, boy. You damn well better be lying to me if you know what's good for you." And he jumped on his bike and roared off.

The girls were sitting in lawn chairs under the big oak tree in front. The Arab was sitting near them. I knew I didn't have much time. There was an old canvas bag filled with tow chains in the shed, big enough to hold a basketball. I dumped out the chains, then I removed the cinch cord and replaced it with a stout zip tie. I stuck a bunch of zip ties in my pocket.

It was a pretty warm afternoon, and late in the day, and the Arab was nodding off. I snuck up behind him, and then I threw the bag over his head and cinched the zip tie tight enough that he couldn't get it off, but not so tight that it choked him. He immediately grabbed the bag and tried to jerk it off, but he couldn't, and he started shouting threats and lashing out with his arms. I got in position while he reached into his jacket and drew out his gun, like I figured he would.

Sailor had taught me this technique to disarm somebody of a handgun, and I had practiced it about a thousand times, so it worked easily. The girls were watching, stunned, and I started yelling at them to get up and move, because the guy was flailing his arms about trying to grab them.

Two of them moved. One didn't. The cult girl lookalike. His hand caught her hair and he jerked her around. I don't know, I had never shot anybody and I didn't want to start, so I took the pistol—it was a heavy .45 caliber—and I just whaled on the side of his head several times real hard until he let go of her and grabbed me. Just right, man. I tossed the gun aside and grabbed his wrist and swung my legs up and over and locked him into an arm bar. I pulled with all my might until his elbow made a nasty "pop" and bent backwards.

He let out a shriek and I was able to jerk free. I picked up the gun and told the girls, "Come with me." Of course, they kinda just looked at each other and hesitated, but I pointed the gun at them and said, "Come on!"

I led them away from New Nod at a run, but these chicks were not athletes, so I had to slow it down to a fast walk. On Wednesdays and Fridays the southbound train came early. I could hear it rumble as we approached the tracks. I saw an open boxcar.

Just as we got close, one of the girls fell down and winced in pain as she held her ankle. As I turned to help her back to her feet I saw the Arab running toward us. I guess the canvas bag had torn where I hit him with the gun, or he had a knife, or maybe he just bit it open with his teeth, because he was looking through this big bloody hole in the bag.

I fired the gun. I didn't try to hit him, I was just trying to scare him off, give us a few more seconds to climb aboard the train. It didn't even slow him down. I picked up the girl with the hurt foot and dragged her to the tracks. By then they were ready to obey me, and as I yelled at them to climb aboard, the two healthy ones did. With all my might I heaved the third girl partway up into the car, and the other two grabbed her and dragged her aboard. I clambered up just as the Arab got there.

I aimed the gun right at his head and yelled, "Stay back! Stay where you are!" He looked right up the barrel and just kept coming. I hit him on the head again with the gun and lost my grip on it. The gun tumbled out into the weeds. He kept coming, running along the tracks, hanging onto the floor of the car, trying to pull himself up. Strong as a bull, smart as an ox, this guy. He had a hard time of it, what with one elbow dislocated, his head bloodied and half stuck in a canvas bag, but he made it up into the boxcar.

I leveled a pretty good spin kick on his jaw, which staggered him, but suddenly he pulled another gun out of his pants or jacket or someplace and pointed it at me with his good arm. He said, "Now you die, American," and he pulled the trigger.

Click, and nothing. He pulled it again. Another misfire.

"I am Cain," I said. "You can't kill me." I kicked him so hard in the groin you could hear his balls crunch and he doubled over and dropped to his knees. I gave him one more spinning heel kick to the temple that knocked him out cold. I turned him on his belly, yanked his arms behind his back and zip tied them. Then I zip tied his ankles together. Then I hogtied his ankles to his wrists behind his back.

Just then wouldn't you know it but Bon Julia and Uncle Pete, who had been cowering in the back of the boxcar all this time, tried to sneak past me and jump out the open door. I stopped them and slammed them against the wall. Then I pulled the switchblade out of my pocket, snapped it open and touched the tip against Bon Julia's cheek just under her left eye.

"All right, you two, listen up," I said. "Here's what you're going to do. You see these girls? They were sex slaves. See that guy? He was their pimp. See this knife? This is the knife that I'm going to skin you with if you don't make sure these people get off this train in Harlington, you hear me? You get off with them. All four of them. And you make sure they get to Sheriff McKenzie in Harlington. Got it?"

They nodded. "Ain't you coming?" Bon Julia said. "Me and Pete, we're old..."

"No, I'm not. But don't think you can weasel out of it. Because I will check up on you. If I find out you screwed up, if you snuck off or something and didn't do your job, I will hunt you down. Do you understand me? I will hunt you down and I will skin you alive. Both of you. You know I will. Got it?"

They nodded again. Uncle Pete was crying.

"One other thing," I said. "Samuel Blue. You seen him?"

"No, young fella, we ain't. Not in a couple a years. I swear."

The train had sped up a good bit by then so my landing was pretty rough when I jumped off. But it was a good landing with a tumble and a roll, and I was able to get back up and jog back home.

Sailor was waiting for me.

"What the hell, Cain? Where's Moe and the girls? You were supposed to be watching them."

I just shrugged and set about working on my bike again.

"Come on, Cain, where'd they go?"

"South."

"South? What the hell? Did he just up and take them away? We got a hundred fifty thousand dollars riding on those girls, man."

"Moe kinda fell asleep. The girls split. He went after them. Maybe he'll bring them back. Maybe not. I wouldn't count on it if I were you, though."

He glared at me. "Did you help them? You did, didn't you? Little punk."

He stepped toward me but I looked at him and gripped my wrench so he pulled up short. Sailor only had maybe ten pounds on me at that point. He and his friends had taught me everything I needed to know to give him the fight of his life. But that wasn't all. In the boxcar, when that Arab pointed his gun at my face and it failed to fire, not once but twice, that's when something clicked in me. My mother was right all along. I really was Cain. I was the killer who could not be killed.

It wasn't a good feeling. It was sour and sick and empty and lost. But it was real enough that when I shot that look at Sailor, he knew. Oh, he tried to brush it off by saying I was the artist's muse and the success of the operation depended on me doing my muse job, and not babysitting canvases and all that crap, but he knew. I could kill him. He couldn't kill me.

Pretty simple arithmetic, huh, Aunt Violet? Yeah, simple and straightforward. But it was nothing compared with what happened next. You're not going to want to hear this. But you asked for the whole story. All I can say is: be careful what you ask for. You just might get it.

24. The Third Panel

FOR A GOOD LONG WHILE it was just my mother and Sailor
and me at New Nod. That's how she wanted it. Sailor at
first busied himself building a blacksmith's forge to
make his brands. I helped him. Carrying stone, mixing
mortar, building the furnace, welding, hammering, and
just general banging around, it was about the only thing
I had to hold on to while this cancer of Cain ate my in-
sides out.

My mother was acting like I had never seen her act
before. Don't get me wrong, it wasn't like that pure
glowing happiness she had as she drew her beautiful pictures on the riverbank. She didn't draw anything, no
pictures and no tattoos, so I couldn't tell by that how she
was really feeling. She wasn't giddy or ecstatic or anything, but she wasn't her gloomy, angry, sarcastic self either. And because there were none of those kind of
things to make her look bad, her natural beauty shone
through so she looked, for lack of a better word (and
there's got to be a better word), happy.

Well, now that I've said it I see "happy" doesn't seem
right at all, but I don't know what else to call it. Samuel
Blue's not around to help me find the right word.

Anyway, she wore her nightgown a lot and walked
around barefoot, and when she walked, she walked slow
and careful, but not like she always did when she had a

migraine. It was more like she was walking on eggshells, hoping not to break any, or like she was carrying something delicate and she didn't want it to fall and break.

Sometimes Sailor would watch her from the shop door with a strange fascination. Like he'd forget for a while his worries about his business venture, and the sheik and the drug lord and Whitey and Estelle and all that, and he'd just stare with awe at her as she stepped softly about the place.

One time I watched him watch her as she watched indigo bunting where he perched on a slender branch and sang his song. The sun was low and the bird's feathers shone as brilliant as could be.

It wasn't a rainbow, though. I had not seen a rainbow since the day I met Samuel Blue. I had come to the conclusion that I would never see one again.

Cain can't have nice things.

At any time I could have taken off. I could have jumped a train and never come back, I could have gone to sea or joined the circus or gone to Arizona and worked on a dude ranch or on cars or construction. I could have chosen not to be a part of all this. But I stayed, and I don't have anybody to blame but myself.

One day, she was pretty far along, my mother got sick. I was out in the yard. Indigo bunting made a strange chirp and flew out of his nest carrying something, which he dropped onto the ground before returning to his nest. Another dead chick. The last one, I figured. I thought how casual it seemed, that he just would get rid of a dead chick like that and get right back to work finding more

food. No mourning, no sorrow, nothing sentimental.
Indigo buntings don't sing the blues, I guess.

And right then my mother called to me from the
kitchen, "Cain!" Her voice was sharp and desperate.

I went in. She had her nightgown pulled up and both
hands on her belly. She was trembling and sweating. I
couldn't help but look, and I saw the movement. I guess
that's what you call it. Looked like something nudged
her belly skin from the inside.

She fell to her knees like she had been kicked by a full-
grown man. She heaved a couple of times, then vomited
on the floor and stayed there on her hands and knees,
shaking. "Take me to the doctor," she groaned.

"Why don't I just call 911?" I said.

"No! No! Here... Take me here..." She had a crumpled
little piece of cardboard in her hand and she pushed it
toward me along the floor. I picked it up. It was a business card. It was for a Doctor Kernell, I think was his
name, and a slogan that said, "Your Body, Your Choice,
Your Time." That, and "We Make House Calls!"

"You've got to help me," she said, and puked again.
"I'm sick..."

I stood there, looking down at her. I looked at the refrigerator. After all these years, the two pieces of refrigerator art were still there: the one with her fishhook and
my blood, and the one with my knife and the cult guy's
blood. Side by side.

I would have had to pick her up and put her in the car.
But I couldn't. She had never touched me in kindness. I
just... I just couldn't. And I remembered what you told

me, Aunt Violet, about how she wanted to abort me when I kicked her. I don't know, maybe I wanted to punish her, but I wasn't about to help her. I said, "No," and I just dropped the business card on the floor.

Just then something swatted me in the face. It was indigo bunting. The kitchen screen door had stuck open when I came in, and he must have flown in. He fluttered about a bit, then back out the door. I followed him.

Don't get me wrong. I knew I was leaving her behind. But I followed indigo bunting out of the trailer, through the woods, all the way to Samuel Blue's place. Samuel wasn't there. Nobody was there but me and indigo bunting. He sang. I listened. I didn't know what he was singing about. I didn't know the words.

Hours passed. The sun got low. Indigo bunting shined one last time, and then he flew away. I was alone. I walked slowly back to New Nod.

I didn't go in through the kitchen, because I didn't want to pass the stench of my mother's vomit. I went around to the front door. I could hear the yelling as I approached.

It was Sailor. Tough guy, coming apart at the seams. Crying. Wailing. Kicking over the furniture. Breaking things. Shouting until his voice cracked and scraped. "What is wrong with you! You crazy bitch! This is not art! This is a human life! What the hell is wrong with you!..."

My mother just sat there on the sofa with her ankles crossed on the coffee table, her hands crossed over her belly, her head back, her eyes half closed, not speaking, not defending herself or responding in any way to Sailor, looking strangely satisfied. As Sailor was fond of saying, "like the cat that ate the canary."

Sailor turned to me. His eyes were red. Tears drained down his cheeks, spittle flecked his lips. "She's all yours," he said. "I'm outta here." As he stepped through the door he stopped and turned back. "Hey, Cain. Your mother the artist finished her triptych. Why don't you check it out?" And then he slammed out the screen door and was gone.

I stepped into the kitchen. There it was, on the refrigerator door. The third bloody panel. I couldn't tell at first what they were. Or maybe I could tell, but my eyes watered at the sight and it was a while before my focus cleared and the reality of it set in.

Blood, smeared in the form of a cross. At the left and right ends, two tiny hands. At the bottom, two tiny feet. Stuck to the paper with pins.

The sun set. I walked back into the living room. My mother wasn't there. I stepped to her bedroom. The door was open, and she was lying on her back on her bed. I stood by the bed and looked down on her. I looked at her for a good long while before I realized I had my switchblade in my hand. The blade was open.

"Just think," she said softly. "Had your father let me do this to you, none of this would have happened. Your father is such a murdering bastard, isn't he?"

My ears whistled and everything tingled such that I couldn't even feel the knife in my hand. I did not wipe away my tears but just looked at her through the water.

Then I turned and walked out of her room. I jammed the door shut so she could not get out. I went outside, got a couple of two-by-fours and nailed them across her window so she couldn't get out. Then I went out to the blacksmith shop.

It was night. I split wood for a while, and I made the fire in the forge. I set to work on my brand, sharpening and bending bands of iron for the design, using whatever nails and screws and other objects to complete it. I worked all night.

The sun came up. Indigo bunting perched on the windowsill, watching, not singing. Finally, I finished shaping my brand. The Christian fish with the baby's head in its mouth, and little X-eyes showing the baby's dead. I left it in the fire and worked the bellows until the brand glowed.

I had taken my shirt off. I was smeared with sweat and soot. I took the brand out of the fire and walked into the trailer. My mother was shaking her door handle trying to get out of her bedroom. I kicked the door in and she backed up and flopped back on the bed. I stepped to her and raised the brand.

"Don't hurt me!" she cried. "What have I ever done to you?"

I jammed the hot brand square into my bare chest with all my might. To this day I can't describe the pain. But I held it there as I screamed, as if I were trying to shove it all the way through my body and out my back. The stench of burning flesh filled the room.

Finally I flung the brand aside and staggered out of the trailer. I kick started the frankenfarmer bike and revved the throttle. As I started down the driveway to the county road I didn't know where I was going. I couldn't think. My whole body felt like it was on fire. But indigo bunting flashed in front of me and I followed him.

I could not retrace my route if you put a gun to my head. All I knew is that whenever and wherever I saw indigo bunting fly, I followed.

Finally, in town, indigo bunting left the road and flew toward a building. I got off the bike and ran after him. He rounded a corner where there was, I don't know, an alley or secluded spot. There were some people there.

One was a kid about my age, but a good bit taller and heavier than me. He had something in his hand—I found out later it was a tennis racket—and he was swinging it around. A couple of other kids were egging him on, and one of them yelled out, "Get it, Catfish, get it!"

Catfish. That's what they called the tall kid. Catfish. And you know what? He looked like one. Oily skin. Pimples. This wide, thin mouth and these wide-set eyes. Just started to grow whiskers, and he had these long black ones by the corners of his mouth. Looked just like catfish whiskers. I guess that's why they called him that.

And Catfish swung the tennis racket and smacked indigo bunting as he flew. Indigo bunting slammed against the brick wall of the building and fell to earth, dead.

25. I Had a Sister

"AND SO THAT'S HOW I WOUND UP HERE," he said. "I lost it. Beat him up pretty bad, I guess. Messed up a couple of cops, too."

"And you had never seen this boy before?" I said.

"Nope."

"And there's no way you could have known that he was the son of the doctor who treated your mother the day before? For the... abortion?"

He shook his head slowly, staring into space. When he spoke again it was in a very soft, distant voice. "They found out she was a girl. I had a sister." He was quiet for a minute, then he said, "Cain can't have nice things."

"Please don't say that," I said. "That was not your fault."

He looked directly at me again. "Yes it is. I put her up to it. I told her: I'm your muse, listen to your muse, let Sailor get you pregnant. She wouldn't have done it otherwise. She would have just gone on tattooing lily white sex slaves for rich art lovers. I knew what she could do. Maybe I knew she would do it, maybe that's why I put her up to it. Maybe I knew she'd call that guy, get her abortion. Maybe that's why I followed indigo bunting. I could have stayed. I could have made her have that baby. But I didn't. Because I'm Cain. It's what I do. I kill."

Maybe, he said. Maybe he knew. Maybe he put her up to it. Those were words of doubt, not delusion, and certainly not destiny. "I don't think you're a killer," I said. "Nothing you've said today indicates that."

He didn't respond, but his eyes didn't waver from their focus on me. And his look wasn't predatory, I realized then, so much as an insistence that I acknowledge and tell the truth. His truth. Then I recalled what his mother had written in his blood on the first panel of the triptych:

TELL

THE

TRUTH

"If you're a killer, then why didn't you kill your mother?" I said. "It seems you had ample opportunity, and came close a few times."

"Maybe the rainbow... distracted me," he said.

"Even the last time? When you branded yourself? I don't think you mentioned a rainbow then."

His focus drifted into the trance stare he had when he was in his memory.

"Was there a rainbow?" I asked.

Still in his trance, he shook his head slowly and whispered, "No." I could see his jaw muscles start to work, and I grew anxious to draw him back out of that memory.

"Do you like it here?" I asked. "At this place? The Lazaretto?"

He took in a breath and blinked. "I hate this place," he said. "I hate that river. It stinks of catfish. All the damn time."

"Do you know what river this is?"

He gazed out the window and nodded. "It's river cat's river. The Prevene. Harlington's about an hour downstream by boat. They told me."

"They told you?"

"Yeah. When I first got here. Guy said, hey, guess what? This is the same river where your little brother drowned."

"Oh my God," I whispered. "What did you say?"

He looked back at me. "He didn't drown. River cat took him."

I began to regret my line of questioning. I wanted him to make a connection with some positive human relationships before we ended the session. I said, "I know you love your Aunt Violet. And I think you respect Sheriff McKenzie. They've both been trying to help you. Can you tell me why you won't let them in?"

He held me in a steady gaze. "Cain can't have nice things."

"What about Laura McKenzie? You know, I talked to her, too. She told me that she really did want you to kiss her that night in Harlington. She only slapped you because her dad had put a camera by your brother's memorial stone to try to catch vandals, and she didn't want him to see you together like that."

"Doesn't matter," he said.

"She likes you, and you seemed to like her," I said. "Do you think about her at all?"

He looked at me for a minute before answering. It was his challenging look. "Sure," he said. "I think about her. When I'm lying in bed at night, alone. I got urges, like any guy. Pretty sure she wouldn't like my thoughts, though. They're not... nice."

"All right. Fair enough. Look..." I almost said his name, but I caught myself. I didn't want to challenge him unnecessarily. So I said, "I have to ask you this: Do you understand the position you're in? I mean, I very much appreciate that you opened up to me the way you did today, but the court order that remanded you to the custody of the Lazaretto had specific conditions, and the therapists here..."

"You'll make sure my Aunt Violet gets that?" he interrupted, pointing to my recorder.

"Yes, of course, if that's what you want. But we really need to..."

"I'm done," he said. He stood and turned toward the door.

"I understand," I said. "It's been a long day. And I think it's been productive. Thank you..." I decided to chance it. "...Richard."

He turned his head toward me. His look was one of tired derision, as if he was disappointed that I hadn't understood a thing he had said all day. He shook his head sadly and turned the doorknob.

"May I ask you one more question?" I said before he opened the door.

He waited, not moving.

"You said that when you were young and living in New Nod you used to go exploring, and you would imagine your little brother was alive and with you. You'd teach him how to throw rocks, and you'd protect him, and all that. And you'd talk to him. If you could imagine your brother here with you now, what would you say to him?"

He stood there, very still, considering. Then he said in a low voice, "I am Cain." He opened the door and was gone.

He had talked virtually without stop for more than seven hours. I had given him a couple lozenges and bottles of water now and again, but I still could hardly believe he did it. By the end I was not afraid of him; I was afraid for him. And I was awestruck by certain things: one was his memory. I was able to check some items in his file, and notes from my conversations with Violet Tyler and Sheriff McKenzie while he was talking. For example, the letter he wrote to Judge Jurlean Witt, asking about his family—it was in the file, and he recited it word for word. The other thing that struck me was the degree of humanity and even sanity he had retained after all he had endured.

But his last words reverberated in that room like a death knell. I was trying to appeal to his rainbow. I was stunned when he answered with darkness.

He would kill his brother. He had become Cain.

I rubbed my temples and said to myself, "Shut up, Lil, you're reading too much into it." And then I realized I had called myself "Lil," what my father used to call me, and my mind dragged up the name "lil Man," and I tapped my forehead with my fist and said, "Stop it, stop it, stop it, there is no connection, just stop it, just... stop."

I was exhausted. I gathered my things and I left the Laz. The walk across the iron footbridge, the swirling river, that damned old leper colony—knowing I was leaving Richard behind in that quarantine worse than any other prison he could be sent to—when I got in my car I took that jar of maternal instinct off the shelf in my mind and I opened it and breathed deeply. And I cried. For a long time.

When I got home I got a call from Violet Tyler. I didn't answer it. I just let it go to voicemail. She had wanted me to let her know how the interview went, but I wasn't ready to talk about it. I was exhausted and confused. I had the strong feeling that Richard—intentionally or not—was trying to tell me something that I wasn't quite understanding. As much as I tried to relax, my mind kept wrestling with it.

That night, as spent as I was, I had a hard time falling asleep. A name crept into my mind, a name my father taught me: Roy G Biv. Red, orange, yellow, green, blue, indigo, violet: the colors of the rainbow. And I thought how Richard Tyler's life had coursed through them, one after another, as if by design. The red house. His orange prisoner's clothes. His mother's job at the sour lemon and the jaundiced look she had. Sailor's green eyes and his saying "I'm all about the green." Samuel Blue. The indigo bunting. And now, Richard's telling of his life story to his Aunt Violet.

Was it by design? His design? Is it possible that Richard Tyler made it all up like some paint-by-numbers story in order to... to what? No, it couldn't be. Violet Tyler told me about the red house herself. Elton Ricks said the cop told him about the indigo bunting and surely Richard didn't have the mental stability after his violent outburst to perpetrate some elaborate lie. Did he?

Did he kill his mother? He said the rainbow saved her, but there was no rainbow the last time he raised his hand against her. Did he concoct a crazy story so that when her body is eventually found he will have established the basis for an insanity plea?

No, that's absurd. Richard is a reasonably intelligent boy, not an evil genius. He's not his mother. But maybe she's not an evil genius either, maybe she's a victim.

A suspicion began to gnaw at me—that Richard was playing me. He was nothing like any teenager I had ever counseled. He didn't act, think, or talk the same way. There was nothing juvenile about the way he told his story, the way he spoke, the phrases he used, his cadence, the way he used slightly different voices for different people, as if he were getting into character like a really good actor or storyteller. He told his story as if he were reliving it from a photographic memory—or a well-rehearsed script.

But that would be expected from a kid who never had the opportunity to socialize with his peers, wouldn't it?

A kid who only ever heard sea stories from the likes of Sailor and his seafaring and biker gang. But what if Sailor didn't even exist? What if Richard made him up? What if...

Shut up, shut up, just go to sleep, for God's sake.

For God's sake. So if he didn't make it up, then what about all these, what, prophetic signs? Is he a religious nut? A prophet? A muse? What? Sarge said it would take a miracle for him to open up to me. It would take God's grace, he said. And then there it was. The rainbow. The sign of the covenant. Richard did not make that up. I saw it myself.

Oh good Lord, just stop. Just get some sleep. You're not his mother. You're not his savior. For Richard prison would be a step up from the Lazaretto. If there was a seventeen-year-old in the world who could handle himself in adult prison, it is Richard Tyler. If you can't do anything about it, you can't do anything about it. You wash your hands of it and...

No. Stop it with the religious stuff. Leave it to Sarge and Violet Tyler. She's a nice lady, loving and caring and good. But she has prayed for her nephew literally thousands of times, and what good has it done? He went from Richard to Cain, from Harlington to New Nod to the Lazaretto. Next stop: prison.

He doesn't need prayers. He needs a good psychiatrist. Or a good mother. Damn. I'm not his mother. I am not this child's mother.

Through all these swirling thoughts and emotions, I could sense that there was one very specific thing troubling me, and I couldn't put my finger on it. I was too tired, too drained. It would come to me if only I could sleep.

I did what I didn't like to do. I took a sleeping pill. As I got drowsy I realized I had not shut my bedroom window. The curtains moved gently in the night breeze. I thought of Eris and her yearning for a mysterious stranger, a holy spirit, to come. I didn't get up to close it.

26. Jailbreak

IT WAS MORNING WHEN I AWOKE. My waking was hard and sudden. I sensed what that specific missing thing was that troubled me the night before. Something about the last color in Roy G Biv was wrong somehow. All the other colors had some dire result, some pain association for Richard. But telling his Aunt Violet his life story? What's dire about that?

Something wrong, something terribly wrong was happening regarding Violet. A fear shivered in me. What if Richard was waiting for that rainbow to tell his story to his Aunt Violet—so he could end it for himself? Suicide? My heart and mind began to race with the fear of a mother about to lose her son.

No, no, no, it's not that. I shook my head and slapped my cheeks. He's playing me. I don't know what his game is, but he's playing me. Or he might be. Just keep that in mind, Doctor.

My ears were buzzing. Then I realized, no, the buzzing was coming from outside. It was coming in through my open bedroom window. It was like the whole world was buzzing. Damn construction crews, I thought. Can't wait for a decent time to start work. I dressed quickly, I didn't wait to put on my makeup, and I stumbled out to my car and sped off to the Lazaretto.

As I approached the place a police car pulled up behind me, lights flashing and siren blaring. I pulled over, but he drove around me and went on. When I finally reached the Lazaretto I was distraught to see several other police cars and ambulances already there.

I ran across the footbridge through the gate, which had been latched open for the police and EMTs. When I entered the building I could see activity down the hall to my right and loud conversation coming from the principal's office. I walked down and peeked in.

Two uniformed cops were in the office questioning Mr. Sanders, the principal, who sounded angry and afraid, almost panicked. One of the cops said, "So let me get this straight. You came in this morning, your door's broken open—by the looks of the door jamb the perp kicked it open, or used a battering ram—and inside you got this display case broken open and—looks like the perp used that chair to bust the glass—and the only thing missing is one knife..."

"Yes, a switchblade."

"And you're saying it was this kid, Richard Tyler, because..."

"Because it was his switchblade! And he's not in his room, we can't find him anywhere."

The other cop said, "You got kitchen knives, homemade shivs, couple of switchblades, hell, brass knuckles... I thought this was a school."

"It is a school!"

"Looks like a prison. I've seen these displays in wardens offices. This one's... pretty impressive, actually. So why do you have it, if this is a school?"

"To let them know who's boss, you know, that we're in control, and they can't just... Look, we take some pretty hard cases here, and this Richard Tyler is the worst of the worst. We were actually trying to get him removed..."

"And you're sure the knife that was taken belonged to this Richard Tyler kid?"

"Yes. It was found on him when he was arrested for nearly killing another kid, and by the way, he also assaulted police officers up in Pico County."

"All right," the first cop said, "You said you have security cameras. Can you pull up video of the hallway, the entrance gate, and all that?"

A man, I figured it was the school's IT guy, was sitting at the computer looking intently at the screen and working the keyboard. "Stanley, have you found anything?" Mr. Sanders said to him.

"Not yet," he said. "This might take a little while."

The first cop said, "Look, Mr. Sanders, the kid's armed with a deadly weapon. Like I said before, if he's as dangerous as you say and he's still on campus, we're going to have to evacuate the other kids and staff, and get the SWAT team in here."

I walked quickly back to the receptionist's desk by the front door. I said, "Where's Richard Tyler's room?"

She looked extremely anxious, and said, "Richard Tyler?"

"He's a student here... you know... Cain."

"Oh." She told me how to get to his room, and as I started that way she called after me, "But you can't go down there, Doctor. I mean, the police said... He could be hiding somewhere. He could..."

The door to that section of the dorm was locked, but I looked through the glass panel and saw Sarge standing among a bunch of teenage boys. I knocked and motioned for him to come and he opened the door for me.

"What the hell did you say to Cain yesterday?" he said.

"Hardly anything," I said. "He did all the talking. Sarge..."

"Cain talked to you? All day? You were in that office all day. Didn't even break for a meal."

"Yes, well, he saw a rainbow and it was off to the races. Sarge, what's going on? Where is he?"

"A rainbow," he said thoughtfully. "Figures."

"Sarge..."

"It was a sign."

"Sarge, listen, we need to find him. The police consider him armed and dangerous. I don't think I have to tell you what could happen if they find him."

One of the boys said, "I hear we're going to be evacuated!"

Another boy yelled, "Road trip!" and the others cheered and high-fived.

"Sarge," I said. "You don't seem to be taking this seriously enough. Richard said certain things to me yesterday that suggest... well, he may be suicidal. We need to find him."

"Cain?" he scoffed. "Cain's not suicidal."

"How do you know?"

He shrugged. "He seemed OK to me yesterday after-noon when I left. How about you boys? Cain seem OK to you?"

They all shrugged and nodded, "Yeah, seemed OK to me... Me, too..."

A voice behind the crowd called out, "He wasn't OK." The other kids all jerked around and one of them ap-proached the boy who yelled and pointed his finger at him. "Shut up, Jasper." Another said, "Snitches get stitches."

Jasper was standing in one of the dorm rooms, peer-ing out the door. "I'm not a snitch. The lady's right, he's in danger. You guys don't care." They yelled back at him to shut up.

He backed into the room as I approached. I went in, and Sarge came in after me, telling the other boys to back off. He shut the door so only the three of us were in the room.

"He wasn't OK after you left yesterday, Sarge," Jasper said. "He read that paper you gave him and he got really, really mad, and he stayed mad all night." He looked at me. "I'm his roommate, Jasper. Are you that shrink?"

"I'm his psychiatrist, yes," I said. "What paper are you talking about?"

"This," he handed me a newspaper.

Sarge said, "I gave him that.   I bring him his hometown fish wrapper once a week. He reads it. I mean, why not? Whatever it takes to keep their reading skills up, right? Hell, none of the other kids here read newspapers."

"I do," Jasper said. "I read the New York Times."

"Yeah, sure you do, kid," Sarge said.

"I do!"

"Jasper," I said, "What was it in here that set him off?"

He shrugged. "I don't know. He just read something and he started rocking back and forth, and..."

"And what?" Sarge said.

"And he was, like, crying... or like whining, you know, like he was trying not to cry. And then he threw the paper down and just started going ape. He kept saying over and over again, 'She did this, she did this, I'm going to kill her... I need to get out... I'm going to kill her."

I looked at Sarge and he looked back and said, "Honest to God, Doc, I didn't know this."

Then I saw it. The headline was: "Body found in septic tank." And the sub-head below it said, "Homicide investigation begun." The story was short, and went like this:

"The body of a man identified by police as Samuel Blue, 71, was discovered Tuesday afternoon in an old septic tank, the top of which had been broken open and covered with plywood. According to police and coroner's reports, the cause of death was drowning, although evidence indicates the victim suffered a skull fracture from being hit with a blunt object.

Police say the man's body was weighted down with cinder blocks tied around his waist, while his hands were tied behind his back, which further indicates this as a homicide.

Found with Mr. Blue's body was a Bible sealed in a plastic bag. The Bible had an inscription inside to someone identified only as "Richard," who police say may be a person of interest in the investigation. Anyone with information is asked to call police at..."

"Oh my God," I said. "Samuel Blue."

"Who's Samuel Blue?" Sarge said.

"A friend of Richard's," I said. "Oh my God, he's going after his mother. He's going back to Pico County."

"Uh-uh, no he's not," Jasper said. "They're going to Harlington."

"Harlington?" I said. "But... wait a minute. What do you mean, 'they'?"

"Cain and that girl," he said.

"What girl?"

"You need to tell her, Sarge," Jasper said. "You need to tell her the truth. Cain could be in trouble."

Sarge had his head down and was pinching the bridge of his nose with his eyes closed.

"What girl, Sarge?" I said. "What's going on? You've got to tell me now."

"All right, all right," he said, looking at me. "Laura McKenzie."

"Laura... What!"

"She's the daughter of..."

"I know who she is! Just tell me what's going on."

"OK, she called me last night and said she had something she needed to tell Cain, and she had to tell him personally, she didn't want him finding out from some damn bureaucrat at the school, as she put it."

"Tell him what?"

"I don't know, I didn't want to be nosy. I told her come up, I'd find a way to get them together so they could talk, that's all."

"It was about the funeral," Jasper said.

"What funeral?" Sarge and I said together.

"She said it was for his Aunt Violet."

A chill went through me. "Oh my God," I said. "Violet Tyler died? Oh my God, that would just crush him. Jasper, are you sure? You heard her say this?"

"Yes. You let her come into the room, Sarge. You didn't even chase me out. It's like I wasn't even there. They always treat me like I'm invisible," he said, looking back at me. "They don't care about me. They roomed me with Cain because they thought I'd be scared of him. But Cain's my friend, and he could be in trouble, Sarge! She came in a boat, Doctor. That girl Laura came in a boat, and Sarge brought her up here from the dock, didn't you Sarge? And they left by boat, too."

"Laura McKenzie drove a boat up here?" I said. "All the way from Harlington?"

"Yeah, and at night, too!" Jasper said. "She knew the jerks here would never let him go to the funeral. So they

busted out. Busted right out of here! Jailbreak, dude!
It was awesome!"

"Good Lord," I said, glaring at Sarge.

"Aw come on, Doc," he said. "It's young love. For
God's sake, doesn't the boy deserve to know love before
they ship him off to prison, or to some nut house?"

"Love?" I said. "Sarge, Richard revealed things to me
yesterday that indicates he might physically harm Laura
McKenzie—not just any girl, but Laura McKenzie specifically, do you understand? And this Samuel Blue thing
tells me he was already in a rage when she got here."

"He didn't act like he was in a rage," Sarge said.

"He just hid it," Jasper said. "You know how he can
do that, Sarge. He's got discipline, you say so yourself!"

"Well, hell," Sarge said.

"And that's not even the weirdest part," Jasper said.
We both looked at him.

"His Aunt Violet? A midget killed her."

"What?"

"That girl, Laura, she told Cain that his aunt died of a
heart attack because she saw a midget."

"You're not making any sense, son," Sarge said.

"That's what she told him! I'm not lying!"

"A midget?" I said, rummaging through my memory
of Richard's story from the day before. "Are you sure
that's what she said? She used that word? Midget?"

"Yeah! Well, no, maybe not midget" he said. "I think
she said a little man. Yeah, that's what it was. She said
that Miss Violet saw a little man and she had a heart attack and died right on the spot."

"Little man... Jasper, did she say it like lit-tle, or like this: lil Man?"

"I guess it was like that. Lil Man."

27. Revival

JUST THEN A VOICE CAME OVER THE INTERCOM instructing everyone to evacuate the premises. Sarge left the room to gain control of the boys in the hallway who had gotten rowdy.

"I'm staying here," Jasper said. "He's not here, anyway. Cain's not. He left with that girl, I saw them go down the river in the boat. You can see the dock from here. He wouldn't hurt me anyway. We're friends, me and Cain."

"The police will make you evacuate," I said.

"That's OK," he said. "They'll protect me."

"From whom?"

"The other guys. They think I'm a snitch."

"You did the right thing, Jasper. Thank you."

As I walked out of the building I became aware again of the buzzing in my ears. It seemed all around me, though, as if the whole world was buzzing. I stopped halfway across the iron footbridge and looked down into the water. I saw a catfish with its mouth wide open take a bug from the surface of the water and dive down. Then I saw another, and another. Then I looked around me.

Cicadas. Everywhere. They had red eyes. They were making an incredible racket. I couldn't believe I hadn't noticed them before.

I passed a police officer sitting in his patrol car listening to a voice over his radio. It said something like, "... You know that body that was found in the septic tank up in Pico County?... Victim's name, Samuel Blue... Pico County police suspect this Richard Tyler kid in that homicide... Also his mother... whereabouts unknown, also possible homicide victim, Tyler kid suspected in that too... We might be dealing with a serial killer here, so consider this suspect very dangerous... Take all due precautions..."

I hurried on and got into my car just as the SWAT team arrived in their armored vehicle. I saw men with black helmets and military style rifles. Students were piling across the iron footbridge and swarming on the parking lot, being corralled by the teachers and therapists and the school's rapid response team, and they were getting rowdy. I heard one of them yell out, "You can't kill him! He's Cain!"

Just as I was about to leave, someone hammered his fist on my window. It was Elton Ricks. He was livid. "I told you!" he yelled. "I told you this would happen!"

I had to swish my wipers to get the bugs off the windshield. Suddenly a throbbing, thumping sound broke through the buzzing of the cicadas. A police helicopter flew over the Laz.

As I drove toward Harlington I tried to call Sheriff McKenzie's cell phone, but it kept just going to voicemail. So I tried his office phone, and a deputy picked up. I told him who I was, and that I needed to speak to the sheriff and that it was urgent. He said the

sheriff was on an urgent matter himself—that a dangerous convict had escaped that morning in their jurisdiction.

I told him to please have him call my cell as soon as
possible, that it was about his daughter Laura and Richard Tyler.

"Richard Tyler?" the deputy said. "You mean the kid
the sheriff knows up at that reform school, what's it
called?"

"The Lazaretto," I said, "yes."

"He's the kid who helped us crack that cult a couple
of years ago."

"Right, I heard about that."

"Damn, is that a coincidence or what?"

"Coincidence... What do you mean?"

"That escaped con we're looking for? That's Aldo-
the- Bear. Aldo Singer-Sanger. He was being transferred to a court hearing yesterday afternoon and he escaped. I guess that Tyler kid's lucky to be in the reform
school. Aldo's kinda got it in for him."

"Oh good God. Look, I'll be there as soon as I can;
can you tell me how I might meet up with the sheriff?"

"Well, he'll be in and out, but he'll likely spend a good
bit of time down at the revival by the river. There's a big
crowd there. We're working security."

"Thank you, Deputy," I said. "If you can contact the
sheriff, please tell him that Richard... well, he's on the
loose too, and he may be heading down your way. With
the sheriff's daughter..." I had lost the cell signal, and I
wasn't sure he caught the last of my message.

My mind was reeling. The whole thing was either a divine reckoning on a biblical scale or a perfect storm of coincidences that could drive anyone over the edge of madness, and I speak as a clinical psychiatrist. The worst of it, though, had to be the reappearance of lil Man. Don't get me wrong, I didn't believe it was really him. Violet Tyler, Laura McKenzie, and Sheriff McKenzie all told me that there had been times over the years when people would impersonate lil Man as a sort of religious hoax to scam money from the gullible and the superstitious, and I fully expected this to be the case here. But if Richard was out to fulfill his destiny as Cain, murdering an imposter wouldn't make it any better for him or for his victim.

I worried about Laura McKenzie, too. I had seen it dozens of times in my work. Good girl falls for bad boy. Good girl gets hurt. Or worse—raped, killed. I did not want to think that Richard had that kind of violence and cruelty in him—no mother can stand... Oh boy... I mean, no psychiatrist can stand to see that in her patient.

I must admit, though, I admired Laura McKenzie. There was a girl with what my father called "moxie." Seventeen years old, and she runs a motorboat up a river by moonlight all by herself, to... to what? Win the heart of a young man who hadn't even spoken to her in more than two years? Prove herself to him? Play Bonnie to his Clyde? Or was it as simple as taking him to his aunt's funeral, knowing the school wasn't about to let him attend? So he could honor the memory of the one woman who acted like a mother, and loved him like her child.

I desperately wanted it to be that. But I knew it wasn't. You don't need a switchblade at a funeral.

When I got to Harlington, a gas station attendant told me how to get to the revival at the river. I was able to park among what seemed like hundreds of other cars at the top of a grassy hill overlooking the river. When I got out I saw I was near a big oak tree and a split rail fence. On the ground under the boughs of the oak, I saw lil Man's memorial stone. It was exactly as Richard had described it, with the cult symbol crudely scratched into it and the place at the bottom where Eris had smashed it with a sledgehammer. There were mounds of flowers, fresh-cut and plastic, around it.

This is it, I thought. This is the place where "river cat took him," where Cain was born.

The broad grassy area on the riverbank where the Tylers and the McKenzies had their picnic so many years ago was full of people. A thousand or more. I walked down the grassy sward into the crowd. Near the riverside was a makeshift wooden stage with loudspeakers, and a voice crackled over the crowd saying, "Let's hear it for the Calamity Creek Choir!" and then the people in the crowd clapped.

A big white banner hung over the stage. In purple block letters it said, "REVIVAL." A man on stage spoke into the microphone. "Ladies and gentlemen, I would like to ask that we all bow our heads in silent prayer in honor of Miss Violet Tyler, a good friend of virtually all of us here, who passed away last evening."

Everybody stood still and quiet and bowed their heads while the only sound was the buzz of the cicadas. And then the man said "Amen" into the microphone and everybody in the crowd said Amen back and started milling about again. Then the man said, "Viewing will be tonight at Quayle's Funeral Home from seven to nine, and the funeral will be tomorrow morning at ten at Calamity Creek Church Cemetery."

I thought of Violet Tyler, what a good and caring woman she seemed to be, how, like me, she was unable to have children of her own, and how, unlike me, she gave her whole spirit to loving one child as if he were her own. I thought of the pain she must have endured living for years thinking some malevolent power had abducted her boy. And I thought of how distraught and guilty Richard must have felt when he found out she had died, knowing how he had rejected her and how he had waited too long to give her what he had promised. And I was nearly overwhelmed with guilt that I didn't answer her call the day before.

Elton Ricks may have been wrong yesterday but he was right today. Richard was a powder keg, and if he exploded in this crowd, it could be a disaster. But was he really here? Or did he explode in some secluded stretch of the river, with only Laura McKenzie to hurt?

I started asking people if they knew where I could find Sheriff McKenzie, but no one had a clear answer. Then the man on stage said something into the microphone and the whole crowd suddenly surged toward him. "They're here! They're here!"

A woman carrying a baby in a blanket rushed by, pushing people aside, crying, and calling out, "Heal my baby! Heal my baby! Please! Oh, praise Jesus!" A lot of the people moving toward the stage were in wheelchairs or crutches or had oxygen tanks, or were being helped along or carried by others.

I moved forward with the crowd toward the stage. A helicopter flew overhead and everyone turned to look at it. It was a police helicopter, and the people started asking each other what it was about. Up on the hill where I had parked, a horn honked repeatedly. A white bus drove up. It jerked to a stop and suddenly I recognized it. It was a Lazaretto bus. The door opened and Sarge jumped out, followed by a bunch of teenage boys who hooted and hollered like they were on the warpath until Sarge motioned for order, as if to a platoon.

Sarge and the boys piled down the hill into the crowd just as several police cars pulled up with their blue lights flashing. Unable to drive through the jumble of parked cars, the officers got out and surveyed the scene below.

The dense, moving crowd carried me along closer to the stage. For a minute I couldn't make out what the people at the microphone were saying because of the sound of the helicopter, but it passed over. And then I heard this weird warbling sound. A human voice, but not speaking in English, and not singing, and not even in anything I could recognize as a language.

She was a woman of medium height, but very spindly and dressed in a threadbare country style farm dress. She was clutching an ancient black Bible that fluttered

as she waved her hands in the air. She was the one making the weird sounds into the microphone.

And then the crowd hushed as she started to speak.

"Praise Jesus, my friends! Amen? Praise Jesus! My
name is Ada Potter and I have come to share my testimony with you. Some thirteen years ago a child went
missing from this very river, taken from his brother's
arms by a great fish. And the people searched for the
babe, and could not find him. They came to where I
lived, down by the river crook, and asked me had I seen
the child. I had not, and I told them so. I spent the rest
of the day in prayer for the child, and that night when
the moon was full and high, the Lord God told me to get
up, Get up, Ada Potter! He said, and go to the riverbank.
So I did. In the water I saw the sign of the covenant of
Noah and a great fish lifted its head above the surface
and opened its mouth. And the Lord told me to reach in,
Reach in, Ada Potter! He said, and receive the child. And
I did. I held the child in my arms and the Lord said, this
child will perform miracles and healings in My name.
But you must remove him from this place, for Satan is
jealous and schemes to corrupt him. For thirteen years
will you wander the wilderness. Go, and educate him in
the Word and the commandments, raise him in the
bosom of the Lord your God and in the name of Christ
Jesus.

"And though I despaired of the sorrow his loss would
cause to his family, I did as God bade me to do, I left this
place with the child and wandered far and wide. We
lived among the poorest of the poor. We slept under

bridges and in homeless shelters. We found food in soup kitchens and garbage cans. I read to him from the Bible and I sat him on my lap as I preached to the penniless and the lost. After a year or so I was tired and I feared I could not carry on, so I fell to my knees and I prayed for the Lord to send me someone to help me in my lonely mission.

"And lo the Lord God answered my prayer, hallelujah! Praise Jesus! God sent me a man who loved the child as his son, a man with a strong back and a warm heart. He sent me a man who was right smart and capable, a man of deep faith, and together we raised the child in the Word and the love of God, and we provided him with shelter and sustenance, thanks be to the Lord. Amen?

"And lo! The Lord did work miracles through this child, and the Lord did heal the sick and the lame through this child! Praise Jesus he did, I am witness! Some of those people are here today to share their testimony with you..."

There were maybe half a dozen people on stage behind her, old and young, black and white, and they were standing, swaying, waving their hands, some looking down with their eyes closed, some looking up to the sky. And then I made out the other two. The man looked a good deal like Richard Tyler, but older, the way I imagined Richard's father might look. He didn't have the wild man's appearance, though. His hair was short and neatly combed, and he was clean-shaven. Like "Ada Potter," the guy was dressed simply and carrying a floppy

Bible. He didn't have the hypnotized look that the gang of "healed" people behind them had. He held his hands in the air like they did, but he had the look of a sentry, or a bodyguard, scanning the crowd for threats. Or marks.

And then there was the kid. He looked to be in his young teens, about the age lil Man would have been had he lived. But for a guy who could supposedly heal people, he looked physically lame and mentally deficient himself, at least from where I stood. He seemed to be staring into space, nodding stupidly. He did not look anything like Richard. His face was... actually quite beautiful. I wondered if he looked anything like Eris.

The man playing Richard's father took the microphone. "My name is Robert Tyus Tyler," he said, "though some of you may remember me as Ty. This is my testimony." His voice was tense and tired, but it rang familiar to me. "Thirteen years ago I was in a boat with my two boys, fishing on this very river, right out there. My older son, Richard, may God bless him, was holding little Emmanuel when the river cat took the baby. I did not see it. My back was turned and I did not see it! And my son Richard was distraught and the poor boy began to scream, "River cat took him, river cat took him!" and he pointed into the water where the fish had gone.

"Immediately I dove in to try to rescue my baby boy. But he was gone. I did not know that the Lord had taken him, that in fact the fish was rescuing him from us, and from Satan who dwelled among us. Desperation and fear seized my soul, and I lost my mind from the terror of not knowing the truth. For a year afterwards I searched the river. In my faithlessness I became like an animal, a fish, living in the river, seeking but not finding.

"I too became tired and crushed by the world and by my selfish, sinful sorrow. I lay down one night in the shack at the river crook that Sister Ada had abandoned. And I lay there thinking I would die in that place. Well, there I did die, my friends, and there I was reborn, for I asked Jesus to take my soul, and Jesus spoke to me. He said, your journey is just beginning, Robert Tyus Tyler! Go, seek out Sister Ada and you will find the boy. Protect them and nurture them, for Satan is jealous and has designs on the boy."

"I cried out, 'but where shall I find them, O Lord?' And the Lord said, 'Have faith and start walking, Ty. I will guide you.' And so it was. I found Sister Ada and together we protected and nurtured the boy as best we could, as humble instruments of the living God.

"O Christians! Can you imagine the joy I felt when I beheld the baby boy alive? Held like Jonah in the belly of a great fish for so long, so long, and yet by the grace of God delivered alive and well to the loving embrace of Sister Ada! It was a miracle! A miracle!

"And I witnessed more miracles, and healings, and I rejoiced, but still my heart cried out with worry for my other son, my Richard. I abandoned him when he needed me, he needed his father."

Here the man started to sob. It was pretty realistic. He was either an accomplished actor or completely crazy, or he really was Richard's father.

"I prayed for Richard! I said, please Jesus let me go to him just once! Let me bring him here! And Jesus said to me, O ye of little faith! Richard is the strong one. He has a role to play. He will draw the forces of Satan to himself and away from the child. Fear not for him. For I will send to him the sign of the covenant of Noah, and it will guide him in righteousness."

Suddenly I felt a hand on my shoulder. It was Sarge. He whispered to me, "You see Cain?"

"No," I said.

"He's right there," Sarge said, nodding forward and to our left.

Richard Tyler was standing right up against the stage. He was glaring at the man speaking in the microphone. His shirt was off and the muscles in his back and shoulders were taut and twitching. Like a predator waiting to pounce, I thought. I tried to move toward him, but Sarge held me by the arm. "Let them be," he said. "Laura's with him, see?"

She was standing next to him, but she didn't seem to be making any effort to restrain him or urge him away from this tense scene that could trigger in him the same kind of violence that almost killed the Kernell kid. She knew what happened then. She had to know it could happen here. I got the dark feeling that she was playing Bonnie to his Clyde.

The man playing "Ty Tyler" broke into hard sobbing. "My sister Violet passed on last night! I know she is in a better place! I hope to see her in heaven one day!"

Richard jumped up on the stage. His eyes were
locked on his prey. He reached into his pocket and
pulled something out and held it behind his hip. Suddenly a blade snapped out of his fist like the claw of a
lion.

28. Baptism

I STARTED TO CALL OUT TO RICHARD, but Sarge placed his hand over my mouth. "Hush," he said. "Let him be. God's in charge." I struggled briefly, but Sarge was very strong, and so I gave up, and he took his hand from my mouth. "Trust in the Lord," he said.

"Ty Tyler" had turned away to shorten the microphone stand for the boy, and did not see Richard. The kid walked with a limp, and his body and face were wracked with little spasms. A line of drool drained over his bottom lip and down his chin. Either this kid really was stuck inside a fish and got brain damage from lack of oxygen, I thought, or these two adults kidnapped him from a short bus somewhere to use in their con game.

Richard stepped toward the boy. Just as he reached him, the kid turned and looked him square in the eyes. Richard's arm twitched, and I braced for the flash of violence. But the boy moved first. He reached up and placed one hand on Richard's cheek and the other hand on Richard's chest, and he said, "Heal!"

They were near enough to the microphone that it resounded through the crowd.

Richard trembled. The kid said, "My brother..."

Richard whispered, "Lil Man..."

The knife dropped from Richard's hand and clattered on the stage floor. There was utter silence. Even the cicadas seemed to hush.

In that breathless moment, someone else jumped onto the stage from the crowd. He had been standing at the foot of the stage, stooped over and covered with a blanket like an elderly invalid. But his movement was sudden and strong. And when he threw off his blanket he was not old.

He seemed to hit the kid in the ribs with his fist, and the kid staggered from the contact, but did not take his eyes off Richard, who was still standing as if in a trance. Then the jumper raised his hands in the air and I could see he was holding the switchblade that Richard had dropped, and he yelled, "I am Aldo the Bear! Reparations for the River! Vengeance for Gaia!"

And then Aldo stabbed the boy a second time with Richard's knife.

Ty Tyler tackled him and they both fell off the stage onto the ground below. Laura threw herself into the fray, grabbing the wrist of Aldo's knife hand, pinning it to the ground as Sheriff McKenzie and a couple of deputies ran up and subdued him. Ty Tyler was on his knees, grabbing his hair in his fists, wailing, "My son! Oh, my son! I have failed! Oh, God, I have failed! Oh God, oh God, oh God!"

Richard looked down at the boy's side. Blood was flowing, soaking lil Man's shirt and down his pants. The boy slumped, and Richard picked him up in his arms. "We need an ambulance!" he cried out.

On the hill above, a voice sounded from a bullhorn. "Richard Tyler! Place the child on the ground and put your hands up. You are under arrest." I could see the SWAT team's armored vehicle. A sniper on top was peering through a rifle scope toward Richard.

"Brother," lil Man said. "Carry me to the river."

Richard was crying. "But you're bleeding, lil Man. You need a doctor."

"Carry me to the river," he said. "I will baptize you."

The cop with the bullhorn said, "People, please disperse and move away from the stage. This is now a crime scene. Richard Tyler! Please put the boy on the ground and let the ambulance crew take him. Then step back and put your hands up. Let's end this peacefully, son. Nobody else has to get hurt."

State police and SWAT team members started moving down the hill and into the crowd.

Sarge whistled real loud and called out, "Boys! Form up! Make a path to the river!" The boys from the Lazaretto scurried in response, yelling to each other. They locked arms in a line facing the descending police force. The people in the crowd saw what was going on, and they joined the boys. They swarmed around the police.

Richard carried lil Man in his arms off the stage and into the river. He kept going until he was waist deep, then he stopped. His skin was slick with lil Man's blood.

Lil Man slid out of Richard's arms and stood on the bottom. The water was nearly to his chest. The blood from his wounds swirled in the current. He seemed so weak and pale, but his face was peaceful.

I realized I was standing knee-deep in the river, watching them. Lil Man looked skyward and said some words in that strange tongue, and they were loud and strong. Then he put one hand on the back of Richard's neck and the other hand on his forehead, and he said one last word and laid his brother back into the water.

As far as I could tell, that last word wasn't in English, but it sounded a lot like this:

Poop!

Then lil Man's eyes rolled back in his head. His body went limp and he disappeared under the water.

Tears were clouding my vision, but this I saw: there was a great swirl in the brown water and something dark and flat like a huge fish's fin broke the surface ever so briefly and then disappeared.

Richard rose from under the water. He stood there looking downstream for a while. Then he turned back toward the riverbank. I saw the scar on his chest. In one way it was far more shocking seeing it in real life than on the photograph in his file. But in another way it was different. Profoundly different. There was the Christian fish symbol with its mouth open and the circle for the baby's head in it as if the fish was swallowing the baby. But in the photo the baby's mouth was turned down and the eyes were X's to show fright and death. Now in real life the mouth was turned up into a beatific smile and the eyes were little round dots. As if lil Man's touch healed Richard all the way down to the stigmata burned into his flesh.

The police helicopter thumped overhead. The bull-horn crackled. All the crowd was shouting and shoving and swirling. This usually staid, law-abiding flock had begun to riot against the police.

Someone called out, "Where's lil Man?"

Richard didn't respond. Amid the chaos, he slowly trudged out of the river.

29. Cain's Testimony

THIS MORNING WHEN LAURA CAME and got me from the Laz, all I felt was pain.

Like the brand was burning my chest and the hook was still in my cheek and the fishers of men were tugging hard on the line, dragging me down from the Laz, fighting all the way, down the river til I was standing there, right there in front of the one that started it all.

My brother, lil Man.

I knew it was him. I had hatred in my heart and a knife in my hand and I was going to end that pain once and for all, and that's the truth of it.

But then lil Man laid his hands on me. Something moved through me with his touch, something warm like a breath, and I saw him, and his eyes were blue like the sky that's home to a rainbow—and now I know where the rainbows go, O God, I know where the rainbows go!—I don't know how to describe it, but he was looking right at me, right into my eyes, and it was like he could see everything, he could see all the pain in me, and he said a word, just one word, he said, "Heal."

And the pain was gone. All of it. In my cheek. In my chest. In my... I don't know, in my heart, my soul... gone.

He took it. Lil Man took my pain. I could see it in his eyes. His eyes were still full of love for me, love I didn't deserve, I'm sorry for crying, I can't help it, but I could see the pain he took from me deep down in his eyes, and there was no end to it. There was no end to it. There was just... no end to it.

I wanted to take him to the ambulance. I wanted him to get better so... so I could teach him how to throw rocks and climb trees, and... but... he wanted me to go to the river, so... so I did. I gave up fighting. I gave up.

Next thing I knew, we were in the river, and he laid his hands on me again and he dunked me. Down there I could see the sunlight shimmer above me. It was warm and beautiful. And then I saw lil Man's face. He had gone under too. He was looking up at the sun shimmering above.

A rainbow appeared in the water, moving toward us. It went from one eye to the other. The river cat, bigger than I ever remembered, opened its mouth, and the water that sucked into it carried my brother along. I reached out to him. He looked back at me. His face was peaceful. He squeezed my hand once, then let go.

River cat took him.

The last word my brother said when he dunked me, and I didn't know this when I was little, but I know now, it means peace and it means love and it means forgiveness, and it means good-bye, but it was spoken in a holy and ancient tongue, and it was the same word as he said to me before, he said:

Poop.

I had a friend once, name of Samuel Blue. He said Jesus could save anybody, even Cain. He didn't tell me, though, what he couldn't know: A saved Cain is still Cain, amen?

I am Cain. This is my testimony.

30. Heal, Mama

I'M SORRY, BUT I STILL CAN'T CALL HIM THAT. Richard gave his testimony in Sister Ada Potter's shack in the woods near the crook in the river. The place looked exactly as I had imagined from the way he had described it to me the day before—even down to the crack in the windowpane, and the way the mottled sunlight broke into its rainbow spectrum if you stood in just the right place.

We were safe there from the state police, who had called in reinforcements in response to the unexpected disobedience of the revival crowd. Sheriff McKenzie took Laura and Richard and led a small group of us to the shack. A couple of his deputies had come to act as sentries. Sister Ada and Ty Tyler were there with several of the people in their group that lil Man had healed. Jasper, the kid who roomed with Richard at the Laz, was there. He had jumped on the hood of the sheriff's car and slipped inside when Tonnie McKenzie got out to shoo him away. Richard put his arm around him and let him come.

Finally, there was a young woman named Brenda. I learned she was the same Brenda who was holding the baby that Richard had saved from the cult when he visited Harlington a couple years before. She cried as Richard talked, and she hugged his neck for a long time after his testimony. She said to him, "You saved me when you saved that baby. I want you to know that. God bless you, young man. God bless you."

Sarge stayed behind to help McKenzie's deputies control the crowd and fend off the state police, and to corral his teenage charges from the Lazaretto. The sound of the police helicopter slowly faded, indicating that our guys were able to misdirect the police while we made our getaway.

But there in Sister Ada's shack, I was still unbelieving. It was as if there was a tiny lawyer, a devil's advocate, sitting on my shoulder, buzzing in my ear:

They're all lying. Life doesn't work this way. Think, Doctor! No baby could survive such a drowning. And no fish in this river could possibly take a fourteen-year-old boy. It's a scam. You're a woman of science, not a superstitious rube. They're playing you. Don't fall for it. That boy, that phony healer, he healed no one and he wasn't swallowed by a fish. He simply swam downstream. He lived to scam another rube another day. Don't let them lie to you. Make them tell the truth! TELL THE TRUTH!

Ty Tyler, or the man who was playing that role, was sitting on the ground with his back to the wall of the shack. I remembered his testimony: He had come to this shack at the bitter end of his life, exhausted from searching for his lost son, and here he spoke with God, and God told him to go find Sister Ada and help her protect and raise the boy. As I looked at him now, I saw a man utterly spent, his face haggard and slouched with sorrow, his shoulders bent under a crisis of faith, and I thought, this is no actor.

Oh, come on, Doctor, I've seen you cry at the movies...

But why would he still be acting now? Where's the audience?

You know what they say. If you walk into a room where there's a scam going on and you can't find the mark, you're the mark. Wake up, Doctor.

No, Sheriff McKenzie vouched for him. This is the real Ty Tyler.

So what? Maybe he was escaping that witch he was married to. Eris. Remember her? A real piece of work! Men have gone to greater extremes to rid themselves of lesser devils. Occam's razor, Doctor. Use it.

What about Sister Ada? She lived in a shack in the woods most of her life, in dire poverty, a religious hermit. She doesn't have the guile or the intellect to run a scam.

All the best grifters have a good backstory, Doctor. Especially the religious ones. The Bible's just their bag of tricks and disguises. Don't let her fool you the way she fools all those sentimental, gullible marks at the revival. Think, Doctor, think!

I turned to look at Sister Ada and found she was watching me. She stood and walked to me. Her step was arthritic and one shoe scraped on the ground. She came very close and her eyes drifted from mine down to my shoulder.

"Look here," she said softly. "You've got a little rider."
She reached up and plucked something off my blouse
and held it between her fingers. It was a red-eyed cicada.
"Get on, little feller," she said, and tossed him aside.

Then she looked me in the eyes again. She placed one
hand on the back of my neck and gently pulled me to her
until our cheeks were touching. At the same time she
placed her other hand on my belly and she whispered in
my ear, "Your baby's all right, good mama, he's all right
now. Heal, mama... Heal, mama..."

I had never felt such a sensation before. It was warm
and tingling, an out-of-body lightness that made me feel
like I was floating and I gasped and my lungs filled with
sweet air like a lifesaving breath given to a suffocating
woman. A brilliant rainbow of colors flooded the shack
through the crack in the windowpane.

The world became blurry with my tears, my body
wracked with childlike sobs. One after another, the people in the shack hugged me or kissed my cheek or
pressed my hand and whispered "God bless..." and one
after another they began to disperse.

Then I heard a loud, sudden roar. Richard had kick-
started his motorcycle. Even I, an ignoramus when it
came to machines, could tell what a gloriously strange
work of art this "frankenfarmer" contraption was—
pieced together with spare tractor parts, pitchfork tines,
scythe blades and other things by Richard with his own
hands.

He yelled out, "Thanks for saving my bike, Sheriff."
The sheriff nodded and touched the brim of his hat.

Richard looked at Laura. She smiled, hopped on the back and put her arms around his waist. As they started off on the dirt path, she turned to wave at her father. Sheriff McKenzie waved back. He kept looking in that direction well after they rounded a turn and disappeared from sight.

Ty Tyler watched them go, too. He said to the sheriff, "What's going to happen to them, Tonnie?"

"Oh, I suspect they'll be all right, Ty."

"He'll be a fugitive and a wanderer forever," Ty Tyler said. "Cain..." He shook his head and sighed.

"As I recall," the sheriff said, "Cain had a wife and a family. He settled down. Ty, Laura's with him now. Don't worry. They're good people. They'll do fine. You gotta believe."

Ty Tyler began to cry. His old friend, Tonnie McKenzie, put his arm around him and walked him to his sheriff's car. Jasper followed behind them. The boy turned to look at me. "You coming?" he said.

"I'll be along in a minute, you go ahead," I said. "I've got my car."

I was alone then. I don't know how long I stood there. A long time, I suppose, not thinking, just staring at the rainbow colors on the floor and wall of the shack as they slowly moved and changed shapes with the sun's path across the sky. Savoring this new feeling of peace.

There was a sound outside as of someone stepping on a dry twig in the leaf litter on the forest floor. A shadow fell over the dusty windowpane. The rainbows went dark. Someone was out there. Looking in. My warm peace turned to a chill, and I ran out of the shack, up the path to my car and I sped off without looking back.

31. Eris

I WAS TOO EXHAUSTED to make the drive back home that evening so I found one of those little country motels that never seem to have any lodgers, and you wonder how they stay in business, but it was open and I got a room for the night.

I'm a psychiatrist. I see young people who are broken by abuse, stunted by neglect, poisoned by chemical and emotional toxins, and sometimes I forget there are young women like Laura McKenzie in this world. I thought about her as I lay in that musty old bed, waiting for sleep to come. With her brown curls pulled back in a ponytail, mud on her boots, her sweat-stained denim blouse with the sleeves rolled up to her elbows, most people would say she had a country girl-next-door prettiness rather than cover girl beauty. But her spirit—the courage and determination and faith it took to do what she did, without which there would have been no redemption that day for Richard or for me—is what made her the most beautiful woman I had ever seen in my life.

I had not prayed since I was a girl, younger than Laura McKenzie was that day. But that night I said a prayer. I said, "God, please take care of Richard and Laura. Amen."

I'm not going to pretend. It felt awkward and faked. But I thought of Sister Ada and Ty Tyler and I knew there would be real prayers offered for the young lovers that night, and I relaxed and fell asleep.

I awoke at sunrise and felt rested enough to drive home. But I decided to stop by the river first, where the revival had taken place. I parked where I had the day before, near the memorial stone Violet Tyler had set in the ground under the oak tree for lil Man, Emmanuel Tyler.

The place was deserted. I walked down the grassy hill to the river's edge and stood there, staring at the brown water drifting by. I recalled the scene of lil Man, wounded and bleeding, laying his big brother back into the water to baptize him. I remembered lil Man going under. I remembered what looked like the tail fin of a huge fish breaking the surface, and the swirl of water, and how Richard stood back up, but lil Man never reappeared. And I knew somehow that I'd remember it in photographic detail for the rest of my life.

I turned to walk back up the hill but stopped short. Up by lil Man's memorial stone stood a woman. She was silhouetted against the rising sun so I could not make out her features. She stared at the stone for a minute, and laid something on it. Then she let out a long, hellish wail that sent a shiver through me. She turned and looked toward me and for a moment I feared she would head my way.

Then the roar of a motorcycle rumbled in the distance and she turned to look that way, as if she recognized the sound. She stumbled to her car, holding her head as if she had a headache, got in and drove away.

I walked up the hill. There, lying atop lil Man's stone was Richard's switchblade knife. It was open. The blade and part of the handle were caked in dried blood.

I thought: it could have been anyone. A member of the cult. Another hoaxer. It couldn't have been her. It just couldn't. But I also thought: it couldn't have been anyone else. I dreaded to think that this display, this installation, could be a panel of her next triptych.

I am Lillian Last. I am a psychiatrist. And I am a mother. This is my testimony.

I'm sorry if it seems unfinished. But no matter how many broken minds or souls I or Sister Ada heal, there will be another to take its place. That's life.

Samuel Blue said that even Cain could be saved. But what about Eris? Where is her treatment, her healing, her redemption? I often wonder if she was there that day at the revival. Or if she came late, and missed seeing her miracle baby alive, missed the chance of being healed by his touch, of finding that happiness she knew when he was a baby. How much deeper into her pain pit of insanity did she fall when she found out that "river cat took him" right out of Cain's hands for a second time?

I worry about Richard as if he were my own son. And I imagine confronting Eris with all my mothering instincts intact, calling her to account for all the rejection and cruelty she showed him from the day he kicked her in the womb. It would be pure fantasy to imagine I would come out on top of such a conflict. I am just not built that way. Laura McKenzie is, though. And that gives me comfort.

I suspect that we have not seen the last of Eris. I fear that she will seek out her muse. Or her muse will find her. And when that day comes, will Richard's healing survive the meeting? Will there be redemption? Or will there just be a reckoning—a final, bloody epilogue to her Book of Cain?

I don't know. Only God knows. All we can do is hope and pray that when that day comes, there will be a rainbow.

Amen?

Made in the USA
Columbia, SC
07 April 2021

35254242R00178